Mr. Pipes

and Psalms and Hymns of the Reformation

Douglas Bond
Christian Liberty Press
Arlington Heights, Illinois

Published by
Christian Liberty Press
502 West Euclid Avenue
Arlington Heights, Illinois 60004
www.christianlibertypress.com

General editorship by Michael J. McHugh
Layout and editing by Edward J. Shewan
Copyediting by Diane C. Olson, Belit M. Shewan, and Carol H. Blair
Cover design and graphics by Christopher D. Kou
Graphics by Christopher D. Kou and Robert Fine
Cover image by Dawn Doughty
Story images by Ron Ferris
Maps by Wendy Tamminga

Hymns are reprinted from the *Trinity Hymnal* (Copyright © 1961, 1990, Great Commission Publications). Used by permission.

ISBN 978-1-930367-52-4 (print)
ISBN 978-1-935796-76-3 (eBook PDF)

Printed in the United States of America

Table of Contents

Mr. Pipes and Psalms and Hymns of the Reformation

by Douglas Bond

Author of

Mr. Pipes and the British Hymn Makers,

Mr. Pipes Comes to America,

and

The Accidental Voyage
(published by P&R Publishing)

Preface

Mr. Pipes and Psalms and Hymns of the Reformation contains more than an interesting story about two young Americans on vacation in Europe. It is a story about the most important subject in the world—the worship of Almighty God.

The worship of God in modern times has too often become shallow and man-centered. Many Christians at the opening of the Twenty-first Century, including young believers, have never understood the importance of approaching God with awesome reverence and majestic praise. As readers move through *Mr. Pipes and Psalms and Hymns of the Reformation*, however, they will not only learn about the fascinating lives of famous hymn writers, but will also be encouraged to cultivate an attitude of humble adoration as they approach their Maker.

Young Christians who grasp the significance of what they read will come to the wonderful realization that their worship is connected with the Church universal—the followers of Christ throughout the world, both past and present. In other words, young readers will understand that true worship is not isolated from believers of the past but is, rather, built upon their godly traditions.

Perhaps the greatest tradition of true biblical worship, aside from scriptural exposition and prayer, is the holy exercise of hymn singing. It is, therefore, the express purpose of this book to rekindle a genuine interest within the lives of young believers in the traditional hymns of the faith once delivered unto the saints. May God be pleased to use this little volume to revive an interest in and appreciation for that which is true and praiseworthy in the realm of Christian worship.

Michael J. McHugh

For Brittany, Rhodri, Cedric, and Desmond

Godly families are
differed from the ungodly
by openly singing the praises of God,
when others sing wanton and idle songs.

Richard Baxter, 1692

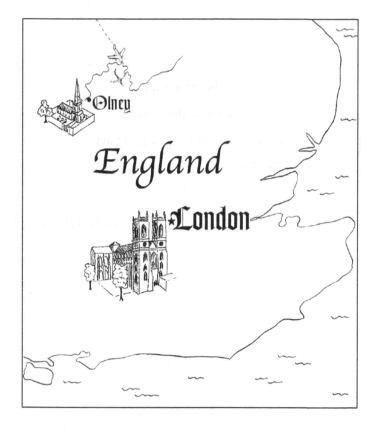

Chapter One

News from England
The Adventure Begins

> Polly was finding the song more and more inter-
> esting because she thought she was beginning to
> see the connection between the music and the
> things that were happening.
> "'old your noise, everyone," said the Cabby. "I
> want to listen to the moosic."
>
> *C. S. Lewis*

The kitchen door flew open with a bang. Lanky, blond-
haired Drew Willis bolted into the house clutching the mail in
his hands, his face flushed with excitement.

"Annie!" he yelled, dropping the pile of letters and tearing
into a thin, blue envelope. "It's from Mrs. Beccles!" he said, as
his sister came rushing into the kitchen.

"Don't read it without me," she said, finishing a braid in
her shiny blond hair, while straining to see over her younger,
but now clearly taller, brother's broadening shoulders.

The children had met Mrs. Beccles last summer when they
traveled with their mother to Olney, an ancient English market
town, where they had expected to spend the most boring summer of their lives. Nothing could have been further from the
truth. Mrs. Beccles owned and operated "Beccles Bakehouse,"
and Drew didn't think anyone made pastries as delicious as
kindly Mrs. Beccles. From their first day in the village she had
become their friend.

Drew read out loud:

> My dears, Annie and Drew,
>
> The most astonishing thing happened today
> in my little shop, and I simply had to be writing

you about it, for as near as I can tell, it concerned you both.

Mr. Pipes and Dr. Dudley called in for tea at half-past four—they often do, as you'll no doubt remember—but very soon their conversation became rather heated, leastwise, heated on Dr. D's part, as you'd be expecting. Your dear friend and companion, Mr. Pipes, seemed to be proposing some adventure, of which Dr. D clearly did not approve. I couldn't be hearing the details, of course, not being given to eavesdropping, but I did hear them mention your names more than once, that's sure, and I'm feeling it in my bones this bodes well for your upcoming summer holidays!

—Oh, you'll have to hold that thought for a moment whilst I pull some of my jelly-fills out of the oven—My, how I do wish I could send you some, Drew, knowing how much you be liking them and all.…

Here, a dark red splotch interrupted the letter. Drew scratched at the splotch, sniffed it, then carefully tasted it.

"Well?" said Annie.

"Currant jelly," said Drew, scratching again at the little splotch. "Umm-m, what I wouldn't do for one of Mrs. Beccles' jelly-fills! What do you think Mr. Pipes has up his sleeve?" he went on.

"Whatever it is," said Annie, "it's got to be good if Mr. Pipes came up with it."

"—And good," said Drew, "if Dr. Dudley doesn't like it."

"Behind his stiff, British way," said Annie, smiling as she remembered Dr. Dudley's jutting chin and long, sniffing nose, "he really means well—I'm sure of it. I think Dr. Dudley just cares so much for Mr. Pipes he doesn't want to see anything— well, you know—anything bad happen to him."

"I guess you're right," said Drew doubtfully.

In the rest of the letter Mrs. Beccles filled them in on all the latest news from Olney:

> Beatrice Faulkner won this year's Pancake Race—the five-hundred-and-fifty-fifth anniversary race—I say, how time does fly! Mrs. Broadwith has new lodgers, imagine it, who flatly refused to eat her stewed tomatoes for breakfast; the local radio station is exerting considerable pressure on the vicar to be placing a ghastly antenna on the very spire of St. Peter and St. Paul's—our parish church, of all places! What would Mr. Newton have thought! English Heritage has threatened to fine the Cowper Museum 100 pounds sterling for repainting dear Mr. Cowper's door the wrong shade of red (how they know it's the wrong shade I'll never know, that's sure!). Lambing season for the Howard family is very busy, as always, but the mild spring weather means fewer lambs are being lost to cold. Bentley and Clara send their love....

Annie and Drew's minds flooded with memories from the narrow, cobbled streets of Olney (cars whizzing by on the wrong side of the street), their fishing and sailing adventures with Mr. Pipes along the Great Ouse, Lulu the white pony, Lord Underfoot the cat, their good friends, Bentley and Clara Howard and all their sheep, the great stone church built so long ago, and Mr. Pipes's stories told around the old organ. Life in Olney was so unlike their life in America, but how they had grown to love that life. What could Mr. Pipes be planning that would involve them? They both wondered.

A week later Annie lay on the floor of her bedroom, her bare feet propped up on her bed, a page of her sketchbook— full of crossed out lines—open in front of her. She looked dreamily at the ceiling, took a deep breath, and sighed. Mr. Pipes told her how to begin writing a poem, but no matter how hard she tried the words seemed to have a mind of their own. How did the hymn writers, that Mr. Pipes had told them about last summer, do it? "Remember, my dear," he had said in his clear, gentle voice, "the rhyme must serve the meaning, not the other way round." Somehow, recalling Mr. Pipes's instruction only made her more discouraged as she gazed at her own efforts—

> There was a man with whitened hair
> Who for his friends so much did care.

—"Ugh!" she groaned.

A clinking sound suddenly interrupted her muse as the mailman dropped letters through the slot in the front door. With regular letters from Clara—some of them written in an elaborate code they'd worked out over months of using dancing paper doll-like symbols, every arm and foot position corresponding to letters of the alphabet—she'd trained herself to listen for the mail every day. After a dash across the hall and a quick shuffle through the pile of mail, she opened, with trembling hands, another blue envelope from England, this one from Mr. Pipes himself. Now, receiving a letter from Mr. Pipes was not so strange. He wrote often, letters filled with reminiscence of their adventures, and filled with encouraging words and helpful solutions to the questions they asked in their replies. But this letter seemed somehow different. Her eyes raced down the page.

"Drew! Oh, my goodness, Drew!" she called, jumping up and down with excitement. She reread the last paragraph of the letter to be sure her eyes had not deceived her.

The piano playing from the den abruptly halted, and a moment later Drew burst into the living room.

"He wants us to come back!" she squealed.

"Who?" asked Drew, scowling at her, irritated that she'd interrupted his practice.

"Mr. Pipes, silly," said Annie.

Mr. Pipes was Drew's long-distance music teacher who assigned hymns through the mail for Drew to practice. He'd just been struggling with learning "Minstrel Boy," the tune Mr. Pipes preferred for Reginald Heber's hymn, "The Son of God Goes Forth to War." Sometimes he wondered about Mr. Pipes's insistence that he begin piano lessons again. It was hard work!

"Let me get this straight," said Drew, the excitement growing in his voice. "Mr. Pipes is inviting us back to Olney?"

"Not exactly," said Annie.

"Let me see that," said Drew, grabbing at the letter.

"Look at the last paragraph," said Annie.

"Naturally, this is all conditioned upon your mother and stepfather's approval...." Drew read aloud. He read on, skimming the rest of the paragraph silently. His heart beat more quickly as he read through the paragraph again. Could it actually be true?

"Annie," said Drew, calming his voice with considerable effort. "Annie, do you realize what this means?"

"You bet I do," said Annie, spinning around on her heel, her pigtails sailing behind her. "If Mom and Dad let us, we are off to Germany and Switzerland for the whole summer—and with Mr. Pipes! Just think—mountains, cowbells, castles—it's too good to be true!"

"Don't forget the Swiss chocolate," said Drew, his eyes rolling back in his head as he flopped onto the couch with a laugh.

"No wonder Dr. Dudley had another of his heated talks with Mr. Pipes," he went on. Sitting up, Drew cleared his throat and jutted out his chin. "I say, old fellow," he began, doing his best imitation of Dr. Dudley's accent. "My dear man, I'll be dashed if you take those American children gallivanting all over the Continent—little blighters! They'll have you in your grave before your time, that's sure."

Annie sank to the floor laughing as Drew continued.

"Of course, I'd simply never dream of interfering—" Here Drew, too, burst into laughter.

Their parents did not entirely understand the change that had come over the children since spending last summer with Mr. Pipes. For a time they tried to discourage it, to divert the children's attention back to their old life and friends, but their mother couldn't help noticing how positive the old man's influence had been on her children. Barring the hymns they almost continually sang—*dirges*, as she called them—they quarreled much less than before, were more helpful around the house, and approached their studies at school with much more enthusiasm. But another whole summer under Mr. Pipes's influence? They did so want their children to be open-minded and free-thinking. However, after some discussion—while Annie and Drew huddled anxiously at their parents' bedroom door—they gave their consent.

The last weeks of the school term seemed to last forever. Annie and Drew spent every spare moment talking excitedly about the adventure that lay ahead. They packed and repacked their knapsacks. Mr. Pipes had written that they needed to travel light, but they would also need sailing and fishing clothes.

"You see, my dears," he explained in his last letter, "one must make every effort to pack clothing that can be used for more than one purpose. For example, I will bring only two neckties—the best one for church and musical performances, and so forth, and my second best one for sailing, fishing, and generally pottering about the countryside."

Annie and Drew smiled. It was so like their dear, proper friend, Mr. Pipes. They repacked again. Drew even experimented with packing a necktie—but only one.

"How can time drag by so slowly," asked Annie the night before their flight to London, "and then all of a sudden what you've been waiting for is here? Oh, I'll never get to sleep tonight."

"Me neither," said Drew, trying on his knapsack for the hundredth time. "But maybe we can get some rest on the airplane—I can't believe we're actually going!"

Annie and Drew swallowed hard as the powerful jet engines roared and the airplane raced down the runway. Suddenly the plane lifted off, climbing steeply into the blue sky above; Annie gulped as she waited for her stomach to catch up. Drew worked his jaw back and forth trying to relieve the popping feeling in his eardrums. Annie scrunched her eyes closed and gripped the armrest as the plane jolted through a layer of fluffy, white clouds.

"Another airline seat bites the dust," said Drew, watching Annie's fingernails dig deeply into the armrest.

In a few moments Annie relaxed as the plane leveled off and flew more smoothly. Seeing the sunlight flash on the shiny wings of the plane, she managed a smile as it carried them north and east toward England and Mr. Pipes.

With a "pling-pling" the fasten-your-seat-belts sign flicked off. After several minutes, a woman wearing a dark blue suit and matching hat stopped in the aisle and smiled at Annie and Drew. Holding something wrapped in plastic toward Drew, she asked, in Dr. Dudley English, "Might I interest you in head-phones for music listening? Here are the selections available." She handed him a little card. Drew scanned down the list: "Garage Mirage, Pragma Magma, and Mr. Wild-Man Band," he read silently. He looked again at the headphones. There was a time when an opportunity to sit for hours soaking up music—this kind of music—would have been like eating his favorite ice cream—with all the toppings.

He looked out the window for a moment and thought of a phrase Mr. Pipes once quoted in a letter: "Worldliness makes sin look normal and righteousness look odd." He turned back to the flight attendant. "No thanks—but—" he hesitated, "—do you have anything to eat?"

Annie scowled at him, "*Drew?*"

But the flight attendant laughed. "I'll be back in a moment with drinks and a little snack. Dinner will follow shortly, after which time dessert will be served, then tea."

"Sounds great!" said Drew, licking his lips.

"It sounds like we'll be eating most of the flight," said Annie.

The flight attendant laughed again. "We do want our passengers happy!" She disappeared behind a little curtain for a moment then reappeared balancing two trays. Annie and Drew flipped down their seat trays in anticipation.

"Here now, this ought to hold you until dinner," she said, setting before them several bags of peanuts, a currant scone each, and an assortment of jams and jellies. "I suppose you prefer soda?" she continued, reaching for two cans of pop from the other tray.

"What's in the pot?" asked Drew.

"Tea—*hot* tea," she said. "We English can't live without the stuff, but I'm given to understand you Americans don't think much of it."

"Oh, but we like tea," said Annie, "with milk and sugar, please."

"How lovely!" said the flight attendant as she skillfully balanced the tray while filling two cups with the steaming liquid.

"May I have more sugar, please?" asked Drew, gazing into his cup before sipping.

◈ ◈ ◈

Darkness spread rapidly as the airplane raced northeast and the sun raced the other way, finally disappearing over the horizon. Annie passed the time by looking at her drawings and poetry written last summer with Mr. Pipes in Olney. She breathed the faint but still fragrant aroma of the dried flowers she'd gathered and pressed in her book. Chewing on her pencil, she scowled at several lines she'd written. Why couldn't she write poetry like Mrs. Alexander or William Cowper? She sighed deeply. Oh well, she'd keep trying.

The hours passed as Drew, a puzzled expression on his face, watched a rugby match on the small TV monitor in the back of the seat in front of him. They both fell asleep somewhere over the frozen wastes of Greenland.

"This is your captain speaking," jolted them awake. Drew stretched and yawned. Annie wiped the sleep out of her eyes with both fists. "Breakfast will be served momentarily," continued the captain. "Do enjoy. We will arrive at Heathrow about 11:00 a.m. London time."

"Oh, no!" said Drew, sniffing the air and looking hungrily down the aisle. "You don't think they'd serve us stewed tomatoes for breakfast, would they?"

"Better get used to it again, Drew," said Annie, who didn't like stewed tomatoes any better than Drew, but who also didn't feel—probably never felt—as hungry as her brother. "Maybe they will ease us back into British cuisine slowly and just serve fried mushrooms and soft-boiled eggs—with a side of baked beans and deep-fried toast. You never can tell." She seemed to be enjoying his distress.

"Ugh!" said Drew.

Breakfast proved to be much more of an American affair than Drew had feared, and after the trays were cleared away the plane began its steady descent through the broken clouds toward London. Drew grabbed the map from the seat pocket in front of him and studied it carefully.

"Where are we?" asked Annie.

Drew glanced out the window at the red, sandy tideland below. "We must be near the Solway Firth just here." He pointed to the map.

"What on earth is a *firth*?" asked Annie.

"Don't know—maybe British for some amount between four and five," said Drew. "But it's the name of this notch of water that marks the western border between Scotland and England—a firth must be like a bay, I'd guess."

Annie looked more closely at the map. "So, if we stay on this route, how close to Olney will we come as we fly toward London?"

Drew traced a line from the border of Scotland and England down to London. "It looks like this time we'll go almost right over Olney!" he said, his excitement growing.

Annie and Drew sat with their faces plastered against the window on the left side of the plane. Green pastures, separated by hedges and low stone walls, stretched below. Sunlight shone through the broken clouds in bright patches on the checkered scene, and tiny, ant-sized cars made their way slowly along winding country lanes.

"Isn't this fun?" said Annie. "I feel like a giant looking down on a miniature world. Look at that little village—it's made all of dollhouses. Everything seems even more beautiful from this angle, don't you think, Drew?"

"Sure, but they still drive on the wrong side of the road," said Drew with a laugh.

"The *other* side of the road," said Annie. "What's that narrow strip of dark green trees zigzagging through the fields?" asked Annie. "Wait! Did you see that flash of sunlight in among the trees?"

Drew scanned his map, calculating how far they might have traveled in the last half-hour. He strained to see below.

"The village is huddled around a doll-house church," squealed Annie, gripping his arm. "Drew, I think it might be—it couldn't be—"

"It's Olney!—maybe," said Drew, "and Newton's church! Remember meeting Mr. Pipes at the organ that first day last summer?—that's the river—The Great Ouse!—I think."

Almost frantic with excitement, and amidst tongue clicking and disapproving glares from nearby passengers, the children searched the scene below for more familiar landmarks.

"I see the bridge—remember when Dr. Dudley watched you get walloped by *Toplady's* boom and fall overboard just below it?" said Annie, only with great effort restraining herself from laughter at the memory.

"Yeah, yeah," said Drew good-naturedly, "and who was at the tiller not watching the wind direction? I certainly never heard a 'Jibe ho!' from you before the sail came swooshing around and the boom thonked me. Boy! How I'd love to go sailing with Mr. Pipes again!"

"Hey! That must be Mr. Pipes's cottage—it has to be!" interrupted Annie.

"No way!" Drew bumped his forehead on the window in his eagerness to see. The village faded into the rolling green fields and hedgerows as the plane sped toward London—and their friend, Mr. Pipes.

Crisscrossed with bridges, the Thames snaked its ancient way through the jumble of church domes and spires, stately buildings, and the sprawling bustle of London. The engines slowed and hissed as the plane, wings dipping, dropped several hundred feet toward the city. Annie looked straight ahead, digging her fingernails into the palm of her hand. She screwed her eyes tightly closed and swallowed.

"We'll be down soon," said Drew, comfortingly. He looked out the window and continued, "Wow! What a view from up here, though. And to think, Mr. Pipes and Dr. Dudley are down there somewhere in among all those grasshoppers!"

"Dr. Dudley would be deeply offended at you calling him a grasshopper," said Annie.

As the runway grew closer below them, the plane seemed to go faster. With a "squilch, squilch," the tires touched down on the tarmac, and the plane taxied to the terminal. After standing in line "forever," as Drew described it, they cleared customs and passed through a security checkpoint. Annie caught sight of Mr. Pipes first, dropped her knapsack, and broke into a run. Drew gathered up her bag and hurried after his sister. Mr. Pipes, wearing his brown tweed suit and necktie, smiled with pleasure at the sight of the children. Annie threw herself into his open arms.

Drew, trailing behind under the weight of their carry-on luggage, arrived a moment later. Looking at Mr. Pipes's sparkling eyes rimmed below by his narrow, little glasses perched on his nose, and crowned above by his white, billowing eyebrows, Drew realized just how much he had missed the old man all these months. Mr. Pipes planted a fatherly kiss on Annie's cheek.

"Words fail me," he said, "in expressing my deepest joy at seeing you. And, my dear Annie, how you have grown!"

Here Mr. Pipes turned to Drew. "And the *little* brother," he winked at Annie, who used to enjoy referring to Drew as little, "one no longer need look closely, Drew, to see that you have grown taller than your older sister. You stand almost a head taller than she."

Drew set down the luggage and extended his hand. Mr. Pipes grasped his hand and with his left arm enfolded Drew's broad shoulders with a hug. A flood of recollection came over Drew as he caught the scent of wool, Earl Grey tea, and something that reminded him of the pipes and keys of the organ surrounded by the ancient stone arches of the parish church where Mr. Pipes had been the organist for more years than Drew knew. He even thought he caught a whiff of the river—and of fish.

"Mr. Pipes," said Drew, looking up at his balding forehead and flowing white hair, "I'm so glad to see you, and we can't wait to see what you want to show us in Europe." Drew paused. "Fishing been good?"

Mr. Pipes threw his head back and laughed. "You're not one to beat around the proverbial bush."

Before Mr. Pipes could answer, a loud and deliberate "Ahem!" came from a tall, dark-haired gentleman standing protectively close to Mr. Pipes.

Annie looked at the man and squealed, "Dr. Dudley! It's so good to see you! And thanks for bringing Mr. Pipes to the airport." She hesitated as he looked coolly down his long nose at her, then timidly extended her hand.

"Delighted, I'm sure," he said with a rather stiff bow as he briskly took her hand. "It has been ever so long since last we ..." he broke off searching for words, "... since last we met."

Mrs. Beccles's letter was right. Dr. Dudley was clearly not pleased about Mr. Pipes taking them on another adventure, thought Annie, looking out of the corner of her eye at Drew. Dr. Dudley had never really gotten over them going with Mr. Pipes on the sailing voyage down the Great Ouse last summer. "But why did he have to always blame us?" she thought. Oh, well, Annie reminded herself that Dr. Dudley only wanted to take good care of Mr. Pipes. She'd do her best to cheer him up.

"And greetings to you, Drew," said Dr. Dudley shortly, and with an impatient twitch of his mustache. "Now then, we must get your things together and into the boot if we are ever to make it out of London and to the boat for your crossing of the channel—that is if you still intend on going through with this ridiculous notion. It's not too late to come to your senses, my dear fellow," he concluded with a sniff and a penetrating stare at Mr. Pipes.

"My dear friend," began Mr. Pipes, "Annie and Drew have not come such a great distance merely to receive a lukewarm welcome from you."

"Oh, mind you," said Dr. Dudley looking more kindly at the children, "mind you, it is nothing, to be sure, of a personal nature toward you, not in the slightest. And I would never dream of interfering—I simply don't approve of elderly gentlemen gallivanting around the countryside when hearth and home would be so much more conducive to—well—to their best interest, shall we say."

Dr. Dudley, nevertheless, called a valet to wheel their belongings toward the exit of the airport, while Mr. Pipes walked ahead, an arm each around Annie and Drew's shoulders. After the luggage was stored in the trunk, Dr. Dudley glanced at his watch and said, "We must be off at once."

"Martin, my friend," said Mr. Pipes after glancing at his watch, "if we departed now for Dover we would arrive hours before sailing time—may I remind you, our tickets are for the evening boat. We have time to see a little something of London, that is if you children are feeling well enough for a bit of sight-seeing?"

"We'd love to!" said Annie and Drew.

Dr. Dudley rolled his eyes, adjusted his lapels with a jerk, and said deliberately, "If we must, we must. But I propose we leave my car in the car park and take public transport to the heart of the city. That way I'll not be required to scour the entire city for a place to park the car."

Moments later Annie and Drew found themselves in the top front seat of a bright-red, double-decker bus weaving its way through the narrow, bustling streets of London. The driver steered the tall bus within inches of the black-iron lampposts lining the way. Drew plastered his face against the cool glass and felt his stomach leap into his throat as the bus careened into a round-about intersection—the on-coming traffic all driving on the wrong side of the road. Annie nearly jumped from her seat as a low-growing branch from a yew tree bordering the street slapped against the roof of the bus just above her face.

"Whoa! That was close," said Annie. "I hope it didn't scratch the paint. Doesn't it seem like he's going a little fast?"

"Chap's been doing this for years, no doubt," said Dr. Dudley. "We all have our place—this fellow's place is clearly behind the wheel of one of her Majesty's buses. It is all for society's good when each person dutifully fulfills his role." With this last comment he looked reprovingly at Mr. Pipes, who simply smiled and said:

"Indeed."

"What river's that?" asked Drew as the bus raced along a broad river lined with tall, stately, and, Drew thought, very *old* buildings.

"The Thames, my boy," said Mr. Pipes, smiling at him, "and, yes, it does have fish!"

"But I've left my pole with our luggage," Drew moaned.

"We'll have plenty of time for fishing later," said Mr. Pipes, chuckling. "Today, I want to show you where some of the great hymn writers I told you about last summer went to school."

Just then the bus screeched to a halt in front of a gray stone building with two massive towers rising above. Annie and Drew followed Dr. Dudley and Mr. Pipes down the narrow, winding staircase from the upper deck of the bus and onto the pavement in front of the imposing structure. Drew looked up at the Gothic arches rising into the sky. He rocked back on his heels, and his neck began to ache.

"This makes St. Peter and St. Paul's back in Olney look pretty small," said Drew.

"It is so—so—majestic," said Annie, gazing at the intricate stone carvings adorning the church. "But *your* church back in Olney, Mr. Pipes, is still my favorite."

"I do love our parish church," said Mr. Pipes, gazing upward at the row-upon-row of flying buttresses supporting the walls and heavy stone ceiling. "But, my dear, it is not my church, it is the Lord's. This church, though really not a church but an abbey—Westminster Abbey—is very important, indeed, to English history. Let's go inside and I'll explain why."

They passed through a massive Gothic door surrounded by sober, saintly-looking statues peering down on them.

"Oh, it's more lovely than I could have ever imagined," said Annie breathlessly, halting just inside the doorway. The nave was lined with dark-ribbed columns, looking more like a cluster of smaller columns than one single one, each holding up enormous Gothic arches shaped from lighter stone. Further up, smaller arches stood pointing to rows of stained glass windows, the light filtering through, illuminating delicate crisscrossing ribs supporting the highest ceiling Annie or Drew had ever seen. Light from rows of sparkling chandeliers reflected on paving stones worn smooth by the feet of centuries of worshipers.

Drew looked around at other visitors gazing about the great abbey; an occasional door shut with a thud that reechoed throughout the massive interior.

"Why does everyone look up in English churches?" asked Drew, almost losing his balance as he tried calculating the weight of the fan-vaulted ceiling.

"The Medieval designers of Gothic cathedrals," said Mr. Pipes, ushering them down the central aisle and past the ornate, gilded quire screen, "wanted everything about the building to point upwards. The narrow nave and magnificent one-hundred-and-three-foot-high, fan-vaulted ceiling compel our eyes, and with them our hearts, to God above—from whence all our blessings flow...."

"Ken! Thomas Ken, the fisherman!" said Drew.

"From the doxology, that's right," chimed in Annie. "Remember singing it around your organ last summer the day we arrived in Olney? I'll never forget that first day we met you, Mr. Pipes."

Mr. Pipes laughed softly. "Of course, I remember that day, my dear, and I'm so very glad you remember my little stories."

They moved down the south transept and into a side chamber surrounded with statues and monuments. Drew studied the many names carved into the paving stones at their feet.

"Who are all these guys?" asked Drew.

"Westminster Abbey is, in actuality, an enormous tomb," said Mr. Pipes. "Nearly all of our great men and kings and queens are buried here. The entire history of England could be told merely by walking through these sacred halls. Ah, yes, and this is the Poets' Corner, where many of our great writers are remembered."

"Great writers," said Annie, "like hymn writers?"

"No, my dear, I'm afraid that most of the hymn writers' bodies rest elsewhere," said Mr. Pipes, "though centuries after their death, their hymns continue to rise in this grand place."

Drew chewed the side of his mouth in thought. "Bunhill Fields had some of them," he said.

"Watts and Bunyan," said Annie, getting their names out before Drew.

"Yes," said Mr. Pipes. "Bunyan is commemorated in stained glass in the north transept—just over there." He pointed off to the left. "And at least three great hymn writers actually studied here at Westminster School—do you remember which ones?"

"Ah, let me see," said Annie. "'The bud may have a bitter taste, but sweet will be the flower'—Cowper—William Cowper!"

"Indeed," said Mr. Pipes with a smile.

"And Charles Wesley—I love his organ!" added Drew.

"Now let me see," said Dr. Dudley, pulling on his ear, his eyes searching the shadows above, "It's coming to me now. Yes, if my memory serves, was not Charles Wesley the King's

Scholar at Westminster School?" He looked smugly at Mr. Pipes. "And you thought I never listened to your stories."

"And didn't Augustus Toplady study here, too?" asked Drew.

"He did," replied Mr. Pipes.

"Say, how is *Toplady?*" Drew continued, referring to Mr. Pipes's little sailboat on which he and Annie learned to row, fish, and sail last summer.

"Oh, I'm afraid the other *Toplady* will be rather lonely with us away. Perhaps you, Martin, will keep her company with an occasional fishing or sailing excursion?"

"I beg your pardon, sir," said Dr. Dudley, "but I do not *do* boating—it simply is not the thing—why, man, people drown when boating, you see, and, I say, a considerable number don't live to tell about it either. Taking care of Lord Underfoot, your over-indulged cat, now that I can manage."

"That's quite all right, my friend," said Mr. Pipes. "*Toplady* is resting snugly on the staithe out of harm's way."

"You will be sure Lord Underfoot gets plenty of warm milk," said Annie. "He especially likes it in a tea saucer—and warm to the touch. Oh, Mr. Pipes, it must be awful leaving Lord Underfoot for the summer. Couldn't you bring him along?"

"No, I'm afraid that would never do with the various countries we will pass through," said Mr. Pipes. "Customs agents, curiously, don't appreciate tourists bearing all their household pets with them."

"Too bad," said Annie.

The sound of chattering voices and shuffling feet caught Drew's attention. Turning, he watched a procession of boys, some his own age, each wearing a suit, white shirt, and tie, filing through the gates into the quire, a sort of sub-chapel in front of the nave.

"What's going on?" he asked.

"It looks as if the students are assembling for a service," said Mr. Pipes.

A clergyman in a blue robe closed the gates after the last boy, and Mr. Pipes, Dr. Dudley, and the children crept closer to watch through the ornate lace-work of the gates.

Annie and Drew pressed their faces against the cold metal, watching the boys settle—some restlessly—into rows of elaborately carved wooden seats lining either side of the room. Gold-gilded spires rose above the seats, and brass candles with little red shades cast a warm glow on the boys' faces.

"I've never seen anything like it," said Drew in hushed tones.

"Like what?" whispered Annie.

Before Drew could reply, the rumbling of a pipe organ filled the sanctuary and rose beyond to the heraldic symbols adorning the vaulting above. He continued gazing back and forth at the rank-upon-rank of gilded pipes lining both sides above the seating in the quire.

"Ah, lovely," said Mr. Pipes, his face glowing as he listened to the organist play.

Drew shook his head in wonder. "It's huge!"

"Indeed," said Mr. Pipes. "Eight thousand pipes does make this one of the largest organs."

"He's playing another tune," said Annie. "Wait! It sounds like—"

The boys suddenly began singing with the organ, "Who would true valor see...."

"It's Bunyan!" cried Drew.

The singing continued: "No lion can him fright, he'll with a giant fight...." The boys' voices echoed off the high-vaulted ceiling; Annie desperately wanted to join them.

"Aren't these guys Anglicans?" asked Drew. "Why are they singing Bunyan's 'Pilgrim Hymn'? I mean, didn't Anglicans throw Mr. Bunyan in jail?"

"Indeed they did," said Mr. Pipes, smiling. "Ah, but nowhere is Christ's church so united as she is in her hymnal. It is glorious testimony to the power of 'psalms and hymns and spiritual songs,' which God calls us to raise to Him in worship, that the Christian church meets in her hymnal." He stooped and peeked through the gate again.

"Do you think they would mind if we joined them?" asked Annie, her eyes wide.

"Splendid idea!" said Mr. Pipes.

Inside the same ancient walls wherein long ago Wesley, Toplady, and Cowper sang, Annie and Drew joined Mr. Pipes, Dr. Dudley (who sang only after some considerable throat clearing), and the Westminster School boys in:

> Hobgoblin nor foul fiend
> Can daunt his spirit,
> He knows he at the end,
> Shall life inherit.
> Then fancies fly away,
> He'll fear not what men say,
> He'll labor night and day
> To be a Pilgrim.

The last chord faded into silence ... when suddenly they heard, from outside the abbey, Big Ben begin its ponderous gonging of the hour. Mr. Pipes glanced at his watch. "I say! We must away! We've a boat to catch in Dover in less than three hours!"

"An absolute—most dashed absolute—impossibility," said Dr. Dudley with a sniff and a hopeful glint in his eye. But he fell in behind the children as they scurried to keep up with Mr. Pipes.

How could someone be so old—Drew wondered, with a backward glance at the nave—and be so hard for a kid to keep up with?

He Who Would Valiant Be

Anyone who does not take his cross and follow me is not worthy of me. Matt. 10:38

1. Who would true val - our see; Let him come hi - ther
2. Who so be - set him round with dis - mal sto - ries
3. Hob gob - lin nor foul fiend can daunt his spi - rit

One here will con - stant be, Come wind come wea - ther.
do but them - selves con - found, his strength the more is;
he knows he at the end shall life in - he - rit.

There's no dis - cour - age - ment Shall make him once re - lent
No li - on can him fright, he'll with a gi - ant fight;
Then fan - cies fly a - way, he'll fear not what men say;

His first a - vow'd in - tent to be a pil - grim.
but he will have a right to be a pil - grim.
he'll la - bour night and day to be a pil - grim.

John Bunyan, *The Pilgrim's Progress*, 1678

ST. DUNSTAN'S 6.5.6.5.6.6.6.5.
Charles Winfred Douglas, 1917; alt. 1990

Chapter Two

Martin Luther
1483–1546

Thou comest in the darksome night
To make us children of the light ...
For this we tune our cheerful lays,
And shout our thanks in ceaseless praise!

After a hair-raising dash through the crowded streets of
London, Dr. Dudley, coaxed gently by Mr. Pipes to "do get on
with it, dear fellow," drove through the countryside. Seagulls
screeched and dipped overhead as the travelers arrived at the
pier in Dover only moments before their sea-going ferry slipped
her moorings for France.

Dr. Dudley stood forlorn on the quay, his face etched with
concern for their safety—well, for Mr. Pipes's safety. He called
after them, "Do be careful, old man. Many depend upon him,
dear children—" Had the wind not swept his words away they
might have heard him add, "—little blighters!" and then something about, "my most troublesome patient. So dashed inconsiderate of his own well being. Oh, why didn't I become a veterinary
surgeon?" The children felt pangs of regret as the large ferry
gained speed and Dr. Dudley's lone figure grew smaller.

Once around the protection of the stone breakwater guarding the harbor, the ferry seemed to shrink. The white cliffs grew
smaller behind them, and the rolling seas grew higher. The
waves, bursting into white on their tops, hissed irritably at the
intruding bow of the little ship.

Mr. Pipes leaned easily on the rail, his white hair twisting
and turning in the breeze. Drawing in a deep breath of salt
air, he sighed. "Ah, there is simply nothing to compare with
the briny main! And this wee stretch of water—The English

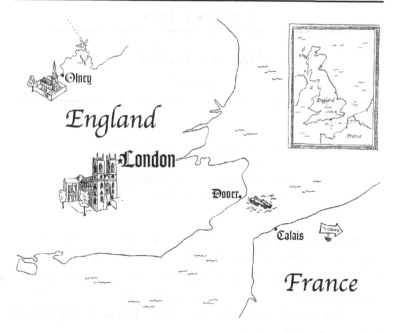

Channel—God placed here to protect our sceptered isle, our jewel set in the silver sea, from any who, envious of our kingdom, might pass this way to our harm." He seemed completely absorbed in the poetry of the moment. "She merely kicks up her heels a wee bit when foes might pass through her to our hurt—Ah, yes, few have had the stomach for her fury." He chuckled and took another deep breath of the sea air.

Annie said nothing. She looked at the gray water swirling below, the wind blowing the frothy tops from the seas, sending splashes of it onto her lips and tongue. The boat lurched under a large swell then dropped into an awaiting trough—then it happened all over again. Twist, roll, lurch, kur-thunk. Twist, roll, lurch, kur-thunk. From bow to stern, the entire boat shuddered in protest. Annie's knuckles turned white as she gripped the rail. A creeping, uneasy feeling rose in her throat.

Meanwhile, Drew had disappeared below decks in hopes of seeing the engine room. Oblivious to Annie's rising discomfort, Mr. Pipes continued. "Oh, the heady days of 1588 when God sent 'Protestant winds' raging over this our grand little moat and the—" His reminiscence was suddenly interrupted when a nearby oval-shaped steel door burst open, and Drew, a green tinge to his face, stumbled onto the deck.

"Oh, I say, my dears," said Mr. Pipes, looking from Annie to Drew. "How inconsiderate of me! I've failed to prepare you for one of England's greatest allies: *mal-de-mer*—the terror of the tummy, the dreaded seasickness. I'm so very sorry. But follow me; there's hope. We'll go amidships—the motion will be least there—and I have bottles of ginger beer." He hurried the staggering children inside. After drinking cautiously from bottles of the spicy liquid, Annie and Drew lay down on seat cushions and escaped from the rumbling nausea into a fitful sleep.

Awakened sometime later by the blast of the ship's horn as it entered the port of Calais, Annie sat up slowly and carefully. She never wanted to feel that way again. Drew lay on his stomach, his head propped on his chin, his jaw set and eyes squinting tightly closed as if sleep under these circumstances required enormous concentration. His left arm and clenched fist extended to the floor for balance. The horn blew again; Drew groaned.

"Is it over?" he asked, without opening his eyes.

"Though often a violent crossing," replied Mr. Pipes, "the passage to Calais, France, is a short one. We have arrived."

◈ ◈ ◈

The salt-sea air mingled now with the sweet smell of cut flowers and the savory aroma of roasting chestnuts. Their seasickness nearly forgotten, Annie and Drew, as if in a dream, gazed around at the bustling port city of Calais. Everything looked and sounded so strange. Drew at first thought it sounded like people spoke through their noses, but Annie thought it sounded like a tender, soft kind of music. To their amazement, Mr. Pipes suddenly started speaking just like the locals.

"Bonsoir, Monsieur," said Mr. Pipes to a uniformed gentleman standing on the pier. "Je voudrais une taxi, s'il vous plaît?"

By this time Annie and Drew felt so numb from jet lag and the aftereffect of seasickness that much of what they saw and heard that evening remained a blur. Mr. Pipes hired a taxi and took them straight to the train station. He had already booked a sleeper car on a train bound for Germany and soon had the children snugly tucked into their bunks. Amidst much hissing, whistle blowing, and general hubbub, the train lurched forward. The great steel wheels gathering speed on the iron rails had a hypnotic effect.

"Where are we going?" asked Annie with a yawn.

"Germany," replied Mr. Pipes. "Just when you awaken, all rested and refreshed in the morning, we'll be there and our adventures will begin. But for now you simply must go to sleep and rest. What a busy day you've had!"

He smiled; the children made no reply.

◈ ◈ ◈

Drew woke with a start to the screeching of brakes on the rails. The train stopped. Drew bolted out of his bunk, landing on the narrow aisle with a thump, and looked eagerly out at the sun-drenched railway platform.

"Oh, my, dear me," said Mr. Pipes, sitting up and groping for his glasses. He positioned them on his nose and looked at his watch. "Drew, what does the sign say on the station house?"

"I can't make it out for sure," said Drew from the window.

Mr. Pipes opened the compartment door and called to a porter, "Bitte, Wie heist dieser Ort?"

"Coburg. Beeilen Sie sich bitte!" came the crisp reply.

"Yeah, *Coburg Bahnhof*—or something like that," said Drew, stumbling over the German name for the railway station. "What else did he say?"

"This is our stop and we must hurry. We've overslept," said Mr. Pipes matter-of-factly. "Very well, then. Can't be helped. We'll just have to get ourselves off the train quickly. Annie, dear, I'm terribly sorry to rush you. And Drew, do let's not leave anything on the train this time. How do you get all of your luggage so scattered about, and in such a short time?"

Just as the whistle blew and the train lurched away from the platform, Annie, Drew (stuffing a pair of socks into his knapsack), and Mr. Pipes stepped off into the sunshine.

Mist drifted above the steep tile roofs of the ancient Saxon village.

"Everything's old," said Drew. "But not old in quite the same way as England."

"It reminds me of an old fairy tale," said Annie, a flush to her cheeks as she spun around taking it all in. "Couldn't you just see Hansel and Gretel walking hand in hand down this winding street? And the front of the houses with all that fancy carving and the little towers on the pointy part of the roofs makes them look like gingerbread cottages. It's all so beautiful."

"I wish they were made of gingerbread," said Drew, rubbing his stomach. "Or anything edible; I'm starved."

Drew thought the ancient buildings lining the narrow streets looked taller and more decorated with fancy trim than the stone cottages of Olney. Almost all of the houses were topped with dull red tile instead of the glassy slate roofs in Mr. Pipes's village.

"Check this out!" said Drew, gazing hungrily through the rippling glass circles of a restaurant window at a couple eating breakfast. The man halted mid-bite, his fork speared into a large bite of sausage, and scowled back at Drew.

"Drew!" said Annie. "It's not polite to stare—even when you are hungry. Yum, it does look good," she added, gazing at the golden bread and butter on the woman's plate.

"Come, my dears," said Mr. Pipes with a laugh. "Let's drop our bags at the hotel, have a bit of a wash, and find a nice place to dine for our breakfast. The hotel is just across the street."

He pointed to a large whitewashed building, crisscrossed with reddish brown timbers, its windows lined with bright red geraniums. A man wearing blue overalls and thick boots vigorously pushed a broom—swish, swish, thud; swish, swish, thud—before the black paneled double door, set deep into the thick-walled entrance.

"We get to stay here?" said Annie, admiring the tidy old building.

"Indeed, my dear, that is the plan," said Mr. Pipes, looking right before leading them across the narrow street.

Weary from their long journey, the travelers tidied up, ate their breakfast, strolled only briefly around the little village, then took a long nap in overstuffed—and very comfortable—beds.

⊠ ⊠ ⊠

"Is that a real castle?" asked Drew later in the afternoon as they paused in their walk at the edge of the village. "It sort of sprawls all over the hilltop," he went on, "and that tallest tower on the left looks more like it's topped with a giant knight's helmet—or maybe a huge metal onion. Come to think of it, the other two towers look almost like church steeples."

"Coburg Castle, built in the twelfth century," said Mr. Pipes, "suffered from fires, enemy sieges, and the ravages of time." He smiled, running his hand over his balding forehead and snowy white hair. "The irregular shape, though, actually makes the castle more difficult to conquer. But, follow me! We'll march up this grassy hillside, through that little wood, and take her by storm! Onward, noblest English!—I mean to say—English and American!"

The children laughed as they trotted to keep up. Dusky gray jackdaws scolded from tree branches, and several of the birds swooped mischievously near the threesome as they approached the wooded border around the castle.

"Can we go inside?" asked Drew in a husky whisper as they passed underneath a canopy of rustling leaves and neared the massive stone walls of the fortress.

"I've forgotten my timetable," said Mr. Pipes, pausing to look upward at the towering stone bower rising above them. "But we'll enter at the main gate and see."

"How could any army ever have broken into this place?" asked Drew. "If I were inside, I'd be shooting at us right now, and I bet the soldiers on that wall would have the upper hand."

"Indeed, they would," said Mr. Pipes. "What with bolts from crossbows raining from those ramparts, the odd boulder thrown in for variety, and your occasional cauldron of boiling oil showering down upon us. Yes, yes, I'd much prefer their position to ours."

"That sounds awful," said Annie, with a shudder.

"A true fortress, this is," said Mr. Pipes. "She has a long—hundreds of years—and quite successful history of protecting her occupants most jealously indeed."

Several tourists emerged from the labyrinth of the castle as Mr. Pipes tried getting the attention of a man sitting in the gatehouse wearing headphones, his head bobbing up and down as he read the newspaper.

"Guten tag," Mr. Pipes greeted the man. "Wann schliest es, bitte?"

The man looked up irritably, pulled one of the headphones away from his ear, said something that sounded like, "Ja, ja. Beeilen Sie sich," and waved them impatiently toward a rough stone walkway. They passed under an arch leading through the massive wall and into the sprawling fortress courtyard. It seemed strangely deserted.

"We don't have much time, I fear," said Mr. Pipes. "So follow me to the north side of this massive stone building." It took some concentration to walk on the large stone pavement. Mr. Pipes led them through an open doorway and up a narrow staircase. Their steps echoed against the ancient walls of the winding stairway as they climbed round and round, and higher and higher up the castle bower.

"Whew!" said Mr. Pipes, wiping his brow as they left the stairway and entered a large room. Late afternoon sunlight shone warmly through the rippled glass of the narrow windows, casting long shadows on the polished timbers of the floor.

"It's like someone's bedroom," said Annie. "Everything is so—so massive. I love this writing desk, and look at the carved legs on that bed. And that fireplace looks tall enough to stand up in."

"Walk-in fireplace, huh?" said Drew, poking his head up into the chimney. "I can see some light at the top of the chimney," he went on, his voice sounding hollow.

"And these blankets hanging on the walls," said Annie. "They have people, horses, dogs, and castles sewn right into them. What a place! Oh, I could get used to this room."

"They're called tapestries," explained Mr. Pipes. "Castles do have a certain charm to them, but I'm afraid they were not the easiest places in which to live. During the winter and at night time they could be dreadfully damp and cold—these lovely woven wall hangings served as a kind of insulation to help keep the chill off. Naturally, the big fireplace helped, too."

Drew had been silently looking around the room and out the narrow windows. "Check out this armor—it's the full suit—and it's holding a real battle-ax. Looks like there might even be a guy inside it."

"Oh, Drew," said Annie, "don't even say things like that."

"Mr. Pipes," said Drew, cautiously testing with his thumb the sharpness of a sword hung on the wall next to the bed, "somebody important must have lived here or you wouldn't have brought us. Who was it?"

Before Mr. Pipes could answer, Annie called from a window, "Look at this view! Whoever lived here had a great view of those mountains and the forest leading to them. I love how the light plays on those shiny leaves."

"It is a lovely spot," said Mr. Pipes. "Drew, you're right. Someone very important did live here for a short time. Do you remember whom Charles Wesley met on the ship to America?"

"Sure," said Drew. "It was some German Christians who sang hymns all the time."

"That's right," said Mr. Pipes.

"And you said the German Christians had been singing hymns for over two hundred years," said Annie, smiling at her brother, "*remember*, Drew?"

"I didn't really think those *same* Christians lived for two hundred years," said Drew, his cheeks flushing.

"Of course, you didn't," said Mr. Pipes. "The leaders of the Protestant Reformation brought the singing of hymns back to Christian worship. And no one man could be more credited with starting the Reformation than Martin Luther."

"So this was Martin Luther's room?" asked Annie, running her hand over the hand-stitched cushion on a trunk at the foot of the massive bed. "Is this his bed—I mean did he actually sleep in it?"

"As far as I know, it is," said Mr. Pipes, glancing uneasily at his watch. "Oh, I do wish we had more time to see it all, and I simply must tell you his story. But it grows late. We must be going."

Annie and Drew reluctantly followed Mr. Pipes to the winding stairway for the long descent to the courtyard below.

"I wish we could stay," Annie's voice sounded hollow against the stone walls.

"Where is everyone?" asked Drew, peering through a narrow opening at the vacant castle ground below. "Hey! There's that guy who was sitting at the gatehouse—he's carrying a huge ring of keys and still wearing his headphones—but I don't see anybody else around."

The uniformed gatekeeper suddenly shook the key ring, spun around, and skipped on one foot backwards across the cobbled castle yard. He threw his head back and sang the way someone sings when no one else is around. It sounded something like, "Darf ich Sie morgen wiedersehen?" He shook the key ring throughout—even throwing it into the air, spinning around, and catching it behind his back—singing louder as he strutted and stomped toward them.

"Can you believe it!" said Drew, about to burst with laughter. Annie crammed her head next to Drew's at the window. Mr. Pipes couldn't help himself—though he tried holding it back—and burst into laughter with the children until tears came to their eyes.

"I say," said Mr. Pipes, "he is having quite a foot rollick."

The dancing German disappeared out of sight directly below them.

"He doesn't know we're watching," said Drew, holding his stomach and wiping his eyes.

"Yeah," said Annie, "he thinks he's alone."

"Indeed, he does, poor chap," said Mr. Pipes. He suddenly grew very serious. "I say, there's the rub. We must hurry. He's forgotten we're inside, and he's locking the castle for the night!"

The patter of their racing feet on the stone steps was suddenly interrupted by an ominous groan as the door turned on its ancient hinges. A loud clang came from directly below. The keys rattled; a pause followed. Then came a decisive "click" as the key turned in the lock.

"He's shut the door to the tower," said Mr. Pipes, halting abruptly. "Quickly, back to the little opening. We'll try to get his attention."

They turned and raced back up the stairs to the window.

"Helfen Sie mir, bitte!" called Mr. Pipes.

"Help! Wait! Don't leave us!" called Annie and Drew, their heads together as they strained to be heard through the little opening. The gatekeeper didn't seem to hear as he spun and sang his way toward the outer gate of the castle.

"Why doesn't he stop?" asked Annie, almost in tears as she watched the man moon-walk toward the exit.

"It's the headphones," said Drew quietly. "You miss a lot wearing those things."

The clanging of the outer gate of the castle echoed decisively across the courtyard. Then, a mysterious silence hung over the ancient fortress. Annie bit her lower lip. No one spoke for several minutes.

"Well, then, my dears," said Mr. Pipes at last. "It looks like we may be spending the night where Luther slept."

◈ ◈ ◈

Back in Luther's room, the streaks of light from the narrow windows cast longer paths of fading light across the polished timbers of the floor.

"Now, then," said Mr. Pipes, sorting the contents of his knapsack on the stout table in front of the fireplace. "We must evaluate our position. Annie, Drew, open your knapsacks and let us determine just what is at our disposal for making a meal. Ah, here are three chocolate bars—"

"—That's a good start!" said Drew, digging in his knapsack.

"—an apple, one bottle of mineral water, and two tins of sardines. Not a great deal—and no tea—however, better than nothing at all," concluded Mr. Pipes.

"And I have a package of crackers," said Annie. "That should help."

"What's in this?" asked Drew, picking up a plain package from the contents of Mr. Pipes's knapsack.

"Oh, that is the wee kit Dr. Dudley insisted I keep with me at all times," said Mr. Pipes. "I don't suppose it has any food in it, but let's open it and see."

A letter inside insisted, in rather irritated terms, that Mr. Pipes get plenty of rest, take his medicine faithfully, and avoid exposure to excessive sunlight. They found bandages, antiseptic, aspirin, sunscreen, a box of matches, a fat candle—"With all these candles about the castle, we'll save Dr. Dudley's candle for another time," said Mr. Pipes. "And what have we here?" He held up a small package. Sniffing the package, he exhaled a satisfied "Ahhh," and with a little smile opened it carefully.

"Three tea bags?" said Annie and Drew together.

"Earl Gray, no less. Bless you, my good doctor," said Mr. Pipes, closing his eyes and breathing in the spicy aroma. "It is not loose-leaf; nevertheless, things are looking much brighter, my dears. Now let's do our best to make tea and have our supper."

"There's wood in the fireplace," said Drew.

"And we can boil water in this old kettle," said Annie, lifting it off its hook and wiping the inside with a clean handkerchief. "Luther's kettle!"

Bustling about their castle, Drew and Mr. Pipes started a fire while Annie lit candles and arranged their evening meal on the thick planks of the ancient table. A warm glow soon came

from the old fireplace, the dry wood crackling merrily as the
last daylight faded over the Thuringian Forest outside.

"This is downright cheery," said Annie.

"What could be better!" said Drew. "We're actually going to
spend the night in a real castle."

After Mr. Pipes gave thanks to God for the meal, he said,
"Now, eat slowly. We must beguile our stomachs into thinking
there's more to eat than there actually is. Annie, let me help you
open that sardine tin, my dear."

Annie felt a wave of nausea as Mr. Pipes wound the key
around the flat container. A fishy smell spread throughout the
room.

"Oh, my dear," said Mr. Pipes, looking from the sardines,
laid snugly head to tail in a bed of oil, to Annie's pale face, "are
you well, my dear? I say, perhaps you're not accustomed to
tinned fish. They're really quite lovely, and you must eat something. Oh, how very unfortunate. I do wish I had something
else to offer you, Annie."

They looked anything but "lovely" to Annie.

"Here, my dear, try one between two of your crackers," said
Mr. Pipes. "Best way to embark on a new delicacy. Yes, yes. Put
one between crackers."

"The poor things," said Annie. "Couldn't they have at least
waited until they grew up? And, look," she continued with a
shudder, "they were in such a hurry they didn't even take time
to remove the skin."

"Try 'em, Annie," said Drew, his mouth stuffed with
cracker and sardine. "They really are great." He held another
slimy little fish by the tail and plopped it into his mouth.

"Water's boiling," said Annie, jumping up and carefully
removing the pot from over the fire. "How about if I make tea.
I think a cup of tea with—with just crackers—sounds delicious."

◈ ◈ ◈

"We will have considerable explaining to do come morning," said Mr. Pipes, with a chuckle, after they cleared away

the remains of their meager meal. With a sigh of satisfaction he settled comfortably into a chair in front of the fire. Annie wriggled into an old quilt on the floor, and Drew straddled a footstool and gazed into the crackling flames.

"So Martin Luther actually lived here?" said Drew, slowly chewing the last bit of his chocolate bar.

"For several months, yes," said Mr. Pipes. "And thirty well-armed soldiers stood guard to protect him."

"Did one of them use that suit of armor?" asked Drew, watching flickers of light play on the shadows surrounding the standing armor. He imagined a real knight behind the visor ready to defend Martin Luther with his life. "The sword and battle-ax might have been one of theirs, too," he concluded with enthusiasm.

"Wouldn't know about that," said Mr. Pipes. "Though you may very well be correct."

"Why was he so important?" asked Annie.

"Yeah, armed guards and all," said Drew. "He must have been some big shot."

"He certainly didn't start out his life as one," replied Mr. Pipes with a chuckle. "Luther was born in 1483 to peasant stock—the working class. Enormous changes, however, were afoot in the world, and nowhere would those changes affect Martin Luther so profoundly as in his education. Only a few years before Luther was born, a chap by the name of Johann Gutenberg converted a winepress into the first European printing press. The rebirth of interest in books and learning was underway with a vengeance." Mr. Pipes swallowed the last of his tea, frowned into the empty mug, and continued.

"After completing his Master of Arts degree, and while walking home to see his family, Luther found himself caught in a violent thunderstorm. The thunder rumbled angrily, and bolts of lightning flashed terrifyingly close to Martin. He fell to the ground, certain that God would strike him, and cried, 'St. Anne, help me! I will become a monk.' His father wanted Martin to make lots of money as a lawyer and disapproved when he kept his vow and entered the Augustinian cloister at Erfurt. There, Luther embarked on a quest to cleanse himself from his sins by all the good works the Roman Catholic Church demanded. Martin later said, 'I was a good monk.... If ever a monk got to heaven by his monkery it was I. If I had kept on any longer, I should have killed myself with vigils, prayers, reading, and other works.' Sometimes he fasted without a crumb for days on end and even lay in his icy cold, monkish cell all night without blankets—all futile efforts to rid himself of his many sins."

Drew's stomach growled and Annie shivered under her quilt.

"He sure understood how sinful he was," said Annie. "But it sounds like he didn't understand the word 'grace.'"

"That's right, I think," said Mr. Pipes. "He never could balance the ledger; the sin column seemed to grow longer the more good works he performed. He neared despair and came to feel that God hated him and would never forgive his sins.

"His confessor at Erfurt, wanting to help Luther find peace with God, sent him to teach theology at the new university in Wittenberg. While teaching through the Psalms, Luther read Psalm 22:1, 'My God, my God, why hast thou forsaken me?' These words, which Christ later cried while dying on the cross, puzzled Luther. *He* felt forsaken by God for *his* sins, but why would sinless Jesus feel forsaken by God? Finishing his lectures through the Psalms, Luther began studying Paul's epistle to the Romans. There, God opened the eyes of his faith. In Romans 1:17 Luther stopped at the words, 'the just shall live by faith.' Understanding came like a flood: man is made righteous not by good works but by faith in God's righteousness, and that faith is not man's work but God's gift. Luther wrote, 'Thereupon I felt myself to be reborn and to have gone through open doors into paradise.' Once the truth of the gospel seized on Luther, he suddenly looked around at the corrupt Roman Catholic Church and could not keep silent about her errors. The pope in Rome loved luxury and worldly pleasures and taught that salvation could be bought with money!—especially if it went to support St. Peter's, his new church building project.

"Outside the borders of Wittenberg, a monk named Johann Tetzel sold papal indulgences, assuring poor peasants that, 'as soon as the coin in the coffer rings, the soul from purgatory springs.' Pope Leo X promised, in writing, that anyone who purchased a certificate of indulgence would relieve the suffering of some loved one in purgatory. Soon people purchased the indulgences, believing they could now sin without repentance. From studying his Bible, Luther knew that indulgences could do nothing to take away sin; moreover, indulgences gave sinners a false security and encouraged further sinning. He sharpened his feather pen and drafted Ninety-five Theses, detailing his biblical objections to this practice. On October 31, 1517, Luther—hammer in hand—marched to the Castle Church and nailed his challenge to the door. After a public debate, wherein Luther was denounced, Luther's views came to the attention of the pope. Eventually, the Holy Roman Emperor, in league with the pope, ordered Luther to the imperial Diet of Worms—"

"—A diet of *worms?*" asked Annie with a grimace. "Why were people so cruel in those days? I'd actually rather eat sardines than worms."

"Let me get this straight," said Drew. "They made the poor guy eat worms?"

Laughing, Mr. Pipes held up his hands for them to stop. "Worms is a city—not too far from here—and a diet was something like a trial. Luther was called to a trial before Charles V, the Emperor, in the city of Worms."

"I'm glad I'm not from a city named Worms," said Annie.

"Might have good fishing bait in a place with a name like that," said Drew. "But, what did the emperor do to Luther?"

"He demanded that Luther recant everything he had taught against the pope and the church," said Mr. Pipes.

"Or what?" asked Drew.

"They would declare Luther a heretic," said Mr. Pipes. "And he would be condemned to death."

"W—what kind of death?" asked Annie.

"Well, burning at the stake was popular then—," said Mr. Pipes, "—alive."

"So, what did Mr. Luther say?" asked Drew.

"Wondering how he could be right and everyone else wrong, he asked to think about it for the night," said Mr. Pipes. "Then, next day he stood boldly before the emperor and the hostile Roman Catholic clergy and declared, 'Unless I am convinced by Scripture and plain reason—I do not accept the authority of popes and councils, for they have contradicted each other—my conscience is captive to the Word of God. I cannot and will not recant anything, for to go against conscience is neither right nor safe. God help me. Here I stand, I cannot do otherwise. Amen.' Luther threw up his arms like a knight who has triumphed over his enemy and slipped from the great hall to his room."

"Bravo, Luther!" said Drew. "Man, I wish I had been there."

"Me, too," said Annie. "What happened next?"

"Too popular among the German people for the emperor to execute, he allowed Luther to leave for his home in Wittenberg. His followers, however, feared the Catholics might try to kill Luther, so the Duke of Saxony arranged for armed knights to 'capture' Luther and take him to the Wartburg Castle for safekeeping. They played hostile abductors well, cursing and wrestling Luther to the ground. Then, leading him on horseback through the dense forest, they deposited him in what would be his 'dungeon' for an entire year. Though not happy about his exile, Luther made good use of it, writing letters, pamphlets, a German catechism, and translating the New Testament into German. Not at all bad for a year's work!

"When released, Luther set about reforming the order of church worship. Luther replaced his priestly robe with a plain black gown, and conducted the service facing the congregation while speaking in German instead of Latin (which few of the common folks had ever understood). He made preaching from the German Bible the central feature of the worship service, and taught the people to sing hymns both in church and in their homes. It is said that Luther gave the German people the Bible so that God might speak directly to them in His Word, and he gave them the hymnbook so that they might answer Him in their songs.

"Luther loved music and said, 'Next after theology I give to music the highest place and the greatest honor.... Next to the Word of God, only music deserves to be extolled as the mistress and governess of the feelings of the human heart. We know that the devil's music is distasteful and insufferable. My heart bubbles up and overflows in response to music.' He sometimes used rather strong language to make his point: after describing the 'perfect wisdom of God in His wonderful work of music,' Luther declared that 'He who does not find [music] an inexpressible miracle of the Lord is truly a clod and is not worthy to be considered a man.'"

"That's telling them!" said Drew.

"Luther, I dare say, always spoke his mind," said Mr. Pipes, crossing his legs and clasping his hands around his knee before continuing. "Called by some 'the nightingale of Wittenberg' for his own skillful singing, Luther wrote thirty-seven hymns and even wrote the musical score for some of the poetry. He played beautifully on the lute and may have plucked out his tunes on catgut strings, pausing between phrases to write them down on paper."

"What's a lute?" asked Drew.

"*Catgut* strings?" questioned Annie. "You don't really mean they used some poor cat's insides for the strings? What if it was Lord Underfoot's?"

Mr. Pipes chuckled. "M'Lord's insides would never do— entirely too unyielding. No, I dare say, it would require a considerably more compliant cat for good lute strings." He rose from his chair in front of the fireplace and reached for a lute hanging against the wall. "This is very like Luther's lute, no doubt," he said, gently fingering the double rows of strings on the wide neck of the instrument. "I say, she's no museum piece; she's fit to play," he said, cocking his head to one side, listening to each string as he twisted the tuning screws.

"It looks like a giant pear—well, half a pear," said Annie, scooting closer to Mr. Pipes, her curiosity overcoming her revulsion at the origin of the strings.

"Please, Annie," said Drew. "You'll make me hungrier. Can you play it, Mr. Pipes?" he asked, pulling his stool closer.

"I might be able to coax a wee tune out of her," said Mr. Pipes, sitting in his chair, the lute resting on his knee. As he plucked, the castle room filled with mellow strains that made Annie and Drew feel transported back in time. "Some historians suggest that Luther wrote his finest hymn right in these walls, perhaps in this very room. It's all about castles, mortal combat, powerful enemies, and great triumphs—but not physical ones. We know for certain that during his stay in this fortress, he often sang in his private devotions the hymn that became the battle hymn of the Reformation."

"What's the hymn?" asked Annie, eagerly.

Mr. Pipes paused for a moment, looking at the beamed ceiling while fingering the strings until he found the right key. "I'll do my best to teach it to you. Listen to the tune; I'll sing the grand words through, then you join me. It goes like this:

A mighty Fortress is our God,
A Bulwark never failing;
Our Helper He amid the flood
Of mortal ills prevailing.
For still our ancient foe
Doth seek to work us woe;
His craft and pow'r are great;
And armed with cruel hate,
On earth is not his equal.

Did we in our own strength confide,
Our striving would be losing;
Were not the right Man on our side,
The Man of God's own choosing.
Dost ask who that may be?
Christ Jesus it is He,

Lord Sabaoth His Name,
From age to age the same,
And He must win the battle.

And though this world, with devils filled,
Should threaten to undo us,
We will not fear, for God hath willed
His truth to triumph through us.
The prince of darkness grim,
We tremble not for him;
His rage we can endure,
For lo! his doom is sure;
One little word shall fell him.

That Word above all earthly powers,
No thanks to them, abideth;
The Spirit and the gifts are ours
Through Him who with us sideth;
Let goods and kindred go,
This mortal life also;
The body they may kill:
God's truth abideth still;
His kingdom is for ever.

After listening to Mr. Pipes's clear voice, and his energetic playing on the lute, they sang the ancient hymn through with him. After a pause, they sang it through again.

The fire hissed as they fell silent. Suddenly Drew, with a set to his jaw, leaped up, grabbed the battle-ax out of the hands of the empty armor, and—swinging it wildly around—jumped up on the table. "I defy that ancient foe—look out, Buck-o; your doom is sure! I'd have fought for God's truth," another swipe of the battle-ax, "I'd have been on his side. Let's sing it again; I'd— I'd shed every drop of blood in my veins for Christ's kingdom!" After a last flourish of the battle-ax, he abruptly stopped; his face grew crimson.

Mr. Pipes raised his eyebrows and smiled. "Many did, my boy. The Protestants not only sang this hymn in worship, more than one battle—real battles with sword and battle-ax—began with several thousand men singing these very words—'His kingdom is forever; we must win the battle!' But, Drew, your battles are no less real. In some ways it was easier in Luther's day when the enemies of God's truth jeered from across the battlefield. But the devil still seeks whom he may devour, and only those who confide their strength in Jesus Christ—the Word above all earthly powers, the mighty Fortress—only through His strength can we defeat the enemies of our souls."

"I love the poetry in our—I can say our, can't I?—our English hymns," said Annie, gazing into the fire. "But there is a—a—strength to Luther's poetry—like no other."

"Yeah," said Drew, "I sure see why they called it a battle hymn."

"Yes," said Mr. Pipes. "Of course, these hymns are for all the church—'from age to age the same.' And as members of Christ's church you must add Luther's hymn to the collection that you claim as your own—his is among the best."

Annie and Drew listened as Mr. Pipes softly played variations on Luther's tune. How amazing, thought Drew, watching Mr. Pipes's fingers skillfully press the strings against the neck of the lute. Luther might have done the same thing in this same room nearly 500 years ago.

"Luther's hymns," Mr. Pipes went on, "played such an important role in the Reformation that one Catholic priest later complained, 'the hymns of Luther killed more souls than his sermons.'"

"He had it all wrong," said Drew. "I bet God used the hymns to save souls—I know He did for us."

"I think you are right, Drew," said Mr. Pipes, strumming a final chord on the lute for emphasis. "Now, we must be off to bed—well, at least Annie will have a bed, Luther's bed."

"I'll take the floor," said Drew. "Mr. Pipes, you can have the cushioned bench—"

"—And my quilt," said Annie. "The bed has plenty of blankets."

"Good night, my dears," said Mr. Pipes, when they'd settled. "It may not be the most comfortable sleeping arrangement, but I'd venture to say we're the first to sleep in this room in—in perhaps several hundred years!"

All Praise to Thee, Eternal Lord

You know the grace of our Lord Jesus Christ, that though he was rich, yet for your sakes he became poor. 2 Cor. 8:9

1. All praise to thee, e - ter - nal Lord, clothed in a garb of flesh and blood; choos - ing a man - ger for thy throne, while worlds on worlds are thine a - lone.

2. Once did the skies be - fore thee bow; a vir - gin's arms con - tain thee now: an - gels who did in thee re - joice now lis - ten for thine in - fant voice.

3. A lit - tle child, thou art our guest, that wea - ry ones in thee may rest; for - lorn and low - ly is thy birth, that we may rise to heav'n from earth.

4. Thou com - est in the dark - some night to make us chil - dren of the light, to make us, in the realms di - vine, like thine own an - gels round thee shine.

5. All this for us thy love hath done; by this to thee our love is won: for this we tune our cheer - ful lays, and shout our thanks in cease - less praise.

Martin Luther, 1524
Tr. in *Sabbath Hymn Book*, 1858

CANONBURY L.M.
Robert Schumann, 1839; arr.

A Mighty Fortress Is Our God

God is our refuge and strength, an ever-present help in trouble. Ps. 46:1

Based on Psalm 46
Martin Luther, 1529
Tr. by Frederick H. Hedge, 1853

EIN' FESTE BURG 8.7.8.7.6.6.6.6.7.
Martin Luther, 1529

Chapter Three

Philipp Nicolai
1556–1608

Nor eye hath seen, nor ear
Hath yet attained to hear
What there is ours;
But we rejoice, and sing to Thee
Our hymn of joy eternally.

Two days later, Mr. Pipes and Annie and Drew rode the train to Wittenberg. As they zoomed past fields of munching cattle, Drew suddenly slapped his knee and burst into laughter. "I'll never forget the look on that poor guy's face in the morning when he opened the door of the castle and saw us."

"I'll never forget sleeping in Luther's castle," said Annie.

"Nor will I, my dears," said Mr. Pipes, wincing as he rubbed his neck. "But just now, I find most memorable the glorious sleep we enjoyed last night in the comfort of our rooms at the guest house. Castles, I still maintain, are not—nor, indeed, ever have been—the most comfortable places in which to sleep."

"It seemed wonderfully comfortable to me," said Annie. "Except the sardines."

"Yeah, that's because you got Mr. Luther's bed!" said Drew. "That was all great, but the feast we had for breakfast at the Royal Sausage, now that was unforgettable!"

"What about the hymn?" asked Annie. "I love Luther's hymn. But, Mr. Pipes, you didn't tell us anything about his family. Did Luther have a wife and kids?"

"You must remember," said Mr. Pipes, "Roman Catholic priests are forbidden to marry."

"So he didn't have a family," said Annie with a frown.

"Ah, but he did," said Mr. Pipes. "You see, the more Luther studied his Bible, the more he came to preach against the many errors of the Roman Church. Forbidding marriage to her priests was one of them. In response to his preaching, Luther watched many monks and nuns leave their cloisters and join hands as Christian husbands and wives. Luther looked on and smiled, but had absolutely no intention of marrying himself. He even declared, 'They won't give me a wife.' In truth, Luther feared at any moment he might be arrested and executed as a heretic. To him, it made no sense to marry one day and leave his wife a widow the next.

"Then, Luther heard of several nuns in a nearby cloister who feared the wrath of the abbess if they tried escaping. He secured the help of a merchant friend of his who often delivered large barrels of herring to the nunnery."

"Is herring anything like sardines?" asked Drew, looking sideways at his sister.

"Very like," said Mr. Pipes. "Though, most generally eaten pickled instead of tinned."

Annie, humming Luther's hymn, steadied herself by looking intently out the window of the train. "Lovely freeways they have in Germany," she said casually.

"*Autobahn*, they're called, my dear," said Mr. Pipes. "Yes, well, the night before Easter, 1523, Luther's friend bundled twelve nuns into his wagon—some may have hidden in the herring barrels—and delivered them to Mr. Luther's doorstep."

"Poor ladies," said Annie. "Imagine the smell!"

"Poor Luther!" said Drew.

"It did pose a bit of a problem," said Mr. Pipes with a chuckle, "for both parties. Luther played matchmaker for all who wanted husbands, and saw them happily married—all except one, Katherine von Bora. Two years passed, but no amount of letter writing and introductions could yield a match that was suitable to her taste. After one particularly disastrous effort to match her with quite an elderly chap, she laughingly refused by saying she'd rather marry Luther himself than the man he'd suggested. He jokingly told his parents about his predicament, and they encouraged *him* to marry Katherine. This got Luther thinking. Bold as ever, Luther proposed marriage, announced his engagement—'to spite the pope'—and married his beloved Katherine. All in a few weeks' time! He declared, 'the gifts of God must be taken on the wing.'"

"Oh, I love this story," said Annie. "Please, go on."

Drew rolled his eyes.

"Luther had lots to get used to when he married," continued Mr. Pipes. "'One wakes up in the morning,' he once said, 'and finds a pair of pigtails on the pillow which were not there before.'"

"I like his Katherine," said Annie, winding one of her pigtails around her finger.

"They lived together in the Augustinian Cloister at Wittenberg, and God blessed them—" Mr. Pipes broke off and gazed out the window, the sparkle in his eyes dimmed, but only for a moment. "—I say, God blessed them with six darling children. Katherine busied herself reading her Bible, raising the children, and caring for the pigs, the garden, and the fish pond."

"Fish pond!" cried Drew. "The Luthers had a fish pond? What kind of fish? Did they use lures or bait—what kind of bait—worms? Where is it? Can we fish there?"

"Whoa! My boy," said Mr. Pipes, laughing. "It's no longer in use for fishing, but Mrs. Luther used a net to harvest—let me see—I believe it was trout, carp, pike, and perch."

"Pike's the best," said Drew.

Mr. Pipes smiled—recollecting how Drew's thirty-pound pike pulled him into the river last summer—and said, "But I doubt Mrs. Luther caught her pike using quite your method, my dear boy."

They laughed together as the train slowed and halted at the *bahnhof* in the city of Wittenberg.

"So this is where Luther nailed his Ninety-five Theses," said Drew, frowning at the bronze double doors of the Castle Church. "Where's the nail hole?"

"Oh, I'm afraid you'll not find the nail hole," replied Mr. Pipes. "In the mid-seventeen hundreds, during the Seven Years' War—I believe you Americans called it, The French and Indian War—the original church and doors were destroyed by fire. These lovely doors, inscribed with Luther's theses, are quite modern—built 1858, I believe it was."

"That's modern?" laughed Drew.

Mr. Pipes showed Annie and Drew Martin Luther's grave, then where Mrs. Luther rests nearby in the oldest building in the town, St. Mary's Church, where her husband preferred preaching. They ate lunch in Market Square under the shadow of the ancient church and Luther's statue.

Suddenly, Annie stopped chewing, swallowed hard, and hissed, "That man with the sunglasses and newspaper, leaning against Luther's statue—I—I've seen him before."

"Annie, there's thousands of tourists in Germany," said Drew, with a snort. "He's just taking in the Luther sights—like we are. Of course, you've seen him before."

"He's clearly dressed like a foreigner—the overcoat looks to be made in London. If it weren't for the American-looking cap, I'd imagine he's English," said Mr. Pipes. "Drew is probably correct, Annie, dear. Nothing at all to fear, I'm sure. Finish your *mittagessen*—lunch, that is—and we'll run along to Luther's house."

After wandering down narrow, cobbled streets and through a massive archway, they arrived at *Lutherhalle*. Drew gazed up at the central tower capped with a bronze dome.

"Look at those windows," he said. "All cockeyed and slant-ing. I wonder—wait! I'll bet there's one of those corkscrewing stairs inside the tower. The builder just set the windows at the angle of the stairs. Clever guy."

Inside Luther's home they wandered through the largest Reformation museum in the world. Mr. Pipes showed them Luther's favorite pulpit; his robe; a copy of his German transla-tion of the Bible; the massive table around which Luther and Katherine entertained many guests and where Luther gave his

famous table talks; and an early hymnal in which the immortal
battle hymn, "A Mighty Fortress," appeared.

"'We lack poets!' Luther once bemoaned," said Mr. Pipes,
pausing before the hymnal. "But by his example, Luther
encouraged generations of Lutheran minister poets to continue
adding to his hymns. His words, indeed, ring true today. How
goes your writing, Annie? And Drew, have you taken my advice
about writing in a wee notebook? I'll tell you what," he continued, guiding them to the exit. "It grows late. Show me what
you've written over supper; then we'll get our rest. Tomorrow
we're off to Erfurt where I shall tell you of the next great German hymn writer who rose at Luther's call for poets."

After dinner in the café in Luther's cellar, Mr. Pipes
adjusted his glasses on his nose and cleared his throat. After
reading a sample of Annie's latest poetry, he said:

"Yes, yes, promising, promising, indeed. But Annie, one
must remember to find the *best* word, not just one that rhymes.
Now then, Drew, what have you written, my boy?"

Drew looked at a page of his notebook and scrunched up
his face. "I kind of wrote this one about—well, about how I
used to think, you know, about things. It's not so good."

"Let us have a look," said Mr. Pipes. He read silently:

> Away with all that's gray and old;
> Begone, all past outdated mold.
> From our own minds we will be told!
> The view from now is good enough;
> Away with all this vile old stuff!

"I didn't mean you, Mr. Pipes," said Drew, squirming in his
seat, "really, I didn't. And, honestly, I don't think that way—not
anymore."

"Of course, you don't, my boy," said Mr. Pipes, smiling
broadly. "You've employed the poetic device called satire—cor-
rective ridicule. Fine work and effective in small doses. However, my dear fellow, poetry used for its highest purpose—the
worship of God—must *adorn* truth and beauty. I'm not so sure

satire does that best." He returned their books, refolded his napkin, and rose from the table. "I am, however, very pleased with both of your efforts; do carry on. Remember, model the great hymn writers, my dears, and find your inspiration where they did—in God's Holy Word."

The bouncing lilt of an accordion broke the stillness of the evening as the threesome strolled from Luther's house to Duke Frederick's palace, where they found their beds at the youth hostel and fell asleep.

◈ ◈ ◈

Dark clouds threatened rain the next morning as they caught the train to Erfurt. When they arrived—though rain fell in earnest—Mr. Pipes insisted that they go for a walk outside of town.

Annie and Drew, their shoes splooshing along in the mud, followed Mr. Pipes down the boggy track. Annie loved the steady beating of the rain on her umbrella.

"It was quite near here," shouted Mr. Pipes over the pelting of the summer rainsquall. "I say, it was on this very road to Erfurt in 1505 that a bolt of lightning crashed from the heavens, nearly striking Luther. Then and there, the terrified young man vowed to be a monk."

Annie and Drew looked up at the massive gray and black clouds bearing down on them.

"Let's get out of here!" yelled Annie.

"Indeed, we must," called Mr. Pipes. "Let's move on to Luther's cloister. It's not at all far from here, and it will be nice and dry."

"Does this mean no fishing today?" asked Drew, as they hurried toward the ancient stone monastery.

◈ ◈ ◈

"Two weeks later," said Mr. Pipes, his now-hushed voice echoing along the stone corridor of the Augustinian cloister surrounding a central garden, "Martin, the bright, young scholar who had just completed his graduate degree at the University of Erfurt, in fulfillment of his vow, presented himself here."

"So, all this was around in 1505?" asked Drew, raindrops splashing on the hand he extended through one of the many windowless Gothic arches opening onto the garden.

"And long before," replied Mr. Pipes. "Just across the garden, you see the window to Martin's cell where he anguished over his sins."

Annie gazed through the rain and mist at the window to Luther's room, looking out of the jumbled black stone walls. "Isn't it something that we're right here," she said, "walking on the same stones that Luther walked on, seeing this place where he lived—and prayed?" They strolled around the cloister for a better view. They gazed up at stone statues lining the passageway leading into the nave of the monastery church. Annie thought the eerie shadows playing on the pained expressions of the ancient images made the faces seem to move. She quickened her step.

"Luther was ordained a priest in 1507," continued Mr. Pipes, "in the Augustinian Church. And he celebrated in these walls— with much fear and trepidation—his first mass. Later, he taught at the monastery and at Erfurt University. Then, off he went to the University of Wittenberg, and you know the rest of the story."

The rain slowed to a drizzle as the children followed Mr. Pipes through the ancient town of tile-roofed houses; covered balconies; half-timbered, whitewashed buildings; and the breathtaking Cathedral Church.

"Hey!" said Drew, halting abruptly as the street ended at an iron railing. "They've got a river here!"

"Yeah, and it almost looks like it goes under those houses," said Annie.

"It's not raining much at all," said Drew, looking eagerly up at Mr. Pipes. "Oh, couldn't we—I mean—isn't there some way we could go fishing on the river? Fishing's better in the rain, isn't it?"

"Well, now, for the moment it has let up considerably, and I do say, it is a warmish sort of rain of the summer variety," said Mr. Pipes. "Follow me. I believe they might have rowing boats for hire on the Gera. And I think I have a plan even if the rain continues."

They walked along the stone pier and down several steps to where a dozen stout boats lay chained together.

"Now where is the chap one pays to use these fine vessels?" said Mr. Pipes, looking around.

Annie pulled out her sketchbook, "I love the pattern these boats make, lying peacefully on the river with all those church spires rising above the town. Was it like this in Luther's time?"

"Very much like," said Mr. Pipes. "And much of the town—that bridge, for instance—had been around for a considerable time before Luther. Barring the electric lights, motor cars, and your fast-food restaurants, yes, yes, it was much the same."

"Fast-food?" said Drew, looking eagerly back at the town. "You mean, like, hamburgers?"

"Yes, indeed, Drew," said Mr. Pipes with a laugh. "A German name, but America's gift to the world."

"There sure are a lot of churches in Erfurt," said Annie.

"Thirty-five, to be exact," said Mr. Pipes.

"That's a lot for a town the size of Erfurt," said Annie. "Oh, I'm getting rain on my sketchbook."

After asking several passersby who scurried along in the drizzle, Mr. Pipes found, sitting on a bench, huddled under a large, multicolored umbrella, the man who was supposed to be renting boats. Mr. Pipes counted out the Deutsche marks; Drew bailed the rainwater. Then they stowed their knapsacks under the thwarts.

"Do you have your torches?' asked Mr. Pipes, sliding the oars into the bronze oarlocks. "And do check your batteries. My plan requires torches—that work."

Drew dug in his knapsack until he found his flashlight. Holding it toward his face, he clicked it off and on several times.

"Yep, mine works," he said.

"So does mine," said Annie.

"Good." said Mr. Pipes, dipping the blades of the oars gently into the river. "After I maneuver us away from the quay and the rest of these boats, you must have a go at the oars, Drew.

Oh, she is a bit heavier than *Toplady*. Not quite so responsive, but seaworthy, nonetheless."

"I haven't rowed a boat since last summer," said Annie, gazing at the raindrops splashing on the river. "Look at the water, Mr. Pipes. There must be hundreds of little rings making miniature waves that just go and go and go." She opened her umbrella as the rings disappeared and the rain changed from a lazy drip-dripping, to a steady shower drumming across the river. Mr. Pipes rested on his oars and pulled his wool cap down over his ears.

"Bit of a deluge," he said. "Can't be helped," he added, resuming his stroke.

Oblivious to the rain dripping off his freckled nose, Drew smiled eagerly as he unscrewed the storage tube he carried his new fishing rod in. With one eye squinted shut and his tongue sticking out the side of his mouth in concentration, he sighted down the eyes of the rod, twisting each section into place until they lined up perfectly. He tightened the fly-casting reel in place at the end of the cork handle, threaded the floatable line, and tied on a hook.

"Well done, Drew," said Mr. Pipes. "You'll be glad you brought along that fine fly-casting reel—so much easier to stow in a knapsack. Now then, we must make for the bridge or be soaked to the skin in the bargain." He made wider strokes.

"It looks awfully dark in there," said Annie from the bow. "And I can't see light at the other end."

"I believe, however, we'll find it pleasantly dry, my dear," said Mr. Pipes over his shoulder.

Drew set a green, worm-like jig on his hook and plopped it over the side, letting out line as Mr. Pipes rowed.

"Do fish bite in the dark?" asked Drew as they neared the gaping mouth of the bridge.

"We shall see, my boy," said Mr. Pipes. "We shall see."

"I'm more worried about what else might bite in the dark," said Annie.

"Not to fear, my dear," said Mr. Pipes, reassuringly.

Half-timbered houses rose four stories above as they passed the first enormous stone column. The noise of the rain and the town outside gave way to stillness, only occasionally interrupted by a reverberating drip into the black water of the river.

"You see, my dears," said Mr. Pipes. "The Kramer Bridge extends under the street and houses above for some 125 meters, making it the longest elevated street in all Europe."

"Wait!" said Drew. "I can do this. Let's see, you convert meters to feet by multiplying by 100; that makes 12,500 centimeters; then, you divide 12,500 by 2.54; that'd be—well rounded off—4,921; then divide that by 12, which gives you about 410 feet—Whew! That's a third again bigger than a football field!"

"All in your head! I can't believe you, Drew," said Annie. Then, peering into the darkness ahead, she added, "That does make it a pretty big bridge."

"Fine calculating, indeed, Drew," said Mr. Pipes, his voice ringing merrily through the growing stillness. "God has coordinated your gifts; mathematics and music can go so very nicely together."

"Drew's good at both," said Annie from the darkness at the bow of the little rowboat.

"How old is this thing?" asked Drew, feeling a little embarrassed.

"These columns date from 1325—constructed at the same time as Olney's parish church," answered Mr. Pipes.

"That's old!" said Drew, letting out his line. "Imagine it! Workers built this bridge at the same time other workers built your church, Mr. Pipes. Huh, all without computers, and they're both still here."

"Yes, indeed," said Mr. Pipes. "Truly wonderful. Now then, Annie," he continued. "You be lookout at the bow—and, hmm, my dear—we're well under the bridge; I don't believe you'll need your umbrella aloft."

Annie laughed as she collapsed her umbrella and flicked on her flashlight.

"And, Drew, let's you and I trade places," went on Mr. Pipes. "I'll settle in the stern and steer with an oar whilst you fish amidships. Ah, yes, that will work just fine. With the rain outside, there's little sense in hurrying our way through."

"It does get light from the other end, doesn't it?" asked Annie nervously. "And just what am I looking out for?"

"Didn't he tell you?" said Drew matter-of-factly. "Big, green, slimy—you know, the Gila monster. Kramer Bridge—this is his home; he lives here. I thought everyone knew that."

"Enough of that, Drew. Nothing at all frightful like that, my dear," said Mr. Pipes. "Just keep us from tripping up on an ancient stone column, or the like—truly, my dear, that's all."

Pigeons cooed softly from their nests in the stone niches overhead.

"They seem happy enough about things in here, I guess," said Annie. "Pigeons make such peaceful songs."

"Music is always like that, my dear," said Mr. Pipes. "It creates an atmosphere and can call us to action and help make us disposed to certain emotions and attitudes. I doubt, Annie, that the screeching of bats just now would reassure you."

"B-bats?" Annie shuddered. "I'll take the pigeons, thanks."

"Music used in the worship of God must follow the same directive," continued Mr. Pipes. "'A Mighty Fortress' would not work if Luther had set it to a lullaby—men aren't called to war with nose flutes! Nor is it appropriate to worship God with music designed to appeal to man's—shall we say—to man's baser nature. Music written for popular entertainment—especially for entertaining people in a decaying culture—is rarely useful in calling men to look beyond themselves to God who is above us. You see, the music must fit the message. If you wanted to write a song about rebellion or hate or lust, you would very naturally choose sounds appropriate to those base themes. Conversely, music written for hymns of worship must fit the grand themes of that worship. Often, moreover, when God gifts a musician and a poet to write hymns and the music with which to sing them, the church is given some of her most appropriate musical settings. Luther's great battle hymn is a good example."

"Are there others?" asked Annie.

"Most certainly, my dear. By the end of Luther's life in 1546," continued Mr. Pipes, "the Protestant cause, preached by Lutheran ministers, had swept through much of Germany. Ten years after Luther's death, Philipp Nicolai—the son of one of those faithful Lutheran pastors—was born. He eventually came here, to Erfurt University, to study theology. Then, as Luther did before him, Philipp moved on to the University of Wittenberg, where he completed his theological training and became a powerful and earnest preacher of the gospel.

"Religious wars raged throughout much of the Protestant European world as Spanish Catholics attempted to regain cities won to Christ through Luther and the Reformation. On several occasions, fleeing for their lives from invading armies, faithful Pastor Nicolai and his congregation went into hiding, worshipping God in secret house churches.

"In 1597, while ministering to a congregation of God's people in Unna in Westphalia—west of here, near Holland—a terrible outbreak of the plague swept through the town. In a few months, Pastor Nicolai saw every household in his parish mourn the death of loved ones; over 1,300 people died from the dreaded pestilence. He daily preached funeral services, and from his house overlooking the churchyard, Nicolai watched as workmen dug new graves, sometimes thirty in one day. He grieved with his flock, and he daily meditated on death, but also on the promise of eternal life through Christ.

"After several days of reading Holy Scripture and meditating on death and the life to come, surprisingly, he found himself full of joy. His own fears calmed, Nicolai wrote down his meditations in a work called 'Mirror of Joy.'"

"With everyone dying all around him," said Drew, "that's quite a name."

"Indeed," continued Mr. Pipes. "One morning in 1597, he rose so filled with the Savior's love and the prospects of eternal

life with Christ that he began writing a poem full of rejoicing
in the Lord, though tribulation and death raged on every side.
Nicolai became so caught up in writing, he forgot to eat his
midday meal."

"That's what I call serious distraction!" said Drew.

"The first line goes: Wie schon leuchtet der morgenstern—
or in English: 'How Lovely Shines the Morning Star.' The
hymn is full of Nicolai's faith in God's undying love and his
ecstasy of longing to rest eternally in heaven. To accompany his
poetry, Nicolai later wrote the lovely tune, which the famous
Johann Sebastian Bach arranged into one of his chorales. I'll
teach it to you as we sing the rest:

> Now richly to my waiting heart,
> O Thou, my God, deign to impart
> The grace of love undying.
> In Thy blest body let me be,
> E'en as the branch is in the tree,
> Thy life my life supplying.
> Sighing, crying,
> For the savor of Thy favor;
> Resting never
> Till I rest in Thee for ever.
>
> Thou, mighty Father, in Thy Son
> Didst love me ere Thou hadst begun
> This ancient world's foundation.
> Thy Son hath made a friend of me,
> And when in spirit Him I see,
> I joy in tribulation....

They finished singing, and as their voices reechoed down
the dark tunnel, Mr. Pipes continued: "What faith; what valor!
I'm all astonishment when I contemplate the simple but deeply
profound poetry of these suffering German saints. But true
faith comes from the Son making a friend of me, and out of
that faith comes joy in tribulation."

"What did Mr. Nicolai mean," asked Annie, "in the part about God loving us before He laid the world's foundation?"

"Yeah," said Drew. "I'm not quite sure I understand that part either."

"Ah, yes. Many stumble here," replied Mr. Pipes. "Nicolai, like all great hymn writers, found the theology for this hymn in Holy Scripture. Paul wrote in Ephesians 1 that God chose us in Christ before the foundation of the world. It is a wonder to think He chose me before all time, not because He saw how receptive I'd be," Mr. Pipes chuckled. "No, no, far from it; that's theological folly, indeed. He loved me, miserable, undeserving wretch that I am, and made me His special favorite by His sovereign good pleasure. Where I deserved God's wrath and curse, through Christ, He lavished upon me grace and forgiveness—truly astonishing!"

Annie turned her flashlight off and blinked into the darkness of the tunnel. "I never thought about it that way before," she said. "I guess I kind of thought I chose God."

"And if you did," replied Mr. Pipes, "good for you, then, you've saved yourself."

"That can't be true," said Annie. "But it all sounds sort of unfair."

"Yeah," said Drew his eyes narrowing. "So, why me and not someone else?"

"Love, my boy, it was love," said Mr. Pipes. "He loved you because He loved you."

"This is a bit hard to understand," said Annie. "But wasn't it Mr. Watts—Isaac Watts, who said 'love so amazing, so divine, demands my soul, my life, my all'?"

"Indeed, it was," said Mr. Pipes.

"Mr. Newton," said Drew, "called it amazing grace. This sounds pretty amazing: I do all the sinning, Jesus does all the righteousness, and I get forgiveness and salvation instead of hell—that is amazing!"

"Yes, it is all of that," said Mr. Pipes.

"Mr. Nicolai wrote a lot about life in this hymn," said Annie. "I think he must have understood that life didn't end in that graveyard out his window."

"And you're right, Mr. Pipes," said Drew. "The music fits—it fits perfectly. I love the way Mr. Nicolai slows the pace and then, at the end, the music seems to—well, almost—to get excited with him about life forevermore with the Lord. Yeah, I like this guy, musician and poet all in one."

"All Germany," said Mr. Pipes, "—I dare say, all the Christian world—should appreciate Nicolai, Drew."

For several minutes they drifted downstream in silence, Annie and Drew thinking about being befriended by God.

Annie flicked her flashlight back on and scanned the foundation stones of the dark structure. "Did you hear something?" she said from the bow.

"No, my dear," said Mr. Pipes. "What did you hear?"

"Bats?" said Drew, grinning at his sister.

"There it is again," said Annie excitedly. She pointed her flashlight along the base of the bridge columns. "Mr. Pipes, can you steer us—let me see—to starboard. I'm sure I heard a faint little squeaking noise—like a cry off to the right."

Mr. Pipes pushed the steering oar to port, easing the boat closer to the foundation stones.

"I see it!" cried Annie suddenly, her flashlight quivering on a wet, motionless form. "It's not moving, Annie," said Drew.

"I think it's a kitten, poor thing," said Annie, reaching toward the drenched animal.

"Looks more like a dead rat to me," said Drew, not intending to be unkind.

Annie bit her lip and drew back. What if it was a rat? She shuddered at the thought. Just then the creature lifted its head and let out a pitiful "meow."

"It's a kitten—a tabby, I think," said Annie. "And I can just reach her," she added, gathering the frail, wet kitten in her arms. "How did you get trapped under the longest bridge in Europe, you poor, poor thing, you?"

"The wee thing looks nearly starved," said Mr. Pipes.

"And drowned," said Drew, frowning at the drenched kitten.

The kitten shivered helplessly in Annie's arms, its wet fur plastered against its scrawny body. Its tail did look more like a rat's tail than a kitten's. Annie dug a dry sweater out of her knapsack and wrapped her new pet in it.

"Mr. Pipes," she said, "please say I can keep her!"

"There is but one thing to be done, my dear," said Mr. Pipes. "We must see the wee thing warmed and filled. Keeping her, however, poses rather serious difficulties. One, of course, is that this is Germany and you live in America. But we will cross that bridge when we come to it."

"Or when we go *under* it," said Drew, reeling in his line with a sigh. Frowning at the empty hook, he stowed his rod.

"Patience, my boy," said Mr. Pipes, handing Drew the steering oar, "learned fishing—"

"—I know, I know," interrupted Drew. "'Patience learned fishing builds character.' Isn't that how you say it, Mr. Pipes?"

"So it is," said Mr. Pipes. "Now then, Drew, take a turn at the oars; we'll have more fishing later."

After fitting the oars into the oarlocks, Drew reached forward with the oars, carefully checking that both blades were in the water, and pulled. "I just wish it didn't take so long," he said. "Then I could get this learning patience thing over and done with right now."

Mr. Pipes chuckled. "I remember long ago feeling much the same way."

As they neared the end of the bridge, an escort of pigeons, frantically flapping their wings, led the little boat and her crew out from under the bridge and into sparkling sunshine. Annie thought she felt her little kitten making feeble attempts at purring. She gently hugged the bundle inside her sweater.

"Oh, good—sunshine," said Annie, shielding her eyes from the brightness all around. "You need sunshine so you can dry out," she added to her kitten. "And some warm milk; we need to get some flesh on those little bones of yours." Annie looked thoughtful for a moment. "I'll call you Lady Katherine after Mr. Luther's wife—maybe Lady Kitty, for short. What do you think, Mr. Pipes?"

"Fitting name, I'm sure," said Mr. Pipes. "I'm certain my cat, Lord Underfoot, would approve."

"And no one will ever make lute strings out of your insides, Lady Katherine," said Annie, holding the pathetic little bundle of wet fur up and rubbing noses with it.

Crowds strolling along the pier in the sunshine watched the little boat and her crew. And young people dangled their legs over the stone breakwater while eating picnic lunches. Nearby a church bell chimed. Drew rested on his oars and squinted in the bright sunlight at his watch.

"Lunch!" he said, licking his lips.

"Wait!" said Annie, cocking her head to listen. "Listen to the church bell; that tune sounds like—like Mr. Nicolai's—but that couldn't be?"

"Oh, but it most certainly is," said Mr. Pipes. "His melody became so loved in Germany that today—hundreds of years later—many church bells are tuned to play his immortal melody throughout every day of the year. Such is the timeless nature of great hymns. What a glorious sound!"

From the stern, Mr. Pipes's eyes sparkled as he looked up at the blue sky; and, unashamed before the onlookers, his clear voice joined the music. Drew didn't notice the stares and jeers of the teenagers watching from the stone breakwater as he and Annie, accompanied by the ancient bells, sang with Mr. Pipes Philipp Nicolai's hymn:

> What bliss is this!
> He that liveth to me giveth
> Life forever;
> Nothing me from Him can sever.

How Lovely Shines the Morning Star!

I am the Root and the Offspring of David, and the bright Morning Star. Rev. 22:16

1. How love - ly shines the Morn- ing Star! The na - tions see and
2. Now rich - ly to my wait - ing heart, O thou, my God, deign
3. Thou, might - y Fa - ther, in thy Son didst love me ere thou

hail a - far the light in Ju - dah shin - ing. Thou Da- vid's son of
to im - part the grace of love un - dy - ing. In thy blest bod - y
hadst be - gun this an- cient world's foun - da - tion. Thy Son hath made a

Ja - cob's race, my bride-groom and my King of grace, for thee my heart is
let me be, e'en as the branch is in the tree, thy life my life sup -
friend of me, and when in spir - it him I see, I joy in trib - u -

pin - ing. Low - ly, ho - ly, great and glo - rious, thou vic - to - rious
ply - ing. Sigh-ing, cry - ing, for the sa - vor of thy fa - vor;
la - tion. What bliss is this! He that liv - eth to me giv - eth

Prince of grac - es, fill - ing all the heav'n-ly plac - es.
rest - ing nev - er till I rest in thee for - ev - er.
life for - ev - er; noth - ing me from him can sev - er.

Philipp Nicolai, 1597
Trans. composite

WIE SCHÖN LEUCHTET DER MORGENSTERN 8.8.7.8.8.7.4.4.4.4.8.
Philipp Nicolai, 1599
Arr. by Johann Sebastian Bach, ca. 1730; alt. 1990

Wake, Awake, for Night Is Flying

Here's the bridegroom! Come out to meet him! Matt. 25:6

1. "Wake, a - wake, for night is fly - ing," the watch - men on the heights are cry - ing, "a - wake, Je - ru - sa - lem, at last!" Mid - night hears the wel - come voic - es, and at the thrill - ing cry re - joic - es: "Come forth, ye vir - gins, night is past!

2. Zi - on hears the watch - men sing - ing, and all her heart with joy is spring - ing; she wakes, she ris - es from her gloom: for her Lord comes down all - glo - rious, the strong in grace, in truth vic - to - rious; her Star is ris'n, her Light is come!

3. Now let all the heav'ns a - dore thee, and men and an - gels sing be - fore thee, with harp and cym - bal's clear - est tone; of one pearl each shin - ing por - tal, where we are with the choir im - mor - tal of an - gels round thy daz - zling throne;

The Bride - groom comes; a - wake, your lamps with glad - ness take;
Ah, come, thou bless - ed Lord, O Je - sus, Son of God,
nor eye hath seen, nor ear hath yet at - tained to hear

al - le - lu - ia! And for his mar - riage
al - le - lu - ia! We fol - low till the
what there is ours; but we re - joice, and

feast pre - pare, for you must go to meet him there."
halls we see where thou hast bid us sup with thee.
sing to thee our hymn of joy e - ter - nal - ly.

Philipp Nicolai, 1599
Tr. by Catherine Winkworth, 1858, 1863

WACHET AUF 8.9.8.8.9.8.6.6.4.8.8.
Philipp Nicolai, 1599
Arr. by Johann Sebastian Bach, 1731

Chapter Four

Johann Michael Altenburg
1584–1640

Fear not, O little flock, the foe
Who madly seeks your overthrow;
Dread not his rage and pow'r:
What though your courage sometimes faints,
His seeming triumph o'er God's saints
Lasts but a little hour.

After securing the rowing boat at the far end of the bridge, Drew begged Mr. Pipes to let them find one of those fast food restaurants he had told them about. Winding through narrow streets with tall, ancient houses looming over the cobbled passages, they found themselves in the central *Fischmarket*. Tracks from commuter trolleys crisscrossed the open square. The Gothic Town Hall, with its stairstep gables and magnificent turrets, rose above shops and restaurants of every kind. Workers and business people enjoyed frankfurters and hunks of bread in the warm sunshine.

"I've gotta have a burger," said Drew, scanning the rows of restaurants hungrily.

"Fine. Just so long as they have milk for Lady Katherine," said Annie, cuddling her new kitten in her arms.

"You pick, Drew," said Mr. Pipes. "It is part of the journey to sample the cuisine of other places. Pick any of these restaurants you want, my boy, but do be quick about it, for the wee kitten's sake—and, I dare say, our voyage under the Kramer Bridge has given me a considerable appetite."

"I see it:" said Drew, pointing excitedly, "'55 billion served'" he read from a sign arched by a large yellow *M*. "They'll have hamburgers and fries and Coke, just like at home."

Mr. Pipes smiled as they approached the restaurant. "Don't expect food in Germany to taste like your food in America; this is an entirely different country, Drew. But let's give your choice a try."

Mr. Pipes looked mildly troubled after viewing the colorfully lit menu above the cash register. Drew seemed to know the menu by heart and helped Mr. Pipes select his order. Annie asked for milk with her order—warm milk. Drew's mouth twitched in anticipation as he led them to a table near the window overlooking the square. Drew tore open the wrapping on his hamburger and, with eyes closed in ecstasy, he opened his mouth to take a juicy bite. Mr. Pipes stared in horror.

"We must offer our thanksgiving first, Drew," said Mr. Pipes, clearing his throat and looking ruffled. Drew reddened, and Mr. Pipes asked Annie to lead in prayer.

When she finished, Mr. Pipes again watched as Drew picked up his hamburger with his hands and took an enormous bite.

"Um, umm," grunted Drew, his cheek bulging with hamburger as he chewed. "That tastes just exactly—munch, munch, swallow—like a hamburger at home." He took another bite then crammed a handful of fries in with it. His straw made a loud "bweep" as he stuck it into the plastic lid of his Coke; he took a long sip on the soft drink. "Now this is real food," he concluded, taking another bite.

After wiping his eyeglasses and fitting them carefully on his nose, Mr. Pipes studied the greasy wrapping on his hamburger. He lifted the tray cover and looked under the napkins.

"Excuse me, my boy," said Mr. Pipes. "But wherever in the world is the silver?"

"The silver?" said Drew, stuffing a handful of French fries, drenched in catsup, into his mouth.

"Forgive me," said Mr. Pipes, "but I simply cannot eat without at least a knife and fork; it's unthinkable for a main meal sitting at table as we are. One simply must use cutlery."

Drew's chewing slowed as he tried to understand the old man.

"I'll get you a fork and knife," said Annie. "But could you hold Lady Kitty for me? She likes it if you dip your finger in milk and let her suck on it."

Annie returned a moment later, set a fork and knife on Mr. Pipes's tray, and resumed feeding her kitten. Mr. Pipes sighed as he positioned the plastic fork, prongs down, in his left hand and the plastic knife in his right. His eyebrows worked up and down as he gazed at the hamburger, his knife and fork poised above it. Then with resolve he set the fork into the bun and began sawing with the plastic knife.

Annie and Drew watched in amusement as the old man carefully carved each bite of his hamburger with his knife and placed it in his mouth with his fork. He occasionally paused and cut a French fried potato in half and placed it—with his fork—into his mouth.

"I say," said Mr. Pipes after he refolded his napkin and placed it carefully on the tray. "A rather messy meal, but tasty in its own sort of way, I suppose. Do you eat hamburgers like these often?"

"As often as I can," said Drew, who had long ago finished his hamburger and had been looking on hungrily, wondering if Mr. Pipes's appetite would hold out to the finish.

Annie tore little bits of her hamburger up and fed them to her kitten.

"Now that she's all dried off and her tummy's full," said Annie, "it's hard to imagine how narrowly she escaped death under that dark bridge."

"They do say cats have nine lives," said Mr. Pipes. "She is a lovely kitten." The kitten purred loudly as he scratched under its little chin. "I just wish I knew how we are to travel about— crossing international borders, and the like—with a kitten. It could, I dare say, become a bit of a sticky wicket. But we'll keep a stiff upper lip, and all that, and do our best for the little orphaned creature."

Dopey from his lunch, Drew slouched in his chair, look- ing out the window at the town square. He suddenly sat up and said, "Hey, Annie, there's that same guy we saw in Wittenberg the other day. I'll bet he's visiting all the Luther sights like we are. Or else," he added with a laugh, "he really is a spy following our every move. I'll bet he bugged us and he's heard everything we said. And maybe—" he grabbed at his throat and made choking sounds, "no, I'm sure of it—he poisoned my burger!" He gasped dramatically; then he slumped in his chair.

"Knock it off, Drew," said Annie, frowning as she scanned the crowds. "He's carrying his overcoat on his arm."

Drew sat up. "That's so he can conceal his automatic weapon—spies need guns, you know."

"Enough of your nonsense, Drew," said Mr. Pipes, his eyebrows lowered in a scowl over his still smiling eyes. "You'll frighten your sister—which is, of course, precisely what you have been trying to do."

Drew mumbled an apology.

"I'm pretty sure I saw him earlier along the pier when we were singing," said Annie. "Mr. Pipes, I'm afraid he is following us."

"I cannot imagine," said Mr. Pipes reassuringly, "why he would be doing anything of the sort." He paused, looking around the restaurant. "But I have an idea. Let's exit through the back door and if—which I doubt—he actually is following us," he winked at the children, "we'll give him the slip!"

"This'll be fun—like in the Cold War," said Drew. "But I think we need arms—weapons—you know, to level the playing field. Lugers, bulletproof vests, a grenade launcher, and a Tommy gun or two. What do you think?"

"Drew, don't be ridiculous," said Mr. Pipes, shaking his head in wonder. He studied the man across the square. "Now, wait to move away from the window until he looks down at his newspaper again. On my signal—he's fumbling with his paper—now! The game's afoot—gather your things and follow me."

They scurried out the back door. This could be fun, thought Annie, gripping Lady Katherine, as long as he doesn't *really* have a gun.

⬧ ⬧ ⬧

After looking both ways down the narrow alley behind the restaurant, the fugitives scurried through a dizzying maze of narrow medieval streets and old buildings, some leaning precariously over the street. Annie glanced over her shoulder at every turn.

"Whew!" said Mr. Pipes, laughing and ducking into a dark doorway. "We *have* taken leave of our senses." He peeked back around the corner. "There, now. We've given the poor chap the slip. I think we can now take a more leisurely pace."

Around the next narrow corner Drew stopped. "Look at that," he said, pointing above a doorway to an iron sign support. "It looks like some kind of helmet, or something. But it's got a brim like a regular hat, only made out of steel." He frowned. "And I don't know if those steel earflaps would do a very good job keeping you warm."

"Not for warmth, Drew," said Mr. Pipes, laughing. "That is a knight's helmet, and the earflaps are for protecting the ears from arrows and the like." Mr. Pipes read the sign hanging above the helmet. "Fancy that. This is a little museum of medieval warfare."

"Let's go in and see," said Drew eagerly.

"I hope they like kittens," said Annie. She buttoned Lady Katherine inside her sweater and followed Mr. Pipes and Drew into the museum.

Mr. Pipes paid the admission fee, and the lady in charge showed Annie and Drew where to set their knapsacks. Annie grabbed her sketchbook. A long row of thick, gray felt slippers lined the wall under the coat rack. The lady told Mr. Pipes they must slip their feet into a pair before going into the main hall of the museum. Lady Katherine wiggled inside Annie's sweater as Annie bent over to put on the cloglike felt slippers. Annie glanced at the lady and patted her sweater reassuringly. If only Lady Katherine didn't meow, all would be well.

Their feet made muffled sliding noises on the polished wood floor as they followed Mr. Pipes into a large room. Full suits of standing armor lined the walls, along with broadswords as tall as

Annie, lances, crossbows, and ancient-looking guns, their stocks
intricately carved and some inlaid with ivory designs.

"Get a load of this," said Drew, breaking the stillness of
the otherwise empty museum. "Imagine guys actually using
this stuff in a battle!" he continued as he walked up to a suit of
armor, comparing his height to it with his eye. "Hey, Mr. Pipes,
this one would fit me. Would boys get suited up and fight in
those old battles?"

"Boys did fight sometimes—for their very lives," said Mr.
Pipes. "But the best evidence suggests that most people in the
fifteenth century were not so tall as we are today. A full-grown
man likely wore that suit of armor."

"I see why they wanted us wearing these slippers," said
Annie, gazing at the wooden floor. "I've never seen such
beautiful wooden designs in a floor. It must be very old." She
dropped to her knees and studied the different kinds of wood
laid in patterns of flowers, linking chains, and delicate knots.

"That took a lot of work," said Drew, glancing at the floor
before returning his attention to the weapons. "But this armor's
different from all the rest," he went on, pointing to a suit of
armor in the middle of the great hall. "Looks like maybe a
horse wore it."

"Precisely," said Mr. Pipes, sitting down on a bench. "The
knight and his well-armored horse were the 'tanks' of medieval
warfare. If your horse was killed from under you ... well, it was
likely the end of the knight himself, so protecting one's horse
was most important indeed."

"But this armor wasn't just for protection," said Annie,
running her hand over the scalelike layers of finely etched steel.
"This is a work of art—it's beautiful." She sat down and began
drawing the delicate designs; Lady Kitty stretched a little paw
out of Annie's sweater and batted at her pencil as she drew.

"Indeed it is, Annie," said Mr. Pipes. "By the time of the
Reformation, armor had become much more for pageantry
than for protection. With the coming of gunpowder, traditional
plate armor was of little use against lead ball, but it was still

used for parades and general strutting about. Now in the battles over religious freedom that ravaged poor Germany in the years after the Reformation," he pointed to a row of shiny breastplates hanging on the wall, "it was armor more of that type that was actually worn by soldiers in battle."

Drew stepped up to the rows of breastplates, and with his knuckles he rapped on the steel. It gonged like a bell.

"Bitte!" said the lady from the front desk.

"Sorry," called Drew, stepping quickly away from the armor.

"*Drew*," said Annie, "you'll get us thrown out."

"I said 'sorry,'" said Drew. "Mr. Pipes, tell us about a battle—a real battle."

"Well, let me see," said Mr. Pipes, clasping his hands around one knee, leaning back, and gazing at the beamed ceiling. "Hmm, those were brutal days, I fear. Desperate fighting nearly destroyed all Germany as the Roman Catholic imperial forces, set on wiping out the Christian followers of Martin Luther, ravaged the land. News of the terrible cruelties of the Roman Catholic soldiers against German Lutherans reached Gustavus Adolphus, Christian King of Sweden. With tears, he left his family for war-ravaged Germany. Though frequently outnumbered, with the help of God, he defended the rights of others to worship freely and gained many victories over the imperial armies.

"But Gustavus couldn't be everywhere at once," continued Mr. Pipes. "At the Protestant town of Magdeburg the imperial commander, Tilly,[†] ordered his soldiers to drag Christian ministers from their homes, dump oil over them, and light them aflame in the streets."

"How awful!" said Annie.

"Worse yet," said Mr. Pipes, a grim set to his jaw, "Tilly directed his army to nail shut the doors of a church filled with terrified women and children—some your ages, no doubt. He

---

† Count Johan Tserclaes von Tilly was a German general in the Thirty Years' War. He led the Catholic Hapsburgs to victory over the Protestants under Frederick, Elector Palatine of the Rhine, in the Battle of White Mountain near Prague, Bohemia, in 1620.

then burned it to ashes. As they watched the inferno, some of his jeering soldiers tossed other children into the flames. Some 30,000 of the 34,000 inhabitants of the town died."

Drew clenched his teeth and looked around at the armor and weapons. "Were these Catholic or Lutheran weapons, do you think?"

"I don't know, my boy," said Mr. Pipes. "I suspect some of both."

"Nearly the whole town killed," said Annie, biting her lower lip. "What did Gustavus do when he heard the news?" she asked.

"Ah, what any true Christian would do," said Mr. Pipes, "thinking on those wives and mothers and wee ones dying so. He wept.

"But, as news of the massacre spread throughout Germany, thousands rallied to avenge the evil and fight on with Gustavus. The king encouraged his men to fight manfully, while trusting in God to fight for them. He led them in singing a hymn and would fall to his knees and pray with his troops before every battle. He prayed something like this, 'O Lord, I have not come for my own glory, but to aid your oppressed church. Protect us and bring victory in this sacred work.'

"Before one battle with Tilly's great army, facing cannons on every side, Gustavus rallied his happy few with the words, 'God is with us, and with the help of the Almighty, victory will be ours!' Amidst the terrifying roar of imperial cannon fire, Gustavus led the attack, charging the Catholic lines. Tilly's troops counterattacked seven times. Each time Gustavus and his valiant army repelled the attacks. While Tilly separated from the Swedish army, the less-experienced German Protestant troops—who then fled in panic—Gustavus led his outnumbered men in an all-out assault and seized the imperial cannon emplacements. He then turned and fired on the enemies of God with their own cannons! Those who survived fled the field for their lives. Gustavus dropped to his knees, removed his helmet, and blessed the Lord for giving them the victory."

"With their own guns!" Drew jumped up and yelled, "Gustavus is our man!"

"Bitte! Bitte!" called the scowling woman from the front desk, this time more loudly.

"Drew, you must contain yourself, my boy," said Mr. Pipes, but with a smile.

"Was it over," said Annie, "the fighting, I mean?"

"Great progress for religious freedom was made that day," continued Mr. Pipes. "But the Catholic Emperor rallied more troops and sent them to crush Gustavus. The armies met November 6, 1632, at Lützen, a place just a bit northeast of Erfurt. Thousands of soldiers prepared their armor and weapons, rank upon rank against each other. A dense mist hung over the battlefield, delaying the conflict. Once again, Gustavus fell to his knees and with all his army prayed for God's deliverance from the enemy. The king rose from his knees, mounted his horse, and rode in front of his men crying together, 'God with us!' Then, accompanied by the blast of trumpets and the rumble of kettledrums, he led them in singing Luther's great battle hymn, 'A Mighty Fortress.'"

"With drums?" said Drew. "That would be quite a sound."

"He then led them in another hymn, 'Fear not, O Little Flock, the Foe,' that some over the years say Gustavus helped write. It is a magnificently tender hymn called in some hymnals, 'Gustavus Adolphus's Battle Hymn.'"

"Did Gustavus write it?" asked Annie. "It would be quite a story if he did."

"Yes, it would be all of that," said Mr. Pipes, with a chuckle. "But he didn't write it, my dears. Johann Michael Altenburg wrote it. He was born very near here in 1584 and ministered in various Lutheran pulpits in and around Erfurt over his lifetime. He wrote the hymn in 1631 after hearing of Gustavus's victory at Leipzig. It goes like this—" he paused, looking out at the lady at the front desk, "—we'd better whisper it here; we'll sing it later.

Fear not, O little flock, the foe
Who madly seeks your overthrow;
Dread not his rage and pow'r:
What though your courage sometimes faints,
His seeming triumph o'er God's saints
Lasts but a little hour.

Be of good cheer; your cause belongs
To Him who can avenge your wrongs;
Leave it to Him, our Lord:
Though hidden yet from all our eyes,
He sees the Gideon who shall rise
To save us and His Word.

As true as God's own Word is true,
Nor earth nor hell with all their crew
Against us shall prevail.
A jest and byword are they grown;
God is with us, we are His own;
Our vict'ry cannot fail.

Amen, Lord Jesus, grant our pray'r;
Great Captain, now Your arm make bare,
Fight for us once again;
So shall Your saints and martyrs raise
A mighty chorus to Your praise,
World without end. Amen.

"What a perfect hymn to sing before a battle," said Drew.

"It does bring powerfully to mind," said Mr. Pipes, "the reality of ultimate victory for God's Word and His saints."

"What did Mr. Altenburg mean by 'the Gideon who shall rise?'" asked Annie.

"Gideon defeated the vast armies of the Midianites with only a small band of soldiers," replied Mr. Pipes. "I think Altenburg may have been referring to Adolphus as Gideon, the great captain in the war that madly raged throughout Germany.

But ultimately his reference to Gideon is a reference to the Lord Jesus, our deliverer from sin and Satan."

"I guess if Jesus is fighting for us," said Drew, thoughtfully, "we don't need to fear the foe."

"Yes, but if we don't realize we're engaged in a battle for our souls," said Mr. Pipes, "then the Devil has already won the victory. One good thing about those terrible days of warfare in Germany was that Christians understood the Bible's use of the military metaphor for the Christian life."

"I wonder if Mr. Altenburg thought of those poor—" Annie shuddered, "—those poor children burned alive in the church when he wrote the last verse about saints and martyrs raising praises to God?"

"He may very well have been thinking of just those martyrs," said Mr. Pipes, "though there have been many others before and since."

"So how did the battle go, that day?" asked Drew.

"After singing the hymn, Gustavus prayed again with his army, then mounted his horse and cried, 'Now we will do battle, if it pleases God. Jesus, Jesus, Jesus, help me today to fight for the honor of Thy Holy Name.' By eleven o'clock the fog had lifted over the fatal field. The king then spurred his horse and without his steel breastplate—which he had refused to put on saying, 'God is my armor'—he charged at full speed upon the enemy.

"It was a furious and bloody battle," continued Mr. Pipes. "And the results were by no means certain, when Gustavus suddenly felt a searing pain as a musket ball shattered through his left arm. Separated from his men in the confusion of the battle, Gustavus found himself surrounded by leering imperial soldiers. 'Who are you?' one of them barked. Though his body was racked with pain, Gustavus replied boldly, 'I am the King of Sweden. This day I seal with my blood the liberty and the religion of the German nation!'"

Mr. Pipes paused, looking at a row of muskets hanging on the wall nearby.

"W-what happened next?" asked Annie.

"Did his men find him in time and rescue him?" asked Drew hopefully.

"I'm afraid not," said Mr. Pipes. "The imperial soldiers opened fire and killed the king."

"B-but I thought," said Annie, "that victory could not fail."

"Oh, my dear," said Mr. Pipes. "The Protestant armies did prevail that day, and the imperial army was again scattered. Though war raged on for many years, Gustavus's victories did secure freedom for the Protestants in Europe. But remember, children, the Devil does seem to have victory over God's saints at times, but those victories are soon over; our Captain has secured for all time our certain victory over all His enemies and ours. What a glorious confidence that gives us in the face of any danger."

◈ ◈ ◈

For several minutes Annie had felt stretching and wiggling inside her sweater. She tried calming Lady Katherine, but the kitten wouldn't be calmed. Suddenly, Lady Katherine poked her little orange head out of Annie's sweater and, with a last wiggle, leaped out onto the floor and scurried out of reach. Annie lunged after her, but it was too late. Drew joined in the chase as they raced in, around, and under medieval suits of armor and ancient weapons. The more they chased, the faster Lady Katherine ran. Once they lost sight of her altogether. She peeked out from around the shiny leg of a suit of armor. Drew spotted her and the chase was on again.

"Bitte! Bitte! Bitte!" demanded the lady, no longer sitting at the front desk but now joining in the chase yelling, "Ein Katze! Ein Katze!"

Mr. Pipes got up and calmly blocked the entrance to the museum. After several more minutes of chaos, Lady Katherine, heading for the exit, ran right into Mr. Pipes's waiting arms. The chase was over.

Mr. Pipes apologized in German, and amidst scolding—Annie decided that kind of scolding sounded pretty much the same in any language—they stepped into the narrow street.

"Oh, Mr. Pipes," said Annie, stroking her kitten. "What a mess; I feel so terrible."

Drew collapsed on the curb and began laughing uncontrollably.

Annie glared at him. "How can you laugh about it? We could have ruined some antique armor, and that lady could have called the police. Worse yet, Lady Kitty could have been hurt!"

"Is she?" asked Drew, still laughing.

"No," said Annie.

"We did make rather a sight in there," said Mr. Pipes, his mouth twitching into what looked nearly like the beginnings of a good laugh. "But we simply must not let that sort of thing happen again or, I dare say, our entire trip will be disrupted beyond recovery. Now, I think a cup of tea would be in order."

Drew looked down the street and suddenly stopped laughing. "Hey, Annie's spy's back."

"What?" said Mr. Pipes.

"Yeah, it's him," said Drew.

At a table in front of a shop sat their spy reading a newspaper.

"He's been waiting for us the whole time," said Annie. "That proves it. I knew he was following us."

"He's good," said Drew. "Annie, maybe you're right and he is actually after us."

"Impudence! I was sure we'd given him the slip," said Mr. Pipes. "But, that's ridiculous!" he added with a short laugh. He ran his hand through his white hair, and his bushy eyebrows made a brim over his eyes as his brow furrowed into a hard stare at the stranger. "Inconceivably ridiculous, I'm sure."

Mr. Pipes stared hard down the street. With a set to his jaw, Mr. Pipes said, "Come, children; we'll settle this once and for all." He marched down the street, leading the children right past the stranger's table. The man rose without so much as glancing at them and walked the opposite way down the street.

Mr. Pipes slowed, studying the man's back, then continued briskly toward the *Fischmarket*.

"No one could have looked more like they belonged," he said with a sigh and a short laugh when they were out of earshot. "It must be merely a coincidence. But if tomorrow he follows us all the way to Strasbourg I'll be inclined to agree with you, Annie. Until then, we must simply consider him a tourist with similar interests—nothing more. After all, he went the other way without even looking at us. There now, that settles it."

Hugging Lady Katherine, Annie looked over her shoulder at the retreating figure and bit her lip. Turning, she scurried to catch up, hoping Mr. Pipes was right.

Fear Not, O Little Flock

Do not be afraid, little flock, for your Father has been pleased to give you the kingdom.
Luke 12:32

1. Fear not, O lit - tle flock, the foe who mad - ly
2. Be of good cheer; your cause be - longs to him who
3. As true as God's own Word is true, nor earth nor
4. A - men, Lord Je - sus, grant our pray'r; great Cap - tain,

seeks your o - ver - throw; dread not his rage and pow'r:
can a - venge your wrongs; leave it to him, our Lord:
hell with all their crew a - gainst us shall pre - vail.
now your arm make bare, fight for us once a - gain;

what though your cour - age some - times faints, his seem - ing
though hid - den yet from all our eyes, he sees the
A jest and by - word are they grown; God is with
so shall your saints and mar - tyrs raise a might - y

tri - umph o'er God's saints lasts but a lit - tle hour.
Gid - eon who shall rise to save us and his Word.
us, we are his own; our vic - t'ry can - not fail.
cho - rus to your praise, world with - out end. A - men.

Attr. to Johann Michael Altenburg, 1584–1640
Tr. by Catherine Winkworth, 1855; mod.

JEHOVAH NISSI 8.8.6.D.
Edward Patrick Crawford, 1846–1912

Chapter Five

Johann Heermann
1585–1647

Keep me from saying words
That later need recalling;
Guard me, lest idle speech
May from my lips be falling.

The next day, after a long train ride to the border city of
Strasbourg, Drew begged to go rowing and maybe fishing again
before they did anything else.

"I've got to get out on that river," said Drew as the train
entered the bustling city. "It looks like it might go all the way
around the city; a boat could be a good way of seeing things,
don't you think, Mr. Pipes?"

Bridges crisscrossed the winding canal encircling the
ancient city, and sunlight sparkled invitingly on the cool water.
Mr. Pipes agreed, and after checking their baggage at a small
hotel near the Rhine, the threesome rented a rowing boat,
agreeing with the boatman to leave it near the *rue de Jean
Cauvin* where they would continue their tour on foot.

"What a perfect day!" said Drew at the oars, glancing over
his shoulder as he steered toward the middle of a low-arched
bridge. "Do you think there's any fish in this river?"

"Well, my boy," said Mr. Pipes from the stern. "This river is
properly part of a network of canals surrounding the old city—
Oh, it connects to the great Rhine River, which is sure to have
fish—but I'm not so sure fish abound in the River Ill."

"*Ill*?" said Drew. "Like, let's go rowing on the 'River Sick'?
What a name! Come to think of it, if you include the Ouse
back in England, Europe has some strange names for rivers."

"Watch out, Drew!" said Annie from the bow. "You're getting awfully close to the column on the—" She held out first her right hand, then her left, and mumbled, "'left' has four letters and 'port' has four letters." Then out loud she said, "—on the *port* side."

As they passed safely under the arch, pedestrians on the bridge smiled down at the orange kitten sunning herself on the floorboards of the little boat near Annie's feet.

"'Twas a bit close," agreed Mr. Pipes. "But you're doing fine; carry on, Drew. After the next bridge, notice to port the magnificent tower of the cathedral. It is truly one of the most grand in all Europe. Just ahead, it is, around the next bend."

Annie dug in her knapsack for her sketchbook. Maybe she could sketch the canal with an old stone bridge and the cathedral spire rising above it all.

Drew pulled steadily on the oars, enjoying the exercise. He was really getting pretty good at rowing—better, in fact, than Annie; he was sure of that. He smiled as he glanced forward, correcting with his starboard oar as the river turned and now, enclosed on either side by a stone wall, looked more like a canal. Further ahead, they slid past the backsides of warehouses and rundown buildings.

Annie had been watching several black-leather clad boys loitering on the crown of the next bridge. She picked up Lady Kitty and glanced forward again. The tallest of the boys grinned down at them, but Annie didn't think it looked at all like a friendly grin. Mr. Pipes frowned. Drew, his back toward the bridge, kept rowing. They came closer. Then Annie noticed the tallest boy kept tossing something back and forth in his hands. Drew's rowing brought them even closer. Annie caught her breath. All five boys stood tossing broken bricks up and down in a menacing way.

"I say, Drew, stop rowing," said Mr. Pipes, "and turn the boat around."

"But you said, 'carry on,' just a minute ago," said Drew. "I want to see the cathedral from the water. Should be a great view from—"

"Guten Tag!" cried the boys from the bridge. And then bricks began splashing on all sides of the little boat. Taunts and laughter came from the bridge as the boys hurled more bricks, hitting the water dangerously close to the boat.

Annie screamed and clutched at her kitten.

"Keep low, Annie," said Mr. Pipes grimly. Spray from the volley of bricks hitting the water splashed in his face. "Drew, we must turn the boat!"

But Drew was no longer listening. The boat drifted closer. Gritting his teeth, Drew turned and stood up on the rowing thwart.

"You lily-livered Cabbage-heads!" he cried, shaking his fist.

The boys laughed harder and picked up more bricks, throwing them closer still. One grazed the side of the boat, and another hit an oar. Drew lunged for an oar. Water poured in over the port gunwale as he desperately tried to maintain his footing. With a heave, he swung the oar upwards toward the boys; it clattered harmlessly against the stones of the bridge. But the effort proved too much for Drew's footing, and as the boat tipped to port, Drew's momentum carried him to starboard.

"You Kraut-breath creeps—" the rest ended in a gurgle as Drew, with a splash, plunged headfirst into the canal.

The boys stopped throwing bricks. One called down at Drew as he sputtered to the surface, "Ja, ja, take a bath, American!" Roaring with laughter, they disappeared down the street.

"Call the cops!" said Drew as he grabbed on to the gunwale of the boat and tried lifting himself back on board.

"Hold on, Drew," said Mr. Pipes, moving to the opposite side. "Now try whilst I counterbalance your weight."

Grunting and red with rage, Drew plopped onto the floor of the boat, dripping all over like a wet sponge. "Can you believe those creeps!" he said through clenched teeth.

"Annie, are you unhurt?" Mr. Pipes called forward.

"I—I think I'm all right," said Annie. "And so is Lady Kitty, no thanks to you, Drew."

"*What!*" cried Drew. "I tried to stop them. They had no business treating us like that. All I did was try to make them knock it off—the creeps!"

"It didn't work," said Annie. She suddenly stopped and looked around the bow. "Oh, no! I can't find my sketchbook. Drew, I'll strangle you if it went overboard!"

Drew looked from Annie to Mr. Pipes. Drew met the old man's eyes for a moment, then looked away.

"There it is, my dear," said Mr. Pipes. He paddled with one oar—Indian fashion—toward the floating sketchbook, then scooped it up. "What a pity. But, I do believe the part most damaged by the water is the blank pages." Annie didn't trust herself to speak as she took the soggy sketchbook from Mr. Pipes. We'll dry it in the sunshine while we have our tea," said Mr. Pipes, reaching for the floating oar Drew had thrown at the ruffians.

"I'll row from here," said Mr. Pipes, fitting the oars into the oarlocks and making effortless strokes down the canal.

After several minutes, Mr. Pipes broke the silence. "You will need to change clothes, Drew. And I think a cup of tea might serve us very well, just now. Do you have dry clothes in your knapsack?"

"Yeah, I think so," said Drew glumly.

As they rounded a bend in the canal, the massive cathedral spire rose above the jumbled houses lining the waterway.

"It just keeps going up," said Annie in wonder. "That spire is so light and delicate-looking. How long has it been there?"

"It is a grand spire, Annie," said Mr. Pipes, resting on his oars and smiling as he looked over his glasses at the reddish sandstone tower. "Completed, I believe it was, in 1439—a bit newer than St. Peter and St. Paul's back in Olney."

"Before the Reformation, then," said Drew. "That makes it about—" he paused, calculating, "—561 years old. Still pretty old. It looks lots taller than Olney's church—let me see. Wasn't your church about 180 something?—no, it was 187 feet, yeah, that's it."

"So how tall is this one?" asked Annie.

"Much, much taller," said Mr. Pipes, guiding the boat toward a pier on the south side of the canal. "This is the rue de Jean Cauvin; let's check our boat in and let Drew get into some dry clothes. Then we'll visit the cathedral, and I'll tell you a most interesting story."

▨ ◈ ▨

Annie and Mr. Pipes sat at a little round table in front of the *Café de Notre-Dame*. Annie carefully opened her sketchbook and propped it open on a chair facing the warm sunlight. It could have been a lot worse, she decided. Most of her drawings were dry or only slightly wet on the edges, and the poems that were wet she could still read. She'd copy them onto dry pages later.

Moments later, Drew, looking dry but still scowling, emerged from a little room marked "W.C."

"Our 'tea' will be coffee and pastry," said Mr. Pipes, looking at the menu. "Thick coffee—like crank-case oil, I fear. The appalling lack of good tea is a trial of foreign travel."

"So how tall is it?" asked Drew, moments later, between bites of braided pastry. "From this angle, looking down this narrow street with all these tall houses on either side, it looks like it goes forever—or nearly so."

"It's breathtaking," said Annie, gazing at the façade filling the end of the street then rising into the single late-Gothic spire. Lady Kitty helped herself to a nibble of Annie's pastry.

"Children," said Mr. Pipes, smiling down the cobbled street at the cathedral, "this spire—rising 466 feet above the street, the highest masonry structure of medieval Europe—is regarded as the Eighth Wonder of the World. For the best of reasons, I'd say," he concluded, taking a sip of coffee, then setting the cup down with a grimace.

"At God's command, Noah built his ark 450 feet long," said Mr. Pipes.

"So if you stood the ark on end," said Drew, shielding his eyes from the sun as he looked up, "that spire would still be taller—sixteen feet taller. Wow!"

"Yes, indeed. But as magnificent as it is on the outside," continued Mr. Pipes, "the inside is a marvel to behold. And it is graced with a most excellent organ. Oh, how I do miss playing my little organ."

"Can we go inside?" asked Annie eagerly.

"Certainly, my dear," said Mr. Pipes, lifting his cup, scowling into it, then setting it down without taking another drink of the bitter brew. "Follow me."

As they came closer to the intricately carved Gothic arched entrance, the vertical lines of the flamboyant pinnacles rising into the enormous rose window forced their eyes upward. Drew nearly stumbled on the cobblestone street as he looked up at layer upon layer of skillfully carved stone. It must have taken hundreds—maybe even thousands of workers—skilled workers, to build this place, Drew decided.

They left the busy street behind them and entered into the hush of the cathedral nave. Multicolored sunlight poured in from enormous Gothic stained glass windows.

"Brilliantly lit interior, though not as lofty in proportion to some cathedrals," explained Mr. Pipes, golden light reflecting off his white hair. "You see, the north transept was built in the early 1200s, in the Romanesque style. But what they lost in height in the interior they made up for in the spire." He paused and rose to his feet. "Now then, follow me over to the pulpit."

They sat on cane chairs across the nave from the stone-carved pulpit, and Mr. Pipes, with a satisfied sigh, continued: "In his student days, the University of Strasbourg was home to another great—perhaps the greatest—Reformation hymn writer, Johann Heermann. During the same years of war and suffering in which Gustavus Adolphus died, Heermann wrote his hymn—a prayer, really—'O God, My Faithful, God.' An amazing first line when one thinks about the wrongs the German Lutheran Christians suffered at the hands of the Roman

Catholics. Drew, I want you especially to listen to the third
verse. It goes like this:

> Keep me from saying words
> That later need recalling;
> Guard me, lest idle speech
> May from my lips be falling....

Drew shuffled his tennis shoes on the worn stones of the
cathedral floor. Mr. Pipes went on:

> When dangers gather round,
> Oh, keep me calm and fearless;
> Help me to bear the cross
> When life seems dark and cheerless;
> Help me, as You have taught,
> To love both great and small,
> And, by Your Spirit's might,
> To live at peace with all.

Drew swallowed and glanced up into Mr. Pipes's eyes.
Mr. Pipes had a way of looking that made Drew feel like he
saw right into his heart. He cleared his throat and was about
to speak when Annie said, "Oh, I need to pray those words,
because this is exactly my trouble." She sounded near tears. "I
say things without thinking all the time."

"You do?" interrupted Drew. "What do you mean you say
things without thinking! No, Annie, this is my problem—I'm
way worse than you are."

"Well, I really do—" replied Annie.

"Listen!" said Drew, his voice getting louder. "You don't
know what you're talking about—" He stopped abruptly, looking first at Mr. Pipes, cradling his elbow in one hand while
stroking his chin in thought with the other, then at Annie, staring intently back at him. He shook his head. "Oh, boy. See, I'm
the one who flies off the handle. What a fool I made of myself

today on the canal. Mr. Pipes, Annie—sorry. And, Annie, I'm really sorry about your sketchbook—it was all my fault."

"That's okay," said Annie and Mr. Pipes together. "But, Drew," continued Mr. Pipes, "you can't take those words back that you yelled to those boys on the bridge."

"Yeah, but they deserved what I said," said Drew, a scowl returning to his face. "And way worse."

"Were your words," said Mr. Pipes, "words of love to both great and small?"

Again, Drew studied the mineral pattern in the ancient paving stones at his feet.

"They weren't loving at all," said Drew at last. "But, Mr. Pipes, it's tough loving cree—I mean—boys like that."

"But are we finally any more deserving of God's love than they?" asked Mr. Pipes. "Compared with God's holiness, Drew, we're all 'creeps,' as you say. And thus we must forgive as we have been forgiven—'Forgive us our debts as we forgive our debtors,' said our Lord. We presume on God's forgiveness when we refuse to forgive those who wrong us. Johann Heermann, whose life was filled with the most profound and continuous suffering imaginable, probably wanted to yell some well chosen words to the imperial troops ravaging his parish—his was a life filled with many wrongs, far worse than a few bricks tossed off a bridge. Let me start at the beginning.

"When he was born in 1585, his faithful Christian parents cherished their fifth child. The other four had died as babies or in early childhood. Johann survived infancy but became gravely ill as a toddler. With tears, his praying mother begged God to spare her son's life. She vowed to see him trained for the ministry if only God would spare him."

"Did God hear her prayer?" asked Annie.

"Oh, come off it, Annie," said Drew, rolling his eyes. "If Heermann died as a kid, how could he write—" He stopped; his face grew red. "I-I mean—well, sorry."

"Ahem, yes," said Mr. Pipes, looking over his glasses at Drew. "God did hear his mother's prayer, and she kept her vow even though the cost of Johann's training in those hard times led her nearly to begging. Johann proved worthy of her sacrifices and made the most of his schooling, distinguishing himself as a poet along the way. In the course of his preparation for the pastorate, he came here to Strasbourg—no doubt overawed as we are at this glorious structure." Mr. Pipes paused, his eyes wandering appreciatively over the stone splendor all around them.

"Did he preach here?" asked Annie.

"No, no, my dear," continued Mr. Pipes. "Eventually he fell ill again—trouble with his eyes—and returned to his home town on the banks of the Oder River."

"The *Odor?*" inquired Drew. "The things they call their rivers around here!"

"During his years as a minister nearby in the town of Koben," continued Mr. Pipes, "the Thirty Years' War trampled its way across Germany. Four times imperial Catholic forces plundered the little village; Heermann lost everything," Mr. Pipes paused in thought, "including his young wife. Twice imperial soldiers nearly ran him through with swords; and, on one occasion, when he was fleeing for his life across the Oder in a boat, bullets whistled dangerously close on every side. On top of it all, he developed such a dreadful case of chronic bronchitis that his preaching was continually interrupted by fits of coughing.

"Through all these trials Johann Heermann continued writing poetry—some of the most tender, passionate poetry in the hymnal."

"After all he suffered," said Annie, "the lines about dangers gathering around and God keeping us calm and fearless make more sense. But how could he be so—so trusting? I mean, with all those awful things happening."

"His poetry expresses the deepest faith in Christ," said Mr. Pipes, "in Christ who suffered. Heermann's poetry is marked by cheerful submission to God's will in all trials. My favorite hymn of his, like Thomas Kelley's, 'Stricken, Smitten and Afflicted,' is based on Isaiah 53. Heermann wrote his as a meditative prayer directly to Jesus, the most afflicted."

Mr. Pipes got up, and the children followed him toward the front of the nave, Lady Kitty nosing her way behind. He paused below row upon row of lovely pipes suspended above stone-carved cornices. Light from the rose window sparkled on the polished pipes.

"How I would love to play Heermann's hymn on this organ," said Mr. Pipes, gazing up with a smile.

"I'll bet they'd let you," said Drew. "Nobody's using it right now anyway. Maybe I could play the right hand?"

"T'would be lovely," replied Mr. Pipes. "But, of course, an entire impossibility, I'm sure," he concluded with a chuckle.

Just then, a short man wearing a blue working coat, wringing his hands and mumbling, walked past them. He paused before the organ, looked at his watch, shook it and held it to his ear, then walked across to the south transept and checked it against the giant astronomical clock.

"Poor chap," said Mr. Pipes to the children. "He's mumbling—near as I can tell; they speak a sort of combination of German and French in Strasbourg—something about the organ tuner. Must be late arriving to tune the organ. Hmm, pity. I'd love to hear it played."

The worried little man returned, talking and gesturing to himself.

"I think I'll ask if he speaks English," said Mr. Pipes. "Alsace German is too much for me." Turning to the distraught man, he asked, "Werzeihung. Wie bitte. Sprechen Sie Englisch?"

The little man stopped mumbling and looked at them as if seeing them for the first time.

"Ja, ja," he said, running his hand through his gray hair.

"Yes, well, I couldn't help overhearing that your organ tuner is running a trifle behind schedule," said Mr. Pipes.

"Ja, ja," said the little man, with emphasis. "It is alvays like dis for me. I am de varder of de cathedral, you understand. Tonight de mayor and other city officials come for de summer festival organ concert in our grand cathedral. De organ needs to be tuned and de mayor, he gotz a very goot ear, ja, a very goot ear for musik. Eek, vhat vill I do if Adolphe, de tuner, him not come?"

Mr. Pipes looked up at the organ pipes then back at the man. Drew pulled on Mr. Pipes's sleeve. "Couldn't you do it?" he said in Mr. Pipes's ear.

"Out of the question, I'm sure," said Mr. Pipes to Drew.

"Vas is dat?" said the warder of the cathedral.

"Oh, nothing at all," said Mr. Pipes. "Merely an unworkable suggestion from my young friend, that is all."

"But you could do it, couldn't you?" said Annie.

"Could do vhat, Mein Herr?" asked the warder.

"Well, I don't know—" began Mr. Pipes.

"What he means," cut in Drew, "is that he could tune the organ for you."

"You!" said the warder, with a nervous laugh, checking his watch.

"He—that is, Mr. Pipes—is an organist," said Drew, "in England. We've heard him play—lots."

"Is dis true, Mein Herr?" asked the warder.

"Well, yes, I suppose it is true," said Mr. Pipes.

"You vill do it for me, den?" pled the warder. "Oh, do say Ja. I am Wolfgang—Karl Wolfgang Kluge, but if you don't help me my name is—how do you say it—'Mud.'"

They all laughed.

"Mr. Kluge sounds much better than Mr. Mud," said Drew.

"Dat settles it," said Mr. Kluge, smiling. "Ve only have time for de reed pipes; ve must get to vork."

Mr. Kluge led them up a very narrow winding staircase to the organ console suspended over the nave of the cathedral. Annie brought up the rear, carrying Lady Katherine in her sweater.

"Great view from up here," said Drew.

Mr. Pipes rubbed his hands together in anticipation and sat down at the elaborate console. "This truly is a lovely organ," he said in wonder.

"All is ready," said Mr. Kluge.

For several hours Mr. Pipes slowly played scales, listening rank upon rank to each pipe, while Mr. Kluge—with Annie and Drew taking turns helping—tap-tapped with his little wooden mallet, adjusting the bronze tuning wires until the reed pressure was just right and the pitch sounded perfect. Lady Kitty slept for a while on the bench next to Mr. Pipes during the low notes but twitched her ears and tail and arched her back during the high ones.

"That about does it, then," said Mr. Pipes, at last.

Drew, with a smudge of pipe dust on his nose, and Mr. Kluge came out from behind the rows of pipes.

"Ant now you must play something for us," said Mr. Kluge, wiping his hands on a rag and putting tools away, "to test your vork."

"As you wish," said Mr. Pipes, pulling stops that sounded like muffled little thuds. He began the single melodic line of a fugue, but as layer was added to layer and the volume increased, Lady Kitty came running from behind the rows of pipes, her hair standing on end. She stopped, arching her back at the pipes and skidding sideways.

Smiling, Mr. Pipes stopped playing. "Curiosity got the cat, again."

Annie gathered Lady Kitty in her arms and stroked her ruffled fur.

"Magnifizent playing, Mein Herr," said Mr. Kluge, rubbing his hands together.

"I'll try playing something Lady Kitty will like better," said Mr. Pipes. He began a meditative tune in a minor key. Drew thought it sounded sad.

"Dat tune is '*Iste Confessor*,'" said Mr. Kluge, humming with the organ, his eyes lifted toward the stone vaulting above. "J. S. Bach, isn't it?"

"Bach did use it in his *St. Matthew Passion*," replied Mr. Pipes. "But the hymn first set to this tune is by Johann Heermann and first appeared in his collection of hymns called *Songs of Tears*. Drew, pull out your little volume of *Hymns Ancient and Modern*; check that it's not in *A and M*—an appalling lack of German hymn writers, I fear."

"You obviously don't need de musik, Mein Herr," said Mr. Kluge, pulling a book off a nearby shelf. "But de vords are here."

Mr. Pipes opened to the hymn. "Ah, yes, but in German—naturally. Annie, let me see your sketchbook. With the German text before me I should be able to faithfully recall the English translation; then, if it is all right with Mr. Kluge, we'll sing it together."

Annie and Drew watched over Mr. Pipes's shoulder as he, glancing occasionally at the German text, wrote down the lines:

> Ah, holy Jesus, how hast Thou offended,
> That man to judge Thee hath in hate pretended?
> By foes derided, by Thine own rejected,
> O most afflicted.
>
> Who was the guilty? who brought this upon Thee?
> Alas, my treason, Jesus, hath undone Thee.
> 'Twas I, Lord Jesus, I it was denied Thee:
> I crucified Thee.
>
> Lo, the good Shepherd for the sheep is offered:
> The slave hath sinned, and the Son hath suffered:
> For man's atonement, while he nothing heedeth,
> God intercedeth.
>
> For me, kind Jesus, was Thine incarnation,
> Thy mortal sorrow, and Thy life's oblation:
> Thy death of anguish and Thy bitter passion,
> For my salvation.
>
> Therefore, kind Jesus, since I cannot pay Thee,
> I do adore Thee, and will ever pray Thee
> Think on Thy pity and Thy love unswerving,
> Not my deserving.

"There we are," said Mr. Pipes. "Now we can sing this magnificent prayer together. Mr. Kluge, won't you join us?"

"Ja, but in German, only. I don't know your English for dis hymn."

"Very well," said Mr. Pipes. "Do notice Mr. Heermann's amazement at the incongruity of Jesus, the Holy One, dying in place of sinners—sinners like you and like me."

Mr. Pipes played *Iste Confessor*, slowly and with feeling, and Mr. Kluge joined them in singing:

> Herzliebster Jesu, was hast du verbrochen....
> ... Alas, my treason, Jesus hath undone Thee.
> 'Twas I, Lord Jesus, I it was denied Thee:
> I crucified Thee.

Drew frowned at the words. Wasn't it Judas that denied Jesus? He thought about his dousing in the river and the temper tantrum that preceded it. Then he thought about his pride, his always wanting to outdo his sister—and everyone else. He swallowed a lump in his throat; maybe he was the guilty one after all.

Annie stopped singing once or twice and bit her lip. She felt so undeserving of the Lord Jesus. Mr. Kluge carried them through, all in German. A group of tourists had entered the cathedral and sat quietly listening to the unlikely quartet. The last chord faded into silence.

"I do adore Thee, kind Jesus," said Mr. Pipes at last.

"Amen, to that," added Annie and Drew quietly.

"Now den," said Mr. Kluge, breaking the quiet of the moment. "I have much to do for de conzert, but I vant to show my gratitude. Ordinarily de steeple is not open to de public," he looked out of the corner of his eye and winked, "but I have de key. Vould you like to climb to the pinnacle of de highest steeple in Europe? De view—how do you say it—takes de breath avay."

"Could we?" asked Annie and Drew.

"Lead the way, Mr. Kluge," said Mr. Pipes.

◈ ◈ ◈

"Whew! Four hundred and sixty-six feet is a long way," said Drew, as they neared the highest observation point of the steeple.

Annie inched cautiously toward the tracery-guarded[†] opening. In a flurry of beating wings, several startled pigeons flew from their perch out over the old town spreading dizzily below.

From Annie's arms, Lady Kitty hissed. "It's okay," said Annie, reassuring herself as much as her kitten.

"That's what I call a bird's eye view," said Drew, watching the pigeons reeling gleefully in circles out over the tile roofs of the medieval houses. The River Ill caught his eye, and he followed it to the canal bridge where he screamed at those boys. How he wished he could take back those words.

"In the Middle Ages, bishops used to have unofficial contests," said Mr. Pipes, wiping his forehead and setting his glasses back on his nose, "to see who could build the highest steeple. Many of them miscalculated, and the steeples plunged to the street below."

"What!" said Drew, backing away from the archway. "Couldn't we talk about something else right now?"

"But Drew, this one's been here for ages," said Annie, leaning out to get a better view. "They did this one right, didn't they, Mr. Pipes?"

"Yes, indeed. The delicate-looking stone work with lots of openings," explained Mr. Pipes, "though it may not look so very solid, actually allows the winds to pass through the steeple instead of battering against it and pushing it over. I say, it has worked quite nicely—so far."

"So far?" said Drew. "What do you mean, 'so far'? Let me see, at thirty-two feet per second per second, and 466 feet, it would take less than five-and-a-half seconds if we fell...."

---

† *Tracery* is ornamental work consisting of branching ribs or bars found in the upper part of a Gothic window—in panels, screens, etc.

"You know," said Annie, ignoring Drew's calculations. "If I were a spy, this would be a good place to spy from." After a pause, she added, "We haven't seen him here at all."

"No doubt his travels have taken him elsewhere, my dear," said Mr. Pipes. "This rather proves he was not a spy after all, I should think. I'm so glad you've come to see it our way, my dear."

"Rats!" said Drew, looking disappointed.

Annie squinted at the antlike people walking the narrow streets below. She wasn't at all sure she did agree. "Oh, I think he's here," she said. "We just haven't seen him."

O God, My Faithful God

The one who calls you is faithful and he will do it. 1 Thess. 5:24

1. O God, my faith - ful God, true foun- tain ev - er - flow - ing,
2. Give me the strength to do with read - y heart and will - ing,
3. Keep me from say - ing words that lat - er need re - call - ing;
4. When dan - gers gath - er round, oh, keep me calm and fear - less;

with - out whom noth - ing is, all per - fect gifts be - stow - ing:
what - ev - er you com - mand, my call - ing here ful - fill - ing—
guard me, lest i - dle speech may from my lips be fall - ing:
help me to bear the cross when life seems dark and cheer - less;

give me a health - y frame, and may i have with - in
to do it when I ought, with all my strength; and bless
but when, with - in my place, I must and ought to speak,
help me, as you have taught, to love both great and small,

a con - science free from blame, a soul un - stained by sin.
what - ev - er I have wrought, for you must give suc - cess.
then to my words give grace, lest I of - fend the weak.
and, by your Spir - it's might, to live at peace with all.

Johann Heermann, 1585–1647
Tr. by Catherine Winkworth, 1863; alt.

DARMSTADT (or WAS FRAG' ICH NACH DER WELT) 6.7.6.7.6.6.6.6.
Ahasuerus Fritsch, 1679
Arr. by Johann Sebastian Bach (1685–1750) in *Cantata 45*

Ah, Holy Jesus, How Hast Thou Offended

Surely he took up our infirmities and carried our sorrows, yet we considered him
stricken by God, smitten by him, and afflicted. Is. 53:4

1. Ah, ho - ly Je - sus, how hast thou of - fend - ed, That man to judge thee hath in hate pre - tend - ed? By foes de - rid - ed, by thine own re - ject - ed, O most af - flict - ed.

2. Who was the guilt - y? who brought this up - on thee? A - las, my trea - son, Je - sus, hath un - done thee. 'Twas I, Lord Je - sus, I it was de - nied thee: I cru - ci - fied thee.

3. Lo, the good Shep-herd for the sheep is of - fered: The slave hath sin - ned, and the Son hath suf - fered: For man's a - tone - ment, while he noth-ing heed-eth, God in - ter - ced - eth.

4. For me, kind Je - sus, was thine in - car - na - tion, Thy mor - tal sor - row, and thy life's ob - la - tion: Thy death of an - guish and thy bit - ter pas - sion, For my sal - va - tion.

5. There-fore, kind Je - sus, since I can-not pay thee, I do a - dore thee, and will ev - er pray thee Think on thy pit - y and thy love un - swerv-ing, Not my de - serv - ing. A - MEN.

ISTE CONFESSOR 11. 11. 11. 5.
Johann Heermann, 1680
Tr. *Yattendon Hymnal*, 1899
Rouen church melody
har. by Healey Willan, 1880-

Chapter Six

Paul Gerhardt
1607–1676

Come, then, banish all your sadness,
One and all,
Great and small;
Come with songs of gladness.

The next morning, amidst the shouting of deck hands and
blaring of horns, Annie and Drew found themselves seated
on the top deck of a large riverboat on a broad expanse of the
Rhine River.

"There, now," said Mr. Pipes, stuffing his knapsack under
his seat. "We've made it on the first boat of the morning." He
breathed in the fresh morning air. "Though not sailing—properly sailing, that is—we've a glorious day for a motor voyage
northward. Annie, dear, do you have Lady Kitty well in hand?
Simply can't have our little feline friend upsetting the punctual-
ity of German river traffic. No, no that would simply not do."

"She should feel right at home on the water," said Annie,
stroking the soft orange fur between the twitching ears. A
steady rumble came from under Annie's sweater as Lady Katherine purred contentedly. "But, Mr. Pipes, doesn't Lady Kitty
need a boarding ticket? We did."

Mr. Pipes seemed suddenly busy adjusting his necktie and
collar. "Well, now, my dear," he paused, clearing his throat and
looking at his ticket. "Ah, yes, I see my way clearly. You see, my
ticket says 'adult,' and may I see yours, Annie?"

She passed him her ticket.

"Ah, just as I thought. Yours says 'child.' Now, Annie, as
much as your affection extends to cats and the like, I don't believe
you would consider her a child—a proper human child, that is?"

Annie looked at Lady Katherine's little orange head poking curiously out of her sweater. The kitten lifted her paw and batted playfully at one of Annie's buttons. "I suppose not," she said, after a moment's hesitation.

"That settles it," said Mr. Pipes triumphantly. "You see, they simply don't sell tickets marked 'kitten.' Therefore, we may confidently conclude that kittens need not pay."

"I hope we don't run into problems later on," said Drew distractedly. In order to catch this first riverboat his breakfast had been cut short. Another hunk of that bulging hot *Brötchen* smothered in butter and jelly, he thought, licking his lips, and one more helping—maybe two—of smoked ham, might have done it.

"We will deal with them as they come, Drew, my boy," said Mr. Pipes, putting his ticket into the inside pocket of his tweed jacket and patting it conclusively. "And, now, let us steer our way into less shoal-bedeviled waters."

A wailing blast came from the ship's horn and echoed across the river; a deck hand cast loose the mooring lines, and with a rumble of powerful engines the riverboat, filled with tourists, left the pier, gaining speed as the captain steered it into the main channel of the river. On the right, dense forest followed the hillside down to the shore, and behind them, Drew watched the great spire of the cathedral grow smaller and finally disappear as they rounded the first bend. Morning sunlight twinkled on the calm expanse of water ahead, and behind them their wake, flecked with white foam, shone a transparent green as it peeled away in a growing V-pattern.

"Guten morgen!" boomed a voice over a loud speaker. "Das ist ..."

"—It is the captain," said Mr. Pipes. "He will be our tour guide as we travel up the 818-mile Rhine River."

"We're traveling 818 miles on this boat!" said Drew. "Even with this fast engine, 818 miles—whew!—that could take a while. I hope they have good food on board—and lots of it!"

Mr. Pipes laughed. "We'll travel only several hours north to Worms today and on north tomorrow. But we'll travel only on the German portion of the Rhine—and not all of that. The mighty Rhine starts in Switzerland, crosses Germany, and, after snaking its way through the Netherlands, empties into the North Sea. She is the lifeblood of German commerce; twenty-five percent of German goods are transported on the Rhine, and 9,000 goods vessels ply her waters every month, making her the busiest river in all Europe."

"Sounds like a happening place to me," said Drew. "And it goes right by that Worms place?"

"Yes," said Mr. Pipes. "We'll spend the afternoon sightseeing, enjoy an evening meal, and retire there for the night."

"Is it a nice place—to eat?" asked Annie with a grimace. "It just sounds kind of—well—kind of slimy."

Mr. Pipes chuckled. "Annie, dear, it is a lovely place, and not at all slimy."

"What's a 'goods' vessel?" asked Drew.

Mr. Pipes walked to the rail surrounding the tourist deck. "I believe we're about to overtake one just ahead."

Drew looked past the heads of other tourists looking forward over the rail. From the broad stern of a black and white tug, water foamed and churned, and the tug's engines made a steady "vrung-thug-thug-thug, vrung-thug-thug-thug." But the tourist boat gained effortlessly on the tug and moved to the right. As they passed, Drew watched in amazement as two enormous barges, piled high with gravel, came into view, stretching like a floating mountain range up the river. From a towerlike wheelhouse, the tugboat skipper waved a salute as they passed.

"Listen to those engines," said Drew. "I guess it takes pretty big ones to push two barges and those heaps of gravel—must be tons of the stuff."

As the tug and barges disappeared behind, Drew spotted a cluster of smaller powerboats just off a point on the left bank.

"What are they doing?" he said.

"Well, Drew," said Mr. Pipes. "Gulls whirling above the water like that, I should think they're fishing."

"No kidding!" said Drew. "For what?"

"Pike do abound in some European rivers," said Mr. Pipes. "Could be pike."

Mr. Pipes watched in amusement as Drew ran back to his seat and frantically pulled his fishing pole out of his knapsack. Glancing eagerly at the fishing boats and at the greenish-brown water, he fitted the pole segments together.

"What on earth are you doing, Drew?" asked Annie.

"Going fishing," said Drew, heading for the stern. "What else?"

"With all these people around?" said Annie, lowering her voice and scanning the crowd.

"Sure, why not?" With a shiny lure tied on the end, Drew let out his line. "If there's a pike swimming down there, I'm going to snag him."

"Drew," said Mr. Pipes. "The powerful engines in this boat are pushing us entirely too fast for fishing. We're not sailing, you know."

"Oh," said Drew, watching his lure bounce and skip with the boat's wake. Puffs of blue smoke swirled at the waterline. Annie wrinkled her nose at the diesel fumes hanging in the air. This was definitely not sailing. The large black, red, and yellow German flag flying at the stern snapped cheerfully in the breeze. "Yeah, I guess you're right." Drew sounded disappointed. Suddenly he brightened. "Do you think the captain would slow her down—maybe even stop?"

"I'm terribly afraid he would do nothing of the sort," said Mr. Pipes. "We'd be forever getting to Worms if he did."

"Maybe when the boat stops at Worms," said Annie kindly. "Maybe you could fish then."

Disappointed, Drew reeled in his line and repacked his rod.

Absently stroking her kitten, Annie looked around at the steep hillsides plunging into the river, the rows of yellow-green vineyards zigzagging between stands of trees, and the sun-drenched bricks of a little village huddled along the banks. She sighed as they rounded a graceful bend in the river.

"It sure is pretty on the Rhine," she said. New scenery came into view farther around the bend. Something on the hillside to the right caught her eye. "Hey, what's that? It looks like some kind of tower sticking up on that cliff to—to starboard."

"Castle!" yelled Drew.

"Get your camera!" said Annie.

"What a perfect spot for a castle," said Drew. "It's perched up there like an eagle's nest. Knights in that place could see anybody coming down the river—and give them big-time grief."

"The Rhine connects Northern and Southern Europe," said Mr. Pipes. "So the fortress that controlled the Rhine controlled Europe. Quite simple, really."

"Looks like maybe those guys didn't do so well," said Drew as they came closer.

"'Tis a bit of a shabby one," agreed Mr. Pipes. "A ruin, in fact. But there are many more castles farther down the Rhine, and some very fine specimens indeed."

"Ruin or not, it is kind of charming," said Annie, gazing back at the disappearing ruin.

"What's that just ahead?" asked Drew. "It looks like some kind of little island in the middle of the river. Maybe another fortress."

"Now that looks like something right out of a fairy tale," said Annie.

"Pfalz Castle, I believe it is," said Mr. Pipes. "A lovely specimen, indeed."

The engines slowed as they admired the whitewashed stone walls and dark turrets rising to a domelike central tower.

"What a place!" said Drew as the castle grew smaller behind them. "You could fish right out the window! Hey, Mr. Pipes, do you think they would—?"

"—I most seriously doubt anything of the kind, my boy," said Mr. Pipes. "One does not generally walk up to the gate of a castle and casually beg admittance. It is just not done."

◈ ◈ ◈

Mr. Pipes busied himself for the next hour writing a long letter to Dr. Dudley and a postcard with an aerial view of Strasbourg Cathedral to Mrs. Beccles.

"There, now," he said, signing his name with a flourish. "Mrs. Beccles will like this photograph, and Dr. Dudley will give me just slightly less 'what for' now that I have told him of our movements about the continent. This trip is an enormous worry to him, so I must be more faithful in my correspondence with the dear fellow."

Annie grimaced as she licked a stamp and put it on her last postcard; Clara would love the picture from one of Strasbourg's gardens. Annie smiled at the rows of dancing-dolls; no fear of anyone reading this postcard.

Drew jotted a quick note to his mother and spent the rest of the time digging in his knapsack for the remains of a chocolate bar he was just sure he hadn't eaten. After emptying the entire contents of his knapsack on deck, including several mismatched and very dirty socks, he found nothing.

"Ugh, Drew," said Annie. "People are watching."

◈ ◈ ◈

After carefully studying every passenger on deck, Annie relaxed: no spy, at least no one looked anything like the man she was sure had been following them. Feeling better, she sketched the river countryside as they continued north, while Drew brooded about fishing and chocolate bars. Around a tight bend in the river, an ancient village with square stone towers came into view.

"Looks like that place has been around forever," said Drew. "Give or take a few years either way."

"Ah, yes, humph, yes, my dears," sputtered Mr. Pipes as he woke from a nap. With the steady hum of the engine and the warm sunshine, Mr. Pipes had folded his hands on his chest, and with a smile and a little sigh, had dozed off, his chin slumped forward. Now wide awake, he glanced from the town to his map, mumbling absently, then, tapping the map with his finger, he said:

"Speyer, the ancient town of Speyer. The great cathedral was built in 1030, nearly 1000 years ago—it's just there, on the hill. They built it on a grand scale in an effort to show the might of the German emperor. During an important imperial diet in Luther's day, while the city filled with papists and supporters of the emperor, Philip of Hesse, a Christian prince, led 200 well-armed horsemen and a crowd of Lutheran ministers into the city. The emperor forbade the ministers to preach in the churches of the city, so, with Philip's encouragement, they preached the gospel from balconies in the streets. Thousands gathered to hear."

"I like this guy!" said Drew.

"What happened next?" asked Annie as the town disappeared behind them.

"Well, Philip's followers grew hungry," said Mr. Pipes, looking sideways at Drew.

"I can appreciate that," said Drew. "By the way, when *do* we get to Worms?"

"Soon, my boy, soon," replied Mr. Pipes with a chuckle. Then he continued, "Roman Catholics are forbidden to eat meat on Fridays, so Philip decided to show his loyalty to the Bible, which nowhere forbids eating meat on any day, and hosted an enormous public barbecue. Germans do like their food, you know. Many people in Speyer enjoyed a tender, well-seasoned ox, cooked to perfection—and served on a Friday."

"Good for Philip!" said Drew, smacking his fist into his palm. "That showed them. Those German Christians—boy, they sure were tough."

"Ah, they lived in tough times," said Mr. Pipes, "times that demanded bold, courageous action from God's people."

"Yes," said Annie slowly, "but their hymns are so full of—well—gentleness. How could they be tough and gentle at the same time?"

"It is a matter of appropriateness, my dears. We are called to stand boldly against sin and evil, but at the same time to submit cheerfully to the hardships and disappointments God has ordained for our good—and we are called to love our enemies. Luther and the German Christians who came after him practiced this rule. One of the features of German hymns is the combination of this bold spirit and a humble submission to the love of God."

While listening, Annie bit the end of her pencil and decided the light was perfect for another sketch of Mr. Pipes. "If only Lady Kitty would hold still and quit trying to chew on my pencil," she thought in frustration. What's more, the vibration from the engine jiggled her pencil, making it still harder to draw, so she closed her sketchbook. Mr. Pipes crossed his legs and continued.

"Luther inspired many other German hymn writers; and by sheer numbers of hymns still included in hymnals, Paul Gerhardt—born in 1607—outwrote Luther four to one. He followed in Luther's steps, studying theology at the University of Wittenberg, where he was regarded as a studious and able young man. But his hopes of marriage to the young woman he loved, and of a church in which to minister, were frustrated by the devastation of the Thirty Years' War. He worked as a private tutor in the home of a Berlin lawyer and kept his hopes alive by writing poetry. Not until Gerhardt turned forty-eight years old and became an assistant minister in Berlin did he and his sweetheart, Anna Maria, finally marry."

Mr. Pipes paused, looking distractedly at the far shore.

"What happened next?" asked Annie.

"What's that, my dear?" replied Mr. Pipes.

"What happened next? Did they have kids?" asked Annie.

Mr. Pipes looked at Annie for a moment before answering. "Yes, yes. God gave them four little ones—" he broke off, adjusting his necktie. "—but they all died in infancy. Anna Maria gave birth to a fifth child—a boy. The child lived, but Mrs. Gerhardt became very ill and eventually, much to her husband's grief, she died, leaving him a widower with a young boy to care for. Differences between local ministers arose, and he finally lost his pastorate in Berlin. He finished out his years with his son in a small country parish, preaching faithfully to a largely unresponsive congregation."

"Tough life," said Drew.

"What do his hymns sound like?" asked Annie.

"I'll bet they're not the most cheerful things on the planet," said Drew.

"Oh, you are most incorrect about that," said Mr. Pipes. "It is said of Gerhardt that he wrote his hymns 'under circumstances that would have made most men cry rather than sing.'

"Though beset by trials and disappointments, Gerhardt's humble devotion to Jesus, the loving Son of God, fills his hymns. His poetry glows with a simple yet hearty sincerity. Perhaps that is why, in Sunday worship, Germans sing Gerhardt more than any other hymn writer."

"Tomorrow's Sunday," said Annie.

"Indeed, it is, and I thought we might worship at *Magnuskirche* in Worms," said Mr. Pipes. "Perhaps we'll sing Gerhardt."

"But we don't know German," said Drew. "What are we going to church for if we can't understand any of it?"

"Well, my boy," said Mr. Pipes, stroking his chin in thought. "We gather in the Lord's House to worship God—to render praise and adoration to Him, not first to receive from Him. We can join our English and American voices with Christians singing in German, and we'll let God sort out the language problem. We'll sing from my English translation of the Lutheran hymnal. But, my boy, we are nowhere nearest heaven in this life than when we are in the Lord's House. And, I say, we must never neglect corporate worship—never."

"So, who translated Mr. Gerhardt's hymns into English?" asked Annie, tickling Lady Katherine under the chin and wondering how she could smuggle her into a church service, especially now that Lady Kitty liked sitting on Annie's shoulder like a parrot.

"Remember Charles Wesley's brother John?" asked Mr. Pipes. "I told you Charles's story last summer."

"Yeah, and the voyage to America," said Drew, "with those Moravian Christians singing German hymns through the big storm."

"Yes, that's it," said Mr. Pipes, obviously pleased. "A number of the hymns they sang with such confidence on board that tempest-tossed ship were written by Paul Gerhardt," said Mr. Pipes. "No sooner did they arrive safely in Georgia and John began translating many of those hymns into English. He actually found himself in a bit of a stew with the Anglican clergy for doing it—remember, before 1861 the Anglican Church sang only from the Psalter. One of Gerhardt's hymns John Wesley translated—maybe while riding his horse between plantations—'Jesus, Thy Boundless Love to Me,' has become a favorite in our English hymnals. His hymns reveal a deep appreciation for Jesus' love for lost and dying sinners, and they remind us that the joy of the Lord is our strength."

Just then Drew heard a change in the riverboat's engines, and the towers and columns of the ancient city of Worms rose majestically into the summer sky on the left bank.

"Fishing time!" said Drew moments later as the boat came alongside the dock. A tall, blond-haired deck hand vaulted onto the pier and looped the mooring lines around anvil-like cleats.

"Fishing is it," said Mr. Pipes, "or lunch?"

"Good idea," said Annie, grabbing her knapsack and cradling Lady Katherine in her free arm. "I'm starved, and so is Lady Kitty."

"Got to keep my strength up," said Drew, returning his fishing pole to his knapsack and heading eagerly for the gangplank leading to town.

◈ ◈ ◈

"So, my dears," said Mr. Pipes, scanning with the children the array of sausages on display in the shop window. "Whatever shall we eat for lunch: weisswurst, bratwurst, Leberwurst—"

"Oh, my," said Annie, gazing wide-eyed at the curved and bulbous mounds of meat. "What could be worse! I don't mean to sound ungrateful, but don't they have anything better?"

"Looks pretty good to me," said Drew. "But how do they keep them in those tubes like that?" asked Drew.

Mr. Pipes looked cautiously at Annie before answering. "Ah, well, now, ah ... let's just say they have conventional ways of creating these lovely sausages that have proven effective for ever so many years. They do have lovely cheeses, Annie, if you prefer, and the local rye bread is delicious."

"Cheese sounds wonderful," said Annie, "and maybe some milk—cold and warm."

"Very well," said Mr. Pipes. "Drew, you might enjoy a frankfurter—or two."

"Sounds great," said Drew. "I'll try a frankfurter, and the bratwurst, and cheese, and bread, and some milk, and some...."

Mr. Pipes ordered Wiener schnitzel along with the children's meals, and they sat down to eat at a quiet table overlooking the Luther Monument.

"That's Luther in the middle," said Drew between mouthfuls, "with his hand on the Bible. But who's the guy on his left in front? The one with the big sword?"

"That is Philip of Hesse," said Mr. Pipes.

"Good guy," said Drew, taking another bite of sausage.

"At Luther's feet are men like John Wycliffe and John Huss on whose shoulders, in a manner of speaking, Luther stood when he took his great stand for gospel truth in this very city," continued Mr. Pipes.

They finished eating and walked across the courtyard for a closer look. Pots overflowing with sun-drenched geraniums and sweet-smelling alyssum lined the stairs leading to the statues. Scenes from the life of Luther, cast in bronze, wrapped around the base of Luther's statue: the nailing of the Ninety-five Theses to the church door, translating Scripture, and preaching. Drew sat on one of a series of little pedestals laid out like giant teeth between the statues surrounding Luther's and gazed through the rustling leaves at the sturdy cathedral nearby. Annie let Lady Katherine down to explore; then she stepped back, frowning in thought as she looked at the whole monument.

"Mr. Pipes," she said, "why is that statue of a woman so sad looking?"

"She is mourning," said Mr. Pipes. "The three statues of women represent important Protestant cities; your sad one is Magdeburg mourning."

Annie felt numb as she remembered what Mr. Pipes told them about that city.

"That's the one where imperial soldiers killed all those children—thousands of them," said Drew, his eyes wide.

"Yes, Magdeburg was besieged and plundered in 1631," said Mr. Pipes. "And many martyrs went to their reward from that city."

"Mr. Pipes," said Annie at last, "why does the whole monument look kind of like a castle? Do you think they meant it to be a castle—a fortress?" She broke off. "Wait! I've got it! It's the hymn."

"What are you talking about?" said Drew, hopping up and taking the steps three at a time to join Annie.

"Annie, dear," said Mr. Pipes, "I believe you're absolutely correct."

"The artist must have designed it all around the words of Luther's hymn: 'A Mighty Fortress Is Our God.' And all these other people," she gestured at the other statues, "trusted in 'That Word above all earthly powers—' and that must be why Luther is on top holding up the Word of God, right?"

"Pretty clever!" said her brother, nodding in approval.

"Indeed," agreed Mr. Pipes, smiling at Annie.

"Yeah, must have been quite an artist," said Annie. "And he had to know the hymn to make a statue of it."

Drew stared at his sister for a moment. "I meant *you're* pretty clever, silly, for figuring it out."

"Oh."

"This may very well be the only statue of a hymn in the entire world!" said Mr. Pipes.

Lady Katherine hopped from cap to cap on the merlons of the fortress walls, making her way around the monument. Reaching the base of a statue, she hesitated; then with all four paws splayed she leaped into a stone flowerpot.

"Uh oh, rescue job," said Drew, as Annie scurried to separate the mischievous kitten from a mass of geraniums.

❖ ❖ ❖

Mr. Pipes led them through a lush garden nearby surrounded by poplar trees, their leaves sparkling merrily in the sunlight and rustling softly with the afternoon breeze. The buzz of a lawn mower came from the far end of the richly manicured lawn. Drew watched a man in blue overalls guiding the mower in perfect diagonal lines.

"Not even a wobble," he said. "The chap's an artist."

Annie closed her eyes and sniffed the air. "Hmm, fresh-mown grass smells like springtime."

"It's summer," Drew corrected.

"I know, but it reminds me of springtime."

"*Heylshofgarten* truly is lovely," said Mr. Pipes. "But it hasn't always been a garden; before fire destroyed it, the Bishop's Palace covered this site. Here, on this very spot, Luther stood before the most powerful ruler in all Germany and boldly declared his loyalty to God's Word. Indeed, it was no small feat, knowing what emperors, kings, and popes did to those who took a stand against them."

Nearby stood the massive Romanesque cathedral, the Dom; and Annie and Drew—Lady Katherine at Annie's heels—followed Mr. Pipes into its grand interior. Drew thought its thick walls, rounded arches, and dark, mysterious atmosphere made it look much older than Strasbourg Cathedral. From there, they visited the Luther Room at the City Museum. Annie felt a tingle of excitement up and down her spine as Mr. Pipes showed them a large German Bible with an entire page handwritten by Martin Luther—signed and dated 1541.

Strolling through town to their hotel, Mr. Pipes stopped at a little shop called *Kleiderhaus Uhrig*. "Ah, very good. I must have them press a shirt for tomorrow."

The shopkeeper stared disapprovingly at Lady Katherine perched on Annie's shoulder batting at her braids, while Mr. Pipes gave instructions about how he liked his shirts pressed. "Do notice this memorial plaque, my dears," said Mr. Pipes as they stepped back into the late afternoon sunlight.

"*Jo-han-nit-er-hof*," read Drew slowly. "What else does it say?"

"In 1521, during his ten days in Worms for the imperial diet, Luther stayed at an inn, the *Johanniterhof*, long since destroyed, but originally on this very site."

"So Luther might have had his shirts pressed on the same spot!" said Drew with a laugh. "They did that sort of thing at inns, didn't they?"

"Maybe," said Annie doubtfully. "But I think Luther still wore a monk's robe—probably didn't need pressing."

◈ ◈ ◈

Next morning, Mr. Pipes, wearing his charcoal tweed suit, newly-pressed white shirt, and best necktie, met Annie and Drew for breakfast. "This is the day the Lord hath made; let us rejoice and be glad in it," he greeted them, as they sat down at the neatly laid table loaded with *Brötchen*—fresh and hot—butter and jam, slices of smoked ham, peaches and cream, and thick black coffee.

After breakfast, Annie—with Lady Kitty trotting at her heels—followed Mr. Pipes and her brother down streets marked with names like *Martinspforte* and *Lutherring*, until they arrived at the arched entrance to the ancient-looking *Magnuskirche*. Rising above the thick stone walls, relieved only occasionally by narrow windows, stood the pointed bell tower. They watched the bell swinging back and forth as it had for centuries, gonging joyously across the city, calling the townsfolk to worship.

"Ah, ancient Romanesque," said Mr. Pipes, smiling up at the plain stone walls. "Though not as fancy, this church is older than the cathedral."

"So that's why you wanted us to come here," said Drew.

Mr. Pipes looked at Drew and chuckled. "Do you still think, my boy, that I like things just because they're old? Surely, by now you know I value what is true and enduring; if that happens also to be old—well, so be it."

Drew smiled up at the old man. "I think I understand, but there's lots of old churches—why this one?"

"Well, Worms was a Roman Catholic city before Luther came. But during the diet, a growing number of Protestant Christians met here and heard the first gospel sermon preached in the city. To this day, it holds special significance to Christians who love the preaching of God's Word. And I'm almost certain that if we're to sing Gerhardt in worship, we'll sing him here. Now, then, gather up Lady Katherine—and, Annie, dear, do keep her quiet in the service."

Seated on a dark, polished pew, Annie stroked Lady Kitty until she curled up into a furry orange ball and fell fast asleep. Mr. Pipes whispered a translation of the minister's call to worship, and directed the children to their English Bibles so they could follow the Scripture readings. Then the strains of a small pipe organ echoed off the ancient walls. Mr. Pipes beamed at the children and quickly found the page in the English hymnal.

"Perfect choice for calling our minds and hearts to worship," he whispered, "and look who wrote it." He pointed to the lower left corner of the hymnal: "Paul Gerhardt, 1653," it read.

"Remember, children," whispered Mr. Pipes, "Mr. Gerhardt was overwhelmed with the love of God and filled with rejoicing that our debt of sin was fully paid by Christ—this hymn overflows with those themes."

The congregation sang in German—a few people looking over their shoulders as Annie, Drew, and Mr. Pipes joined them singing:

O Lord, how shall I meet Thee,
How welcome Thee aright?
Thy people long to greet Thee,
My Hope, my heart's Delight!
O, kindle, Lord, most holy,
Thy lamp within my breast
To do in spirit lowly
All that may please Thee best.

Love caused Thine incarnation,
Love brought Thee down to me;
Thy thirst for my salvation
Procured my liberty.
O love beyond all telling,
That led Thee to embrace,
In love all love excelling,
Our lost and fallen race!

Rejoice, then, ye sad-hearted,
Who sit in deepest gloom,
Who mourn o'er joys departed
And tremble at your doom.
Despair not, He is near you,
Yea, standing at the door,
Who best can help and cheer you
And bids you weep no more.

Sin's debt, that fearful burden,
Let not your souls distress;
Your guilt the Lord will pardon
And cover by His grace.
He comes, for men procuring
The peace of sin forgiv'n,
For all God's sons securing
Their heritage in heav'n.

During the incomprehensible sermon—preached, of course, in German—Drew read back over the hymn, and without actually planning to, he found himself memorizing it:

> ... O, kindle, Lord, most holy,
> Thy lamp within my breast
> To do in spirit lowly
> All that may please Thee best....
>
> ... He comes, for men procuring
> The peace of sin forgiv'n,
> For all God's sons securing
> Their heritage in heav'n.

As the meaning of the immortal words made their way more deeply into Drew's heart, he felt an overwhelming sense of wonder in his soul: "Lord Jesus, I am one of God's sons; help me to do only what pleases You best. Amen."

All My Heart This Night Rejoices

The Word became flesh and made his dwelling among us. We have seen his glory.
John 1:14

1. All my heart this night re- joic - es   as I hear   far and near
2. Forth to - day the Con-qu'ror go - eth,   who the foe,   sin and woe,
3. Shall we still dread God's dis- plea - sure, who, to save,   free - ly gave
4. He be - comes the Lamb that tak - eth   sin a- way   and for aye
5. Hark! a voice from yon- der man - ger,   soft and sweet, doth en- treat:

sweet - est an - gel voic- es. "Christ is born," their choirs are sing - ing
death and hell, o'er - throw- eth. God is man, man to de - liv - er;
• his most cher- ished Trea- sure? To re - deem us, he hath giv - en
full a - tone- ment mak - eth. For our life his own he ten - ders;
"Flee from woe and dan - ger. Breth- ren, from all ills that grieve you,

till the air ev - 'ry- where now with joy is ring - ing.
his dear Son now is one with our blood for - ev - er.
• his own Son from the throne of his might in heav - en.
and our race, by his grace, meet for glo - ry ren - ders.
you are freed; all you need I will sure - ly give you."

6. Come, then, banish all your sadness,
one and all, great and small;
come with songs of gladness.
Love him who with love is glowing;
hail the star, near and far
light and joy bestowing.

7. Dearest Lord, thee will I cherish.
Though my breath fail in death,
yet I shall not perish,
but with thee abide forever
there on high, in that joy
which can vanish never.

Paul Gerhardt, 1653
Tr. by Catherine Winkworth, 1858; alt.

WARUM SOLLT' ICH MICH DENN GRAMEN 8.3.3.6.8.3.3.6.
Johann G. Ebeling, 1666

O Lord, How Shall I Meet You

Here's the bridegroom! Come out to meet him! Matt. 25:6

1. O Lord, how shall I meet you, how wel-come you a-right?
   Your peo-ple long to greet you, my hope, my heart's de-light!
   O kin-dle, Lord Most Ho-ly, your lamp with-in my breast
   to do in spir-it low-ly all that may please you best.

2. Love caused your in-car-na-tion, love brought you down to me;
   your thirst for my sal-va-tion pro-cured my lib-er-ty.
   O love be-yond all tell-ing, that led you to em-brace,
   in love all love ex-cel-ling, our lost and fall-en race!

3. Re-joice, then, you sad-heart-ed, who sit in deep-est gloom,
   who mourn o'er joys de-part-ed and trem-ble at your doom.
   De-spair not, he is near you, yea, stand-ing at the door,
   who best can help and cheer you and bids you weep no more.

4. Sin's debt, that fear-ful bur-den, let not your souls dis-tress;
   your guilt the Lord will par-don and cov-er by his grace.
   He comes, for men pro-cur-ing the peace of sin for-giv'n,
   for all God's sons se-cur-ing their her-i-tage in heav'n.

Paul Gerhardt, 1653, cento
Trans. composite; mod.

ST. THEODULPH 7.6.7.6.D.
Melchior Teschner, ca. 1615

Chapter Seven

Johann Franck
1618–1677

Those who love the Father,
Though the storms may gather,
Still have peace within.
Yea, whate'er I here must bear,
Thou art still my purest pleasure,
Jesus, priceless treasure.

Translated by Catherine Winkworth, 1863

"I just know it's the same guy," hissed Annie in Mr. Pipes's ear, her fingers gripping his sleeve.

Mr. Pipes looked at Annie's wide eyes and terrified face and checked himself before dismissing her fears with a light jest. Clearly, she believed that someone was following them. He had just been thinking that Monday morning, as they boarded the boat for an excursion north on the Rhine, how pleasant it was to have Annie's fears of someone following them behind her. He looked around the deck of the riverboat; it looked like an ordinary mixture of foreign and German tourists. But he saw no one who looked at all like the young man they had seen earlier.

"I beg your pardon; to whom are you referring, my dear?" asked Mr. Pipes patiently. "I can't see anyone who looks like— well, like a spy."

He felt Annie's fingers grip his arm more tightly, and her eyes begged him to believe her. "Two rows back, near the German flag at the stern," she whispered, trying to keep her voice from quavering. "He's reading a newspaper. And, of course, he doesn't look like a spy—that's just the point: they try not to look like they're spying."

"Wait a second," said Drew, overhearing. "So if you're right, Annie, everyone who doesn't look like a spy is one." He rolled his eyes.

"*Might* be one," said Annie defensively. "And that guy we saw before, who used to wear the overcoat and cap, is sitting right by the flag—same guy, I'm sure of it."

"But there's nobody around who looks anything like him," said Drew, standing up conspicuously and craning his neck for a better view.

Mr. Pipes turned around deliberately. "But, my dear," he said at last. "You can't mean that young man—yes, yes, reading a newspaper—but wearing a black leather jacket, thick-soled combat boots, with shaved head, and all those earrings—and, I say, that ghastly ring in his nose. How could you possibly recognize him as the same fellow? Furthermore, my dear, one cannot fail to observe, that fellow looks like a rather high percentage of Germans we've seen under the age of thirty. How can you be so sure that he's the same chap? I'm morally certain there are large segments of society who read newspapers but who are never drawn into the cloak-and-dagger life of the common spy."

"It's him," said Annie. "He's only shaved his head and dressed like that to try and fool us—he looks pretty embarrassed about it all."

"As well he should," said Mr. Pipes.

"I'm more convinced than ever," said Annie, "that he is following us."

"The plot thickens," said Drew, obviously enjoying himself.

"Drew, I think you'd actually like it if he was a spy—or worse," said Annie.

"You bet!" agreed Drew. "Hey, I'm going to try and get a photograph of him—they did that kind of thing in the Cold War—he's probably already got ours. And the KGB, no doubt, has had us on file for years." He grinned eagerly as he dug his camera out of his knapsack. Turning it over in his hand, he frowned. "I sure wish this was a spy camera—what did they call them?—a Minox, yeah, that's it. German made, too, I think."

He narrowed his eyes and looked side to side. "Now, you just leave this all to me; the name's Willis—Andrew Willis."

It was Annie's turn to roll her eyes.

"Drew," said Mr. Pipes, smiling indulgently, "you clearly have an overworked imagination. Now, Annie, my dear, we are approaching some of the loveliest scenery on the Rhine. Do try to forget our young friend back there—I'm absolutely certain he's harmless."

Annie bit her lip and stroked Lady Katherine's chin. "I'll try," she said, glancing once more back at the man. She broke into a little smile then almost giggled. "He does look awfully ridiculous, dressed like that."

"About that we agree," said Mr. Pipes.

The hills along the Rhine seemed to level and melt away into a broad, populated city.

"Ah, yes, the incomparable city of Mainz," said Mr. Pipes. "Do look to our port; the many towers of the Cathedral of St. Mary and St. Martin rise within full view of the river. She is a marvelous example of late Romanesque with hints of Gothic on her newer arches and towers. Here, Annie, look through my opera glasses; they bring every detail so wonderfully close."

"Look at all those arches," she said, peering through the little binoculars. "I—I don't know what to say; it's all so beautiful."

"Can I have a peek?" asked Drew.

Drew studied the stonework and scalloped gables, the rows and rows of arches and lofty turrets. "You're right, Mr. Pipes, those lower round towers look lots older. Churches must have been pretty important to people back in the old days." With the opera glasses, he scanned slowly along the sun-drenched rooflines. "I can't imagine how long it took them to build a place like this—whew! and how much money it must have cost!"

"Indeed, it does tell us something about the shifting priorities of people then and now," said Mr. Pipes.

"I wish churches in America looked beautiful like these," said Annie wistfully.

"Yeah, our fanciest buildings are for sports and government—maybe banks, too," said Drew. "This place looks even better; was it an important city in the Reformation?" asked Drew.

"In a most profound way it was," said Mr. Pipes. "Mainz was the home of Johann Gutenberg, the inventor of the first printing press. He revolutionized the printing of books, and his press greatly enhanced the spread of the gospel throughout Europe."

"How did they make books before Gutenberg?" asked Annie, nuzzling noses with Lady Kitty, settled in her perch on Annie's shoulder.

"In the Middle Ages, every word of every page of every book monks laboriously copied by hand, my dear," said Mr. Pipes.

"Oh, there must not have been very many books, then," said Annie.

"And hand-copied ones cost the big bucks, I'll bet," added Drew.

"Yes, so only the very wealthy owned books," said Mr. Pipes. "And, of course, if books were scarce and expensive, only a very few learned to read them. Gutenberg helped change all that. Now, what book do you suppose he first printed on his new invention?"

"I don't know," said Drew, "a cookbook?"

They all laughed.

"Gutenberg gave history wonderful testimony to his priorities in 1456 when the first book produced in the Western world by movable-type printing was the Holy Bible—God's Word, not man's. Later, Luther's German Bible, his books, pamphlets, and hymns were printed in large quantities and at affordable prices. As a result, schools grew and more people learned to read. Yes, I would certainly say, thanks to Johann Gutenberg, that Mainz was an important city, helping spread the gospel during the Reformation."

They left behind the broad valley surrounding Mainz and, once again, hills covered with vineyards and terraced with ancient stone retaining walls met the banks of the Rhine.

Hoping no one saw him, Drew slowly turned the opera glasses back toward Annie's spy, sitting only yards behind. The spy's face leaped into view as he focused. Wow! He's really got a nose—wait, he actually *does* look sort of like.... Drew refocused the little binoculars. Maybe Annie was right about this guy.

Annie, gazing at the changing scenery, didn't notice Drew's spying, but she couldn't help peering nervously toward the stern.

Then it happened. Perhaps the fluttering of the colorful German flag caught the kitten's attention, but in any case, Lady Katherine suddenly sprang from Annie's shoulder, onto the shoulder of a large German woman in the row behind. Frightened by the woman's shrieking and her flailing arms, Lady Katherine leaped onto the shoulder of the next passenger, and then, with a crouch-and-spring motion, she landed on the cap of a gentleman in the next row. As the man clawed at his head, Annie realized with horror that her kitten was about to vault onto the stern rail next to the flag. If she missed, Annie realized, Lady Kitty would plunge into the swirling wake of those powerful engines—and most certainly be lost forever. Annie did what any self-respecting girl would do in the same situation—she screamed.

With all four paws spread out, Lady Kitty did leap. Annie felt her heart sink. But what was that? Suddenly springing from his seat, the man in the black leather jacket, like a wide receiver, caught Lady Kitty only a hair's width before she would have plunged into the foaming wake.

"What a catch!" said Drew.

Annie felt weak in the knees, but mumbled her thanks as her spy handed the spitting and hissing Lady Kitty to her. Mr. Pipes spoke to the man in German, thanking him, and offered apologies to the ruffled passengers before they returned to their seats.

"That was so close," said Annie when she finally recovered her voice. "Oh, but why did it have to be the spy who rescued you, you naughty kitty?"

Mr. Pipes, wearing a puzzled expression on his face, pulled out his map and thumbed through his little notebook.

"What're you looking for?" asked Drew.

Mr. Pipes glanced back at the leather-clad, earringed man before answering.

Annie looked at the frown on Mr. Pipes's face. "What's wrong, Mr. Pipes?"

"Oh, I'm sure it's nothing—really I am," he paused. "It's just that he spoke to me in German—but he is not German; I know that from his accent—it's nothing, surely not."

Drew looked at Annie and raised his eyebrows.

With a "Hmm," Mr. Pipes resumed studying his notebook and map. "Ah, here it is. Just ahead is the village—home of a most extraordinary pipe organ builder. Mind you, Germany is filled with organ builders, but I've had the privilege of playing one of Herr Fritz's organs, and, I dare say, he is the very best. What would you say to—" he glanced quickly over his shoulder, "—to a detour, an unplanned stopover at his workshop? We could hail a taxi at the next stop and be there in a few minutes time. It will be most interesting, I'm sure."

"That sounds great!" said Drew.

Annie looked over her shoulder. "Oh, let's go. But, can we do it without—" she gestured with her head, rolling her eyes toward the stern of the boat, "—without you-know-who following?"

"That, my dear," said Mr. Pipes, unsmiling, "is precisely my desire."

At the next stop, Mr. Pipes, looking out of the corner of his eye, said, "Make no move until the very last minute; that's it, look casual and unhurried."

"What if we miss getting off?" hissed Annie, behind a casual-looking smile. "The last passenger just stepped off."

"Patience, my dears," said Mr. Pipes. "Grip your knap-sacks—do you have Lady Kitty well in hand? Stay seated; stay, stay." He glanced casually back at the spy. "He remains seated; this may very well work." The deck hand began pulling the plank aside.

"Now," said Mr. Pipes, rising swiftly from his seat. Annie and Drew scrambled after him.

"Bitte!" called Mr. Pipes, smiling and waving. The children followed Mr. Pipes across the gangway; then they turned and watched as the deck hand cast off lines. With a roaring of engines, the boat finally pulled away from the dock—their spy still on board.

Drew turned with a big grin and waved at the boat.

"Come along, Drew," said Mr. Pipes. "Surely we've given him the slip this time, but we mustn't gloat." He hailed a taxi waiting at the pier, and they sped away from the river, Annie straining to watch the disappearing boat out of the back window.

The moment the taxi disappeared from sight, the young man on the boat sprang into action. Peeling off his leather jacket and yanking off his boots, he then moved casually to the port quarter of the boat, the side closest to the pier. He glanced back at the passengers, stepped nimbly over the rail, and slipped silently into the water. To avoid detection from the boat, he swam underwater. A minute and a half later he gasped to the surface, paused for only a second, and with strong, steady strokes made his way to shore.

Moments later he stood barefoot and dripping in a phone booth. "I'll not beat around the bush—I've lost them. —Yes, yes, I know all that. —No, of course not, I wouldn't dream of it. —Well, yes, as a matter of fact, I believe my cover is blown. —Now just you wait a minute. I'll simply not dress like a German peasant woman—ridiculous idea. Leave my next disguise to me. —Yes, yes, this clearly is not on their original itinerary; I'll intercept them at stop F." He slammed down the receiver, and with eyes narrowed, looked both ways and walked into a clothing shop across the street.

Meanwhile, several miles away, on the outskirts of a nearby village, Mr. Pipes paid the taxi driver, and the children followed him down a scalloped stone walk past a carved sign that read *Fritz Kirchenorgelbau*. The pathway wound through neatly trimmed red and yellow roses and took them to the front steps of a large brick house crisscrossed with white timbers that reminded Annie of hopscotch patterns. Above the sturdy double doors in the center of the house rose a high gable, the two lower wings of the house forming shoulderlike additions to the imposing center. Mr. Pipes pushed a button next to the door, and a sustained, reedy bass pipe sounded from inside.

"He's rigged a pipe organ doorbell," said Drew. "That's a nice touch."

Once inside, Mr. Pipes introduced himself and the children to a young man sweeping a pile of curly wood shavings and asked to speak with Herr Fritz.

A moment later, the room filled with the bustling presence of Herr Fritz, a broad smile on his fleshy face.

"Guten Tag, Mein Herr," said Herr Fritz, shaking Mr. Pipes's hand warmly. The two men spoke in German for several minutes before the big German turned to Annie and Drew: "Dis is a most velcome distraction. Your friend has said very nice tings about my organs, and asked me if I vould mind showing you my little vorkshop—mind? I say to him, I vould be delighted! You must come vith me."

They followed Herr Fritz to the pipe rooms down a narrow hallway—at least it seemed narrow as Herr Fritz lumbered ahead, gesturing and explaining, sometimes in English, sometimes in German.

"Swish, swish," went a block plane as a worker shaped a long wooden pipe lying on saw horses. Paper-thin shavings, curling like ringlets, fell to the floor.

"Dis pipe vill make a lovely low G," said Herr Fritz, bending and eyeing down the long pipe. The woodworker stood aside nervously for the impromptu inspection. Suddenly, Herr Fritz hefted the enormous pipe; his cheeks puffed out, and with red face he blew a long blast into the pipe. A low, clear tone ended in a gasp as Herr Fritz, helped by the workman, lowered the pipe back in place. "Ja, ja. I believe you may fit dis one into de vind chamber."

Next, Herr Fritz led them into a room lined with dull metal pipes, each one slightly bigger than the last, and some taller than Mr. Pipes. He showed them trays of tiny little pipes, the smallest no bigger than a pencil. Drew watched in fascination as one worker cut thin sheets of lead and tin alloy, another hammered them with a wooden mallet over pipe forms, and another cautiously soldered them into their completed pipe shape. In a much quieter adjoining room, a worker with a magnifying glass attached to his glasses and a sharp cutting tool in hand bent over a small pipe.

Mr. Pipes spoke softly to the children. "This is, perhaps, one of the most critical parts of the entire process."

"True, indeed," added Herr Fritz. "Hans, my voicer, is an artist."

"Why is he cutting the pipe all up," asked Drew, moving closer.

"He is cutting de mouth of de pipe, and den he vill shave a little here and shape a little dere. His vork finally determines de qvality and character of de entire organ and of my reputation as an organ builder! Good man, Hans!"

Hans gave them a shy smile; then in halting English he said, "Herr Fritz, teached me all."

Next, Hans put the foot of the pipe to his lips and blew. A clear, reedy tone came from the little pipe.

"Ah, Hans's pipes almost alvays speak de first time."

Hans, still blowing, cocked his head, listening critically. He picked up a tiny hammer and, tapping around the mouth of the pipe, shaped the voice of the pipe.

"He vill do dat vith every pipe in dis organ," said Herr Fritz.

Drew eyed Hans with interest as he blew in the pipe. "I never realized you could blow in a pipe with just your own breath," he said, eyeballing up the pipe at Hans. "How many pipes in this organ?" he asked, counting the pipes lined up on Hans's workbench.

"Dis organ vill have only 2,600," said Herr Fritz. "Not de very biggest. And each one ve make by hand—every step by hand. Come vith me. I vill show you how ve make de lead for de pipes."

Annie scrunched up her nose and covered her ears in the next room. Steam drifted from a sinister-looking gray cauldron where a worker, shrouded in what Drew thought looked like a space suit, adjusted the temperature.

"Several hundreds of degrees," shouted Herr Fritz, "very hot!"

Next, the workers poured out the molten lead and tin onto a long table, while another man pulled a wooden squeegee-like device over it, spreading the lead evenly.

"No, no, Drew," said Mr. Pipes. "Watch from right here, my boy; any closer and you might very well end up a permanent part of this organ."

Drew obeyed.

"What's all the banging?" asked Annie, now covering Lady Kitty's ears.

"Trip hammer," said Herr Fritz. "Ve use it to vork harden de lead. It does make an awful racket; ve vill go."

Finally, Herr Fritz led them into a room with a soaring ceiling and, rising to the rafters, its grandeur already evident, stood a partly completed organ.

"What a lot of work goes into one of these," said Drew, looking at the row upon row of wooden and lead pipes already in place. "Look at all these keys and levers and pedals."

"It's a work of art, Mr. Fritz," said Annie quietly.

Herr Fritz beamed.

Mr. Pipes took off his glasses, blew the dust off, wiped them on his sleeve, eyed through them, and placed them back on his nose. He nodded and smiled appreciatively up at the instrument. "Magnificent."

"You vould like to play it, I tink," said Herr Fritz.

"Surely it is not ready, though," said Mr. Pipes.

"Part of it is ready to play," said Herr Fritz. "Ve play each pipe on de little voicing organ, den ve install de pipes here and try dem out. De entire organ is built here in de vorkshop, played, sometimes by de organist who vill play it vhen it is finished—I vould never allow an imperfect organ to leave my shop—and den ve take it all apart, move it to de church, and put it all back together again." He paused for breath. "It vould be an honor if you vould play it for me; please, play vhat every you like."

He cleared away a chisel and some wood shavings from the bench, and Mr. Pipes, stroking his chin in thought, sat down in front of the keyboard.

"Well, then, this being Germany," said Mr. Pipes, digging in his knapsack and handing his hymnal to Annie and Drew. "I'll play Paul Gerhardt; the children and I have talked recently about your grand hymn writers, of which he is among the very best."

Several workers gathered around as Mr. Pipes played Gerhardt's, "All My Heart This Night Rejoices."

"Try dese pipes," said Herr Fritz, hovering over Mr. Pipes and pulling stops on the console.

Mr. Pipes added more bass and the music swelled. Soon the workshop filled with singing:

> Warum sollt' Ich Mich Denn Gramen....

Annie and Drew flipped pages until they found Gerhardt's hymn. Not sure where to put in singing, Annie and Drew read through the words as they listened to Mr. Pipes and Herr Fritz and his little workshop choir. Drew especially liked the words of the third verse:

> Shall we still dread God's displeasure,
> Who, to save,
> Freely gave
> His most cherished Treasure? ...

Annie smiled as she realized how characteristic short poetic lines were in German hymns. It adds to the simple grandeur— Mr. Pipes taught them that word last summer—of German hymns, she decided. On the bottom of the page under Paul

Gerhardt's name she saw a woman's name: Catherine Wink-worth. Maybe she helped write it, Annie decided.

When the music stopped, Herr Fritz applauded Mr. Pipes's playing. "Do play for as long as you like—I insist. But ve must return to our vork. I vill check vith you presently," he said. With a sharp clap of his fleshy hands, his workers dispersed and he was gone.

Mr. Pipes and the children found themselves alone with the grand instrument.

"Is it just me," said Annie at last, "or do the lines of German hymns all seem shorter than most English poetry?"

"Quite right, my dear," said Mr. Pipes. "German hymns—so often passionate prayers, really—reflect these earnest Christians' immediate relationship and constant conversation with the Lord Jesus. Even the structure of their poetic lines shows this."

"Maybe with all the troubles they suffered through," continued Annie, "they had less time to think about longer, eloquent lines. This way it sounds more like they were really crying out to the Lord."

"Yeah," agreed Drew, "if you were busy dodging bullets and running for your life, you'd cry out for help, too."

"But there is considerable eloquence, though of a different kind, in their passionate plea to the Lord," said Mr. Pipes. "Those punctuated lines help create a tone of utter dependence on the Lord and faith that He will answer their cry."

Drew looked again at the hymnal. "'His most cherished Treasure.' Hmm, Mr. Gerhardt must have meant Jesus, God's Son—the Treasure, I mean."

"Yes," said Mr. Pipes. "By the late sixteen hundreds German hymns had taken on a more personal, devotional character. And increasingly, Jesus, the second Person of the Godhead, was the object of that adoration."

"I wonder," said Annie, a faraway look in her eyes, "if it was because Jesus suffered so terribly, German Christians felt that He understood *their* suffering—it's just a thought."

"And a very good one, perhaps, my dear," said Mr. Pipes. He turned back to the keyboard. "I'm reminded of another lovely hymn, also a passionate adoration of Jesus 'though the earth be shaking and every heart be quaking.' Remember, these were extremely difficult days. A lawyer, Johann Franck, wrote a hymn in 1655, full of tender resting in the arms of Jesus and at the same time a defiance of the Devil and a determination to find the purest pleasure—come wind, come weather—in Jesus. Follow along while I play the tune; then we will sing it together."

A tender melody filled the workshop with notes descending contemplatively in the first lines, then rising to a resolving crescendo, and finally returning to quiet adoration at the finish.

They sang:

> Jesus, priceless Treasure,
> Fount of purest pleasure,
> Truest Friend to me:
> Ah, how long in anguish
> Shall my spirit languish,
> Yearning, Lord, for Thee?
> Thine I am,
> O spotless Lamb!
> I will suffer naught to hide Thee,
> Naught I ask beside Thee.
>
> In Thine arms I rest me;
> Foes who would molest me
> Cannot reach me here.
> Though the earth be shaking,
> Ev'ry heart be quaking,
> Jesus calms my fear.
> Lightnings flash
> And thunders crash;
> Yet, though sin and hell assail me,
> Jesus will not fail me.

Satan, I defy thee;
Death, I now decry thee;
Fear, I bid thee cease.
World, thou shalt not harm me
Nor thy threats alarm me
While I sing of peace.
God's great pow'r
Guards ev'ry hour;
Earth and all its depths adore Him,
Silent bow before Him.

Hence with earthly treasure!
Thou art all my pleasure,
Jesus, all my choice.
Hence, thou empty glory!
Naught to me thy story,
Told with tempting voice.
Pain or loss
Or shame or cross
Shall not from my Saviour move me,
Since He deigns to love me.

Hence, all fear and sadness!
For the Lord of gladness,
Jesus, enters in.
Those who love the Father,
Though the storms may gather,
Still have peace within.
Yea, whate'er
I here must bear,
Thou art still my purest pleasure,
Jesus, priceless Treasure.

Mr. Pipes's voice quavered slightly on the last line, and
Drew cleared his throat and coughed. No one spoke for several
moments.

"I-I don't think I have ever heard anything more beautiful," said Annie at last. "Life must have been very hard in those days, but he sounds like he really did have peace within. I think I'd be scared."

Mr. Pipes blinked rapidly before speaking. "My dears, Mr. Franck made the very best use of his troubles. 'Pain or loss or shame or cross,' he resolved, as ought we, never to give over to fear or despair, and why? I'll tell you why: since Jesus, the Lord of gladness, deigns to love us."

"I think this one might come in handy," said Drew. "I think it'd be a good one to memorize—you know, for if, well, if troubles ever come to us."

"Oh, not *if*, but *when*, my boy," said Mr. Pipes sadly. "This world is not heaven, filled with sin and sorrows and disappointments as it is." He paused, looking at the children but not seeing them.

Annie studied the old man's usually cheerful face. Was he thinking of his wife who years ago grew sick and died? Annie remembered how pretty Mrs. Pipes looked in the pictures filling the walls of the old man's cottage back in England. Or was he thinking of the children they never had? Annie's mind traveled back to their home in America; she felt an ache inside for her mother and father: all they had was earthly treasure—but then it must not be enough, she mused, because they always seemed to need more. She longed for them to know Jesus.

A smile began to reappear on the old man's face, and the sparkle returned to his kind eyes. "Whatever we here must bear, Annie and Drew, remember that Jesus is our purest pleasure— He, our priceless treasure."

◈ ◈ ◈

Annie and Drew followed Mr. Pipes into Herr Fritz's office a few moments later to thank him and say good-bye.

"Ah, my friends. If you must go, let me present you vith a gift to remember my little organ building vorkshop."

Drew heard rustling and clanging as Herr Fritz bent down behind his desk.

"Here ve are," he said. "I hope you do not mind; dese vere not qvite perfect. For you, Mr. Pipes, a Fritz pipe in C; and for you, my dear," he said to Annie, "a Fritz pipe in E; and for de young man, a Fritz pipe in G. Now, vith practice, you can play something—maybe a hymn—vhile you continue your journey. That's it, blow dem all together now."

Lady Kitty's tail twitched, and she arched her back as the threesome blew a chord in thirds.

"This is great," said Drew. "It's like we're a human organ." He blew another long blast as they said farewell to Herr Fritz and walked down the cobbled lane, leaving the workshop behind.

As they got into the cab, Annie looked cautiously up and down the narrow street.

Mr. Pipes saw her, and said, "You were right all along, my dear. I'm absolutely convinced of it, and I'm most awfully sorry I didn't believe you. I do hope now we have finally given him the slip. I wonder if I ought in my next letter to mention our spy to Dr. Dudley—No, no. That would never do. We mustn't worry him further. Caution, that's the rule, and we must keep our wits about us, indeed we must."

Jesus, Priceless Treasure

To you who believe ... [he] is precious. 1 Pet. 2:7

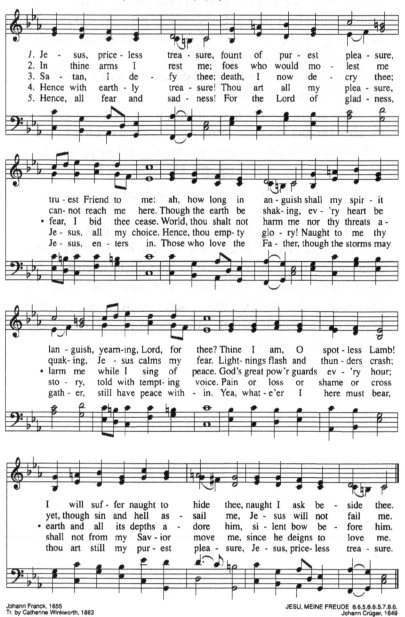

1. Je - sus, price - less trea - sure, fount of pur - est plea - sure,
2. In thine arms I rest me; foes who would mo - lest me
3. Sa - tan, I de - fy thee; death, I now de - cry thee;
4. Hence with earth - ly trea - sure! Thou art all my plea - sure,
5. Hence, all fear and sad - ness! For the Lord of glad - ness,

tru - est Friend to me: ah, how long in an - guish shall my spir - it
can - not reach me here. Though the earth be shak - ing, ev - 'ry heart be
• fear, I bid thee cease. World, thou shalt not harm me nor thy threats a -
Je - sus, all my choice. Hence, thou emp - ty glo - ry! Naught to me thy
Je - sus, en - ters in. Those who love the Fa - ther, though the storms may

lan - guish, yearn - ing, Lord, for thee? Thine I am, O spot - less Lamb!
quak - ing, Je - sus calms my fear. Light - nings flash and thun - ders crash;
• larm me while I sing of peace. God's great pow'r guards ev - 'ry hour;
sto - ry, told with tempt - ing voice. Pain or loss or shame or cross
gath - er, still have peace with - in. Yea, what - e'er I here must bear,

I will suf - fer naught to hide thee, naught I ask be - side thee.
yet, though sin and hell as - sail me, Je - sus will not fail me.
• earth and all its depths a - dore him, si - lent bow be - fore him.
shall not from my Sav - ior move me, since he deigns to love me.
thou art still my pur - est plea - sure, Je - sus, price - less trea - sure.

Johann Franck, 1655
Tr. by Catherine Winkworth, 1863

JESU, MEINE FREUDE 6.6.5.6.6.5.7.8.6.
Johann Crüger, 1649

Chapter Eight

Joachim Neander
1650–1680

Praise to the Lord, the Almighty, the King of creation!
O my soul, praise Him, for He is thy health and salvation!
All ye who hear,
Now to His temple draw near,
Join me in glad adoration.

Translated by Catherine Winkworth, 1863

After spending the night in a quiet guest house overlooking the Rhine, and after boarding the same riverboat making its short trips back and forth between villages on the central Rhine, Mr. Pipes and Annie—with Lady Kitty perched smugly on her shoulder—admired the sparkling morning from the starboard rail.

"I'm not so sure about this noisy riverboat and its smelly exhaust," said Annie, crinkling her nose. "It's not quiet like sailing," she broke off. "But that sounds like complaining; I do love this scenery," she went on, the sunlight flashing on her blond hair as she looked anxiously at Mr. Pipes and back at the river. "The mountains seem to come right down into the water."

"Yes, it is a most lovely stretch of the river," agreed Mr. Pipes. "Now don't go reminding me of *Toplady*," his feigned scolding made Annie giggle. "Ah, yes, my little slow-moving river. Oh, you know how I love sailing, my dear, and we shall sail, soon we shall." He turned to Drew, who sat with one arm buried inside his knapsack. Drew bit on his lower lip and gazed upward, blindly feeling for something among the dubious contents.

"Drew, you must come enjoy the view," said Mr. Pipes. "I say, what is it you've lost, my boy?"

"Well, I'm not sure if it's lost," said Drew, grunting with frustration as he dug. "But I haven't seen my notebook for a while." He pulled out his Fritz pipe and set it carefully on the seat; then he plopped a wadded-up shirt on the deck. A spare pair of tennis shoes followed with a thud, and before Annie could stop him, the entire contents of his knapsack flew through the air, landing in disordered heaps all around him.

Lady Kitty sniffed at a stiff, wrinkled sweatshirt and broke into a fit of sneezing, rubbing her paws again and again over her nose and whiskers.

"Oh, Drew," said Annie, her hand on her forehead. She glanced quickly around at the other passengers.

"That is, indeed, one way of finding out if you've lost it," said Mr. Pipes, staring with raised eyebrows at the cluttered mounds of knapsack contents. "While you two make an effort at tidying up a bit, I'll trot along to the lost and found; if you left it on board it should be found there. Be back in a jiffy."

❖ ❖ ❖

Mr. Pipes waited at the counter of the purser's desk while a crewman ambled off to look for Drew's notebook. His eyes wandered over several larger items behind the counter, apparently left on board and waiting to be recovered: a knapsack, large purse, stroller, two umbrellas, a raincoat, black leather jacket, and a pair of thick-soled black combat boots. His heart skipped a beat: leather jacket and combat boots? That is precisely what Annie's spy wore yesterday when they gave him the slip and left him on board—or did they?

The man returned carrying Drew's notebook.

"Is this it?" he asked in German, holding the notebook toward Mr. Pipes.

"Yes—yes, thank you," said Mr. Pipes absently, taking the book.

He turned to go ... and then looked again at the jacket and boots; they simply had to be the spy's.

In German Mr. Pipes asked, "Excuse me, sir, but when did that black leather jacket and those boots get left on board?"

The German looked for a moment at Mr. Pipes standing there in his proper tweed suit and necktie. His face broke into a wide grin, and he replied incredulously in German, "Your boots, sir?" he gave a short laugh. "From time to time we have people who try to claim things that are clearly not theirs. You, sir, it is impossible that these are yours." He roared with laughter.

"Surely, sir—" Mr. Pipes tried explaining. He stopped. How could he expect the man to understand—especially about the spy; he'd laugh all the more. Mr. Pipes, his dignity slightly ruffled, politely excused himself and returned to the children. There was only one conclusion to be drawn: The owner of the heavy boots and jacket must have left them on board—Mr. Pipes's face grew serious—so he could swim ashore. He looked into the churning water as he walked along the deck. His hand shielding his eyes, he squinted at the distant shore. His troubled frown softened imperceptibly. What if the poor chap—what if he didn't make it all that way?

"They didn't have it?" asked Annie, looking at Mr. Pipes's furrowed brow as he approached.

"What a bummer," said Drew.

"Oh, on the contrary, my dears," said Mr. Pipes, handing Drew his notebook. He forced himself to smile. "It is right here, safe and sound." The children looked curiously at Mr. Pipes. "I, incidentally—" he began.

"Thanks, Mr. Pipes!" said Drew. "Incidentally, what?"

"Well, Ah—" stammered Mr. Pipes. "Ah—ah, do be more careful in the future." No, for Annie's sake, he'd say nothing of the matter to the children. After all, it was still entirely possible that they had indeed evaded the spy—entirely possible, Mr. Pipes assured himself. No sense arousing new fears; no, no sense at all.

The day grew warm, and Mr. Pipes and Annie and Drew made their way below decks in hopes of escaping the heat.

"Whew!" said Drew, wiping perspiration from his brow, "It's even hot down here."

"One does have the impression of being broiled by the sun's rays blazing on the deck above," agreed Mr. Pipes, refolding his handkerchief. "However, make yourselves as comfortable as you can; we arrive in Dusseldorf in a few hours, where we'll spend the night. Tomorrow we'll make our way into a shady forest for a bit of tramping in the native bush. Should be cooler, and, ah, yes, I could do with a good stretch of the old limbs."

"*Dusseldorf*?" said Drew incredulously.

◈ ◈ ◈

Next morning after breakfast—a four-sausage breakfast for Drew, and after packing fresh bread rolls, cheese, more sausages, chocolate bars, and soft drinks (Annie did not want any of the food going in Drew's knapsack), Mr. Pipes, the children, and Lady Katherine boarded a train for a short trip to the tiny village of Neanderthal. Within minutes of the little station, they entered a pathway bordered by tall, slender trees—their pale, smooth bark reflecting patches of morning sunlight creeping through the canopy of rustling leaves. Finches sang cheerfully overhead, flittering from branch to branch. From her perch on Annie's shoulder, Lady Kitty's ears twitched, and her head darted from side to side and all around as she followed the flight of the tiny birds.

"It's like a tunnel," said Drew, adjusting the straps of his knapsack. "You know, Annie," he added, looking at Annie's and Mr. Pipes's bulging packs, "I could carry the food that's packaged."

"Not on your life," said Annie. "The chocolate is the only food that's packaged."

"No kidding?" said Drew with a grin.

"This is a beautiful valley," Annie continued, "and it's cool and shady! What's it called?"

"The Neanderthal. And just ahead we will encounter the Dussel River," said Mr. Pipes, breathing deeply of the mountain air. "The little Dussel cuts its way through the Neanderthal—

thal means 'valley,' so, this is Neander's valley—then empties itself into the Rhine. It is truly a wonder to think of God's perfect wisdom—His skill in fashioning such natural beauty that lifts our hearts and minds to great thoughts of our Creator." Looking at the forest scene, Mr. Pipes took another deep breath and exhaled appreciatively.

As they continued down the wide path, wide enough that they walked side by side, Drew realized he rarely thought about God making woods and rivers; he just thought about playing in the outdoors—and fishing.

On their right, just visible through the trees, rose a gray wall of sheer rock. On their left, sunlight sparkled on the Dussel, winding and gurgling its way through the valley floor.

"I sure am glad," said Drew as they paused where the path came alongside the river, "they didn't name it the Dorf."

Mr. Pipes laughed. "*Dorf* simply means 'village,' in German."

"So *Dusseldorf* just means 'village on the Dussel?'" asked Annie.

"Right you are," said Mr. Pipes.

Drew studied the water, looking for any signs of fish. "Hey, look at that twisty branch," he said. "It must have fallen into the edge of the river during a storm. Hold on, I'm going to get it."

He yanked his sneakers off in a flash.

"Drew, you'll get soaked," yelled Annie.

"It'll make a great walking stick for you, Mr. Pipes," he said, wading into the cool water.

"Mr. Pipes doesn't seem to need help walking," said Annie as Drew rejoined them, holding his prize stick in hand. "We can hardly keep up with you as it is, Mr. Pipes."

"Ah, I do love a good ramble," said Mr. Pipes, smiling at Annie.

Drew opened his pocketknife and began shaving off bark and whittling away small branches. "This'll make you look like Moses, or somebody."

"'Tis a curiously shaped stick, knobby and twisted like that," observed Mr. Pipes.

In spite of her objections, Annie moved closer. "You might have found something, Drew. It is sort of pretty."

Drew's knife stopped, and he held the stick at arm's length for a moment. He scrunched his face at Annie. "Pretty?" he said, his knife scraping again at the bark. "Nifty, maybe."

"Onward we go," laughed Mr. Pipes, stepping back onto the path. "I'm sure Drew will make something of it."

"This would be a good fishing spot," said Drew, looking back.

"Plenty more further up the valley, my boy," said Mr. Pipes. Then, with a twinkle in his eye, he added, "And, I say, further on there's something else of particular interest to you both."

"What is it?" said Annie and Drew.

"Oh, I'll show you; simply follow me—but, Drew, do close your clasp knife while walking."

After several hundred yards the path narrowed, and they heard a clanging noise down a still narrower path branching off through the undergrowth to the right.

"What on earth is that?" asked Drew.

"It sounds like a not-very-well-tuned bell," said Annie. "And I hear voices—German voices."

"Shocking," said Drew, "this being Germany."

"Let's go have a look," said Mr. Pipes, casting a disapproving glance at Drew.

The little path ended in a clearing at the base of an enormous granite wall, cracks and fissures making great scars up the face. Annie's eye fell on a mound of bright yellow and red rope lying carelessly at the base of the rock. A knapsack, its contents scattered, lay limp and crumpled on the ground.

"Guten Morgen!" echoed from somewhere high above them.

Annie gasped as the threesome, their heads thrown back gazing up and up the rock face, caught sight of two multicolored, spandex-clad figures, connected by another rope, and waving down at them.

Drew smiled. "Boy, does that ever look fun!"

"Yeah," said Annie, "fun until the rope breaks and you fall." She shuddered.

"Looks like pretty strong rope to me," said Drew, walking closer to the rock wall.

Mr. Pipes had a faraway expression on his face, perhaps remembering the allure of Ben Nevis and the Scottish Highlands in his youth.

"Is it safe?" asked Annie, stepping back.

Mr. Pipes took off his wool cap and ran his fingers through his white hair. His scraggy eyebrows formed their familiar brim over his eyes as he looked up at the climbers. When he replied, his voice was somber. "Of course, it is not safe, my dear. If there were no risks involved, much of the attraction would disappear. Outdoor activities are good and well when a greater appreciation of God and His creation is gained." He stroked his chin in thought. "But some outdoor activities remind me of Satan tempting Jesus to throw himself off the Temple. I'm convinced that this," he nodded upward, "is one of those activities, my dears. Remember our Lord's reply, 'You shall not tempt the Lord thy God.'"

In spite of Mr. Pipes's words, Drew felt an almost overwhelming thrill pass over him as he watched one of the climbers swinging like a clock pendulum across the face. "It sure does look fun," he said again, a kind of awe in his voice.

"W-what would happen," asked Annie, her voice hushed and her eyes wide, "if one of those thingamajigs holding the rope pulled out right now?"

"That chap, like most all climbers," replied Mr. Pipes, "is certain it won't happen to him; a sort of invincibility takes over in high-risk outdoor activities like climbing." He paused, his kind eyes studying them intently. "Drew and Annie, the Christian is called to make his stand—to take risks, to live recklessly, to hazard all—but, to do so for Christ's Kingdom. Life is too precious to willfully risk on dangerous entertainments with mere selfish, temporal thrills in view. Join those who have found their greatest pleasure in giving what they cannot keep to gain what they cannot lose, as one Christian martyr so aptly put it. He is no fool, my dears, who lives for eternal thrills."

They watched for a moment longer before Mr. Pipes said, "We'll move farther up the valley now."

◈ ◈ ◈

As the children followed Mr. Pipes back onto the main path, Lady Kitty, still perched on Annie's shoulder, arched her back and hissed.

"What's the matter, Lady Kitty?" cooed Annie. "Ouch! Your claws are digging into my shoulder."

A high-pitched yapping came from down the path. Halted on the path and staring at them, stood a man holding at bay a short-legged wiener dog. In a frenzy of excitement, the dog strained at its leash. Drew nearly burst out laughing, not only at the vicious little dog not much bigger than Annie's kitten, prancing and growling, but at its master.

"Now there's a real German," Drew whispered under his breath.

The dog's master wore green leather walking shorts with suspenders joined across his chest by a wide strip of colorfully decorated leather. He wore wool stockings pulled up to his knees, and leather tassels hung from under a thick fold on their tops. The sleeves of his red and white checkered shirt he'd rolled up to his elbows, and a goose feather protruded from a green felt hat that reminded Drew of Robin Hood.

"Guten Tag," the man greeted them shortly; then, adjusting his hat, he hurried past.

"What kind of get-up was that?" asked Drew.

"Lederhosen," said Mr. Pipes, as they watched the man drag his dog, still lunging and straining at its leash, ahead of them up the valley path. "Traditional German costume—quite popular with some."

"He doesn't seem to have a particularly good relationship with his dog," said Annie, stroking Lady Kitty, whose unblinking eyes stared distrustfully after the agitated animal.

"Yes," said Mr. Pipes, stroking his chin, "quite so."

Drew, not particularly interested in the man, had plunged off the trail toward the river. A few moments later his voice, though muffled slightly by the chattering of the river, echoed off the walls of the gorge through the trees: "Perfect fishing spot! Come check it out!" As they came closer, he added, "There's these huge, smooth rocks like stone couches for giants!—great for relaxing while I catch us some fish. I'm sure I saw one jump—there goes another! This spot's swarming with fish!"

By the time Annie and Mr. Pipes found Drew, he'd put his pole together, chosen a fly, and stood knee deep in the river. He held his mouth half-opened in expectation, and his lower jaw shifted to one side as if fly-fishing depended in large part on the precise positioning of the face. Eyes intently piercing the surface of the river, he gathered line in his left hand, lifted his pole over his shoulder and, with a quick movement of his wrist, cast the fly into a shady backwater on the opposite side of the river.

"This is a beautiful spot," said Annie, climbing onto a sun-warmed slab of rock worn smooth and comfortable.

"Splendid!" said Mr. Pipes, reclining into a stone chair. With a sigh he crossed his legs and clasped his hands behind his white head. "One can hardly imagine a prettier spot."

Annie lay down on her back and gazed into the blue sky framed by rustling trees rising from the banks of the river but not quite joining overhead. With her white-tipped paws, Lady Kitty batted at a yellow butterfly drifting lazily in the sunshine. "It is lovely in this valley," said Annie dreamily.

"Shhh!" hissed Drew from his stance only a few feet away. "I think I've ..." His voice trailed away in concentration.

Drew felt another nudge on his line; his pole suddenly waggled and bent nearly double.

"Got one!" he yelled, reeling in as the furious fish broke the surface. The shimmering brown body writhed and danced before diving underwater, desperate to get away.

Annie felt sorry for the fish, but Lady Kitty's ears stood at attention and she licked her lips several times as Drew played the fish onto the bank.

"Jolly good catch, Drew!" said Mr. Pipes, inspecting the fish. "Looks like a brown trout to me. Try for another; maybe we'll have enough for a lovely midday meal at the hut."

For the next hour, while Annie sketched the lush river scene, Lady Kitty chased beetles along the bank, and Mr. Pipes lay very still, breathing deeply with his hat pulled over his face, Drew landed two more trout.

Refreshed from his nap, Mr. Pipes stood—a little stiffly—stretched, and said, "Extraordinary success fishing, Drew. I say, most wonderful fishing, indeed."

"They are beauties, aren't they?" said Drew, looking proudly at the three plump trout lined up on the bank. "But what are we going to do with them until lunch? By the way, Annie, how about some chocolate? You know, to hold us over."

Annie dug in her pack and set out a snack on a smooth rock.

Moments later, Mr. Pipes washed his last bite of chocolate down with a swallow of soda pop. "Now then, my boy, let's string your fish onto a short line and immerse them in the shallows and secure them to a branch on the bank. Just here should do fine. They'll stay nice and fresh that way, and we'll return presently and retrieve them."

"For lunch!" added Drew, beaming with pleasure as he tied the stringer securely.

"Now follow me; just down the way," said Mr. Pipes, leading them back onto the path, "is an ancient grotto—a cave with a most interesting history."

Annie and Drew followed eagerly after Mr. Pipes. He led them over a narrow bridge, its stones covered in thick moss. The trail narrowed, and tree branches shrouded the path, making Annie wonder where Mr. Pipes could possibly be taking them. The forest ended abruptly; the gray wall of the gorge rose above the trees.

"Ah, yes, here it is," said Mr. Pipes, pausing and studying his map.

"Here is what?" said Drew. "I don't see a thing, except a dead end."

"Indeed, it is a bit hidden," said Mr. Pipes, "which, naturally, contributes more charm to the place."

The path did seem to end at the wall, but neither Annie nor Drew saw any opening that looked like a cave. Mr. Pipes turned abruptly at the wall, rounded a rocky bulge, and led them through a natural archway into total darkness.

"It's pretty d-dark," said Annie, gripping Mr. Pipes's sleeve. Her words sounded hollow and seemed to linger in the air of the dark cave.

"Not at all, my dear," said Mr. Pipes, snapping on his flashlight. "Do get out your torches, and we'll illuminate Neander's cave and explore."

"What a place! It's much bigger than Dragon's Grotto back in Olney," said Drew, running his flashlight beam along the ceiling rising higher than Mr. Pipes could reach.

"And this cave's more like a big living room," said Annie, feeling better with the light from three flashlights shining off the walls. "Look! Someone's even cut furniture into the walls."

"Yeah," said Drew, "this low shelf might have been a sleeping berth, big enough for a man."

"Somebody chiseled this chunk of solid rock," said Annie, "into some kind of desk, least that's what it looks like."

"Looks to me like somebody lived here," said Drew, "a long time ago. Did they, Mr. Pipes?"

"Live here?" said Mr. Pipes, propping his flashlight so it cast its light against the wall, illuminating more of the room. "I don't know about someone actually living here, but I do know that someone often retired here for contemplation and writing." He unwrapped Dr. Dudley's emergency package and set the candle upright on the stone desk. Striking a match, he lit the candle and a warm glow shone on his face.

"Who?" said Annie and Drew in unison, gathering around the candlelight.

"His name was Joachim Neander, born in 1650," said Mr. Pipes.

"Neander?" said Drew in surprise. "Like Neanderthal—this valley?"

"Precisely."

"So his mother and father named him after the valley?" asked Annie.

"On the contrary, my dear," replied Mr. Pipes. "The valley was named after him."

"Wow! Another big shot," said Drew. He tested his pocket-knife on his thumb and scraped the last of the bark off of Mr. Pipes's walking stick.

"Joachim certainly thought so about himself in his youth," said Mr. Pipes. "While a student in Bremen, he and his friends decided to go visit St. Martin's Church and poke fun at the new minister, a gentleman named Theodore Under-Eyck. But while sitting in the worship service that Lord's Day planning his wise-cracks and critical comments, Joachim heard the Word of the Lord in Pastor Under-Eyck's words; his conscience was awakened, and he later met with the earnest preacher in private. Through the minister's counsel, the Spirit of God brought Joachim to repentance and faith, and his life as a student began to change."

The flame from Dr. Dudley's candle flickered as Mr. Pipes paused.

"Isn't it wonderful how different people come to know the Lord?" said Annie, smiling at Lady Kitty as she batted at Mr. Pipes's shadow, quavering in the candlelight against the wall of the cave.

"Indeed, God in His all-wise Providence draws His elect out of the most unlikely of sinful circumstances. Joachim, like all new Christians, still had much to learn of the life of faith and obedience. And a near tragedy while climbing proved a major turning point in the process of his spiritual maturity."

"Tell us," said Drew eagerly.

"Not a great deal to tell, except that while out scrambling on rocky cliffs and ledges, shadows deepened and he found himself hopelessly lost in the dark. Climbing blindly about for some time, he suddenly felt overwhelmed by a sense of horror; he froze in his tracks, unable to move—I believe mountaineers call this being 'gripped.' Inching forward, he found himself teetering on the brink of a craggy precipice, over which if he had fallen, certain death would have awaited him in the blackness below."

Drew thought about the climbers that they had seen earlier. "W-what did he do next?" he asked.

"I'll bet he prayed," said Annie with a decisive nod of her head.

"Most earnestly, indeed," said Mr. Pipes. "Moreover, he vowed that if God granted him deliverance, he would devote his life wholeheartedly to the service of God. He tells us that from the moment of that prayer he felt the invisible hand of God guiding him safely off the mountain and home."

"Did he keep the vow?" asked Annie.

"Indeed, he did. He pursued theological studies in preparation for the ministry, during which time he met Johann Schütz— I'll tell you his story another time. Upon completion of his studies he was appointed Latin teacher at a school in Dusseldorf, where his students quickly grew fond of their zealous instructor. He frequently preached in the town but soon grew troubled by the cold formality of some in the Lutheran Church. Unconverted churchgoers lived sinful lifestyles without discipline, even partaking of the Lord's Supper without censure. In his youthful zeal to correct this and other problems in the church, he offended the elders, who finally called Mr. Neander himself before them for discipline. In the summer of 1677, he was released from his teaching duties until he conceded to their demands."

"Ouch! Poor Neander," said Drew, cutting away the last stray branch on his stick. "What did he do next?"

"Wait!" said Annie. "I think I know." She looked around the cave with a smile. "He came here."

"Yes, some say he even lived in this cave for several months. But it is certain he wrote many of his seventy-one hymns here, surrounded by the beauties of the Dussel River and his beloved valley."

"So maybe he sat here," said Annie, "and wrote on this stone desklike ledge?"

"Almost certainly so," said Mr. Pipes.

"Teach us one of his hymns," begged Annie and Drew together.

"Gladly, my dears," said Mr. Pipes, the candlelight flickering on his smiling face and casting feathery shadows from his eyebrows onto his forehead. "Many of his hymns written immediately after his ouster are rather harsh; however, as he made good use of his trial, a glowing depth and sweetness filled his musical lines that eventually overflowed in exalted praise to God.

"My favorite of Neander's hymns," said Mr. Pipes, opening his hymnal and holding it near the candle, "is simply bursting with adoration to God the Creator. In it he enumerates all the blessings for which the Christian ought ever to praise God. Neander wrote some of his own tunes. Though this one is not his, it is wonderfully suited to his poetry as a triumphant call to worship."

"Hey! Look!" said Drew, studying the hymnal. He suddenly tore into his knapsack and pulled out his pipe. "It's in the key of G!" Eyes wide and cheeks bulging, he raised his pipe to his mouth and blew. A long blast echoed throughout the cave.

"Music really rings off these walls," said Annie. "What's the tune sound like, Mr. Pipes?"

Mr. Pipes hummed the tune, and Drew followed the musical score, blowing his G pipe every time that note appeared in the melody. He held the dotted half note at the end much longer than three beats. No one seemed to mind.

"You know," said Drew, breathing hard. "If you each blew your pipes here and here—" he pointed to the E's and C's in the melody, "—and on the last syllable of 'Almighty' in the first line; Mr. Pipes, you and Annie could play together; and again on 'King,' two beats later. Oh, this is great! I'll play two G's for 'Praise to,' and we'll hum in between pipe blasts. Can we try it?"

"Drew, you are most extraordinary," said Mr. Pipes, shaking his head in wonder but, nevertheless, bringing his pipe to his lips. His clear C sounded deep and solid against the walls.

For the next several minutes the unusual orchestra, alternating between human humming and rich organ tones, filled the ancient cave with its textured melody. Drew directed their efforts like a Carnegie Hall conductor.

"Most extraordinary, indeed," said Mr. Pipes at last, merriment in his voice.

"How about if we sing for a change," suggested Annie, stroking along Lady Kitty's back and onto her twitching tail. "The words remind me of reading in the Psalms," she added, studying Neander's lines.

"Yes, great hymns are Psalm-like. After all, what better model for our poetic compositions in praise of God than God-breathed poetry from Holy Scripture itself? Join Mr. Neander, and the saints from all ages, praising God:

> Praise to the Lord, the Almighty, the King of creation!
> O my soul, praise Him, for He is thy health and salvation!
> All ye who hear,
> Now to His temple draw near,
> Join me in glad adoration.
>
> Praise to the Lord, who o'er all things so wondrously reigneth,
> Shelters thee under His wings, yea, so gently sustaineth!
> Hast thou not seen
> How thy desires e'er have been
> Granted in what He ordaineth?
>
> Praise to the Lord, who doth prosper thy work....

A thrill at God's goodness and mercy filled Annie until she felt she might burst. And Drew thought of God's marvelous wisdom making him—Andrew Willis—for a life of adoration and

obedience to God. He wondered at the line: "... If with His love
He befriend thee." Right then, no task seemed too demanding
when done in the service of the God of all the universe who had
befriended him. Their voices rose higher and more fervently:

> Praise to the Lord! O let all that is in me adore Him!
> All that hath life and breath, come now with praises before Him!
> Let the Amen
> Sound from His people again;
> Gladly for aye we adore Him.

When the last echo died away, Annie was first to break the
hollow stillness. "'The King of creation,' I wonder if Mr. Neander's love of the outdoors—this beautiful valley—made him say
it like that?"

"It would appear from this hymn," replied Mr. Pipes, "that
Mr. Neander no longer sought enjoyment in nature merely as
an end in itself, but as a means of private contemplation and
worship of the Ruler of all nature, God Himself."

After leaving the cave, and as they crossed the mossy bridge,
the Dussel gurgling merrily below, Drew suddenly stopped,
shielding his eyes from the midday sun. "It's a hawk! A big one!"
With his eyes he followed the large bird soaring against the blue
sky, and wondered about flying. Gripping his stomach in mock
agony, he added, "He must be looking for his lunch, too."

"Carry on, Drew," said Mr. Pipes. "We'll retrieve your
lovely trout and have them prepared at the alpine hut only a
short distance down river. We'll settle there for the night—
lovely spot, I'm told—and if you please, we'll stay on longer,
enjoying this most agreeable valley.

"But, I say, while walking let me teach you another German hymn extolling the God of creation. Its origin is a mystery,
though some insist German children sang it while marching
boldly across Europe to help drive the Muslims out of Jerusa-
lem—an entirely disastrous crusade, I fear. It was written in
1677 by a poet who clearly reveled in the beauties of nature,

but in his hymn, he contrasts that beauty with the surpassing splendor of Jesus. Feel the sunshine bathing your faces, feast your eyes on the forest charms along this wooded pathway, inhale the clean summer air, and sing along with me:"

> Fairest Lord Jesus, Ruler of all nature,
> Son of God and Son of Man!
> Thee will I cherish, Thee will I honor,
> Thou, my soul's glory, joy, and crown.
>
> Fair are the meadows, fair are the woodlands,
> Robed in the blooming garb of spring:
> Jesus is fairer, Jesus is purer,
> Who makes the woeful heart to sing.
>
> Fair is the sunshine, fair is the moonlight,
> And all the twinkling, starry host:
> Jesus shines brighter, Jesus shines purer
> Than all the angels heav'n can boast.

Tramping along the path, they approached Drew's fishing spot as the hymn came to its close. Drew scrambled eagerly ahead.

Annie and Mr. Pipes held companionably onto his new walking stick, swinging it jauntily together between each stride. "You know," Annie began, so captivated by the purity of praise that only a faint smile shone on her lips, "whoever wrote that hymn had to have been thinking about a place just like this. It seems perfect here, almost like heaven—"

"Oh, no!" cried Drew, sounding as close to tears as Annie could remember. "My fish—my precious fish, all three of 'em, they're all gone."

Annie and Mr. Pipes joined Drew on the bank of the river. It would be difficult to describe a more forlorn boy. With sagging shoulders he stood biting his lower lip, staring at the empty stringer in his hands.

"Some dirty rotten thief stole 'em," he said with a sniff.

Mr. Pipes put his arm tenderly on Drew's shoulder and looked closely at the knots on the stringer. Then, he squinted through the trees at the patches of blue sky above. Drew followed his gaze.

"That hawk?" asked Drew.

"Almost certainly," replied Mr. Pipes sadly. "I'm most awfully sorry, Drew. But I'll tell you what. We'll spend an extra day at the alpine hut and come fishing here tomorrow. Annie, you can finish your drawing, and when we catch our trout, we'll cook them over an open fire on the bank and eat them, then and there—"

Annie swallowed and her cheeks grew slightly pale.

"—Leastwise, Drew and I will eat them."

Lady Kitty rubbed against Mr. Pipes's leg and meowed pitifully.

"—Yes, yes, of course, you, Lady Kitty, shall have some, too!"

Fairest Lord Jesus

You are the most excellent of men and your lips have been anointed with grace, since God has blessed you forever. Ps. 45:2

1. Fair - est Lord Je - sus, Rul - er of all na - ture,
2. Fair are the mead - ows, fair are the wood - lands,
3. Fair is the sun - shine, fair is the moon - light,
4. Beau - ti - ful Sav - ior! Lord of the na - tions!

Son of God and Son of Man! Thee will I cher - ish,
robed in the bloom- ing garb of spring: Je - sus is fair - er,
and all the twink- ling, star - ry host: Je - sus shines bright- er,
Son of God and Son of Man! Glo - ry and hon - or,

thee will I hon - or, thou, my soul's glo - ry, joy, and crown.
Je - sus is pur - er, who makes the woe - ful heart to sing.
Je - sus shines pur - er than all the an - gels heav'n can boast.
praise, ad - o - ra - tion, now and for - ev - er - more be thine.

Münster Gesangbuch, 1677
Tr. 1850, 1873

CRUSADER'S HYMN 5.6.8.5.5.8.
Silesian folk song
Schlesische Volkslieder, Leipzig, 1842

Praise to the Lord, the Almighty

Praise the LORD, O my soul; all my inmost being, praise his holy name. Praise the LORD, O my soul, and forget not all his benefits. Ps. 103:1, 2

1. Praise to the Lord, the Al - might - y, the King of cre -
2. Praise to the Lord, who o'er all things so won - drous - ly
3. Praise to the Lord, who doth pros - per thy work and de -
4. Praise to the Lord, who with mar - vel - ous wis - dom hath
5. Praise to the Lord! O let all that is in me a -

a - tion! O my soul, praise him, for he is thy
reign - eth, shel - ters thee un - der his wings, yea, so
• fend thee! Sure - ly his good - ness and mer - cy here
made thee, decked thee with health, and with lov - ing hand
dore him! All that hath life and breath, come now with

health and sal - va - tion! All ye who hear, now to his
gent - ly sus - tain - eth! Hast thou not seen how thy de -
• dai - ly at - tend thee; pon - der a - new what the Al -
guid - ed and stayed thee. How oft in grief hath not he
prais - es be - fore him! Let the a - men sound from his

tem - ple draw near, join me in glad ad - o - ra - tion.
sires e'er have been grant - ed in what he or - dain - eth?
• might - y will do, if with his love he be - friend thee.
brought thee re - lief, spread - ing his wings to o'er - shade thee!
peo - ple a - gain; glad - ly for - e'er we a - dore him.

Based on Psalm 103
Joachim Neander, 1680
Tr. by Catherine Winkworth, 1863; alt. 1990

LOBE DEN HERREN 14.14.4.7.8.
Stralsund Gesangbuch, 1665
Arr. in Praxis Pietatis Melica, 1668

Chapter Nine

Martin Rinkart
1586–1649

Now thank we all our God
With heart and hands and voices,
Who wondrous things hath done,
In whom His world rejoices; ...
Translated by Catherine Winkworth 1858

Mr. Pipes, Annie, Lady Kitty, and Drew stayed at the alpine hut in Neander's valley for several more days. Due to the fine weather, good hiking trails, beautiful scenery, daily visits to Neander's cave, and good fishing—when it came time to leave and return to the train, they made slow, reluctant regress ... lingering often with comments like: "I say, what a simply lovely stand of forest lies here;" or "I've never seen alpine flowers so pretty; I could stay here forever;" or "Now this stretch of the river's gotta be just flip-flopping with fish."

As they, with long faces, boarded the train, Mr. Pipes said, "Lovely though it was, think what adventures now lie before us. Several hours on the train, and if all goes well, a wonderful surprise awaits us in the tiny village of Dinkelsbühl—where, I dare say, the town boasts a most excellent bakery."

"Race you to our seats," said Drew, brightening considerably.

◈ ◈ ◈

"Something's going on here," said Drew, hours later, as they stood outside the ancient walls of Dinkelsbühl.

"I feel like I've been transported back in time," said Annie.

"Yeah, the castle wall even has a real moat," added Drew.

"But look at the way everyone's dressed," said Annie.

Just then a man and woman strode past, pulling a wooden cart filled with yellow flowers and two small children snuggled on a woolly sheepskin. The man wore brown knickers, a white shirt, and a vest with two-tone puffy rolls extending like little brims over the armholes; his wife wore a full-length burgundy colored dress with billowing split sleeves. The boy looked like a miniature version of his father, and the little girl wore a dress like her mother's and a little oval cap clipped to her blond— nearly white—hair. Jostling along in the cart, the little children smiled shyly and pointed up at where Lady Kitty sat snuggled against Annie's neck. Looking wistfully at the family, Annie felt a pang of envy.

"It's like everyone just jumped out of a history book," said Drew, watching the laughing crowds going in the city gate.

"Indeed, this *Kinderfest* is an important—and most happy—historical celebration," said Mr. Pipes, leading Annie and Drew through the gateway of the walled village.

Just inside, Drew, gazing upward, stumbled into Mr. Pipes, who had stopped to take in the scene.

"Hey! Will you look at that chimney," he said, pointing at a round brick chimney jutting above a row of steep roofs. "It's got a giant nest on top—with giant birds in it!"

"Those are *some* beaks," added Annie, following Drew's gaze at the white and black birds peering down at the festivities from the jumbled sticks that made up their nest.

"Storks," said Mr. Pipes. "German legend insists that storks bring children—babies." He paused. "Not a shred of truth in it, of course."

Their attention drawn again to the merrymakers, Annie and Drew looked at the crowds and felt as if long ago time must have stopped. Smiling children of every age, all wearing medieval costumes, jammed the narrow, cobbled streets. Bright red geraniums filled the window boxes of the tall houses, and colorful banners fluttered over the streets. Mr. Pipes, Annie, and Drew found a vantage point on the top steps of the old church. The earthy smell of horses hung in the air, and the children watched villag-

ers spreading hay while several men saddled two enormous draft
horses. An air of expectation hung over the village.

Annie scanned the costumed crowds. "You know, if our spy
did catch up with us," she gave a short nervous laugh, "we'd
never spot him if he dressed like all these folks."

Drew looked around hopefully. Mr. Pipes's smile faded as
he too scanned the happy faces all around them.

Suddenly, from nearby they heard music. Annie and Drew
watched with expectation as four young people played different
sized wooden pipes. The delicate sounds accompanied by the
jingling of tambourines drifted throughout the town square.

"They're going to dance!" said Annie, watching a group of
flower-bedecked children join hands in a large circle. Jumping and yapping excitedly, a shaggy brown dog tried following
the dancers; the children laughed as they dodged around the
intruder.

Drew stood up and studied the musicians with interest. "It
sounds sort of—sort of medieval."

"Charming, isn't it?" said Mr. Pipes.

"The instruments look like Fritz pipes with finger holes,"
said Drew. "What are they?"

"'*Blockfluten*,' the Germans call them," said Mr. Pipes.
"'Recorders,' we call them. Lovely, ancient instruments, and
they do, in fact, work on the same principle as organ pipes."

The dancers whirled merrily to the enchanting music. Villagers encouraged the dancers by clapping hands and stomping
feet with the rhythm; everyone applauded heartily when they
finished. Then the musicians changed tunes, and several adults
broke into another song. Soon, everyone joined in.

"It's Newton!" said Drew. "They're singing John Newton!
How do these Germans know 'Glorious Things of Thee are
Spoken'?"

Mr. Pipes laughed. "That tune, my boy, is Franz Josef
Haydn's 'Austrian Hymn'—the melody for the German
national anthem. Not Newton's words, but, of course, everyone
in Dinkelsbühl would know their national anthem. The great

hymn tunes are like that—timeless and universal in appeal. Alas, much of church singing today is enslaved to a popular and, I fear, superficial expression that tends to trivialize Christian worship. Music produced by the shallow appetites of transient worldliness cannot adorn and define the noble, enduring truths of the gospel. One simply cannot make a silk purse—it is said—out of a sow's ear. The function of music, therefore, my dears, must determine the sound of music—wise men have known that for ages."

The anthem ended, and the festive dancers and villagers cleared a path in the street as a trumpet call sounded from over the fortified village wall. Drew scurried up a nearby lamppost and, peering through the blues and pinks of a hanging flower basket, he called down to his sister and Mr. Pipes.

"Check this out!" he said. "I can just barely see. Yeah, there's two knights in full armor—with swords, big hulking ones—riding those huge draft horses up to the gates. We're talking real swords, here."

"Oh! What's going to happen?" squealed Annie, unable to see over the crowd pressing up the steps for a better view.

"They stopped," continued Drew, his legs hugging the lamppost. "They're just waiting."

"Here come some villagers," said Annie, looking back at the procession coming from the town square.

A black-robed minister led a group of somber adults, dressed in their finest medieval costumes, out to the gate. A hush fell over the crowd as the small procession stopped before the knights.

"What are they saying?" asked Annie.

"I don't have a clue," said Drew, "it's all in German, and too far away to hear anyway. Wait! The soldiers are shaking their heads angrily, and the townsfolk are following the minister back this way. They don't look happy about something."

"What's it all mean, Mr. Pipes?" asked Annie.

"This entire festival celebrates the preservation of Dinkelsbühl from the ravages of the Thirty Years' War. Those mounted knights represent the imperial armies; and, of course, the villagers represent the minister and town officials attempting to negotiate with the greedy troops eager to plunder the village."

"Doesn't look to me like the negotiations went so well," said Drew, still watching from the lamppost but straining to hear Mr. Pipes.

"Fact is, the soldiers rejected any terms but total surrender of the village and all her inhabitants," went on Mr. Pipes.

"So why are they celebrating?" asked Annie.

Just then a group of more than a hundred beautifully clad children—little blond girls with braided pigtails and flower crowns, and little boys with rosy cheeks and caps of green and brown—joined hands and made their way toward the soldiers. As they grew closer, one knight's horse snorted nervously and pranced in circles.

"Watch and see," said Mr. Pipes with a smile. Then under his breath he added, "'All pity choked with custom of fell [*deadly*] deeds'—but, such lovely children. Who would *not* be moved?"

The children halted before the knights, who looked sternly down at them. A little girl stepped forward, and the crowd strained to hear. Her high-pitched German rang along the narrow street.

"What did she say?" asked Annie.

"She has asked for mercy," said Mr. Pipes, "for the children's sake."

"Don't count on it," said Drew, remembering Magdeburg. "My arms are killing me," he added, dropping on the steps beside them with a thud.

A great cry suddenly went up from the entire village. Drew scrambled back up the lamppost. "The knights are galloping into the distance, and the children are dancing and shouting—everyone's shouting."

"We can hear them, Drew," said Annie. "So it worked."

"Yes," said Mr. Pipes. "This commander was so impressed by the courage of the children that he left the village unharmed without even entering her gates. Great cause for thanksgiving 350 years ago—and today."

The cheering gradually subsided; the musicians began playing another tune, and soon the entire village sang a lofty melody together.

"Now, I don't understand much German," said Drew. "But the tune—it has that sound, like a hymn—it sounds like praise to God; it just sounds like it's got to be for praising God."

Mr. Pipes dug in his knapsack and pulled out his hymnal. "'Nun danket alle Gott.' Martin Rinkart's great text, 'Now Thank We All Our God,' set to Johann Crüger's thanksgiving melody—an exquisite, near-perfect hymn."

Drew pulled out his *Hymns Ancient and Modern* and turned to the index. "Hey, it's in here!" he said, flipping pages until he found the text.

"This hymn is used at most German festivals, and it appears in every single German hymnal and nearly all our English hymnals; it has definitely stood the test of time. Follow along as they sing."

> Now thank we all our God
> With heart and hands and voices,
> Who wondrous things hath done,
> In whom His world rejoices;
> Who from our mothers' arms,
> Hath blessed us on our way
> With countless gifts of love,
> And still is ours today.
>
> O may this bounteous God
> Through all our life be near us,
> With ever joyful hearts
> And blessed peace to cheer us;
> And keep us in His grace,
> And guide us when perplexed,
> And free us from all ills
> In this world and the next.

All praise and thanks to God,
The Father, now be given,
The Son, and Him who reigns
With them in highest heaven,
The One Eternal God
Whom earth and heav'n adore;
For thus it was, is now,
And shall be evermore.

The music came to a close, and Annie and Drew watched the crowds slowly drift away.

"Mr. Rinkart must have had lots to thank the Lord for," said Annie at last. "His hymn is so full of joy, and with words like 'bounteous' it just sounds content and even cheerful. Please tell us more about him, Mr. Pipes."

Mr. Pipes raised his eyebrows and looked thoughtfully at the departing villagers before replying. "How about a visit to that bakery before I begin?"

"Now you're talking!" said Drew. "Lead the way."

Mr. Pipes led the children along the pavement bordering the sandstone wall of the ancient Lutheran Church. The remaining merrymakers tidied the streets, and one young girl offered her flower crown to Annie.

"Danke," said Annie, beaming with pleasure as she bent over and the little girl placed it on her head. Lady Kitty batted playfully at the colorful wreath.

Moments later, pausing in front of a window filled to overflowing with pastries to stop the heart, Mr. Pipes said, "Ah, splendid, here is just the place."

Inside the little bakery they ordered three golden, flaky, raspberry crisps smothered in whipped cream, and a mug of coffee each. Behind the bakery, they mounted the ancient battlements of the town wall and found a bench overlooking the rolling Bavarian countryside just outside the village. Near the bench stood a cannon poking ominously through the crenelated battlements.

Drew bit hungrily into his pastry and, closing his eyes, emitted little groans of ecstasy as he chewed. "Not quite—gulp—a Mrs. Beccles," he said, pausing only briefly between bites, "but not bad—chomp, hmm—no, not bad." Mr. Pipes and Annie laughed at him as they began eating theirs.

When the last crumb had disappeared, Annie asked Mr. Pipes if he would finish Martin Rinkart's story.

"I love the sounds of his words," she said. "'Bounteous' and 'wondrous'—he clearly had lots to thank the Lord for."

"Yes, he did," said Mr. Pipes slowly. "But you and I will marvel at the trials and devastations out of which he offered such thanksgiving. Martin was born in 1586 in the walled city of Eilenburg. As a young, musically gifted teenager, he went on to be a scholar and chorister at St. Thomas School a few miles away in the city of Leipzig, where years before Luther first debated his Ninety-five Theses. Nearly 125 years later, the great German composer and Christian, Johann Sebastian Bach, would become the Kapellmeister, or choir director, at St. Thomas. There, he wrote most of his immortal cantatas—nearly one per week," he paused. "Drew will learn Bach's cantatas soon."

"I will?"

"Naturally, my boy."

"Where did Martin go from St. Thomas School?" asked Annie.

"He secured a music teaching position at a school in Luther's birthplace, the town of Eisleben. Poetry and music were his passion, and in 1614 he received public acclaim as a poet. In 1617, the year before the outbreak of the Thirty Years' War, he was called as pastor to a pulpit in his hometown of Eilenburg. He died there in 1649, the year after the war ended."

"So his whole ministry was during a war?" asked Annie soberly.

"And a most devastating war, indeed, my dear."

Drew walked over to inspect the cannon. The gaping barrel projected through a notch in the wall over the moat far below.

"You must understand, my dears, that the Thirty Years' War was, root and branch, a religious war waged for the survival of Protestant Christianity in Germany. Mr. Rinkart's walled village became a place of refuge for Christians who survived the ruin of their homes in other towns destroyed by imperial Catholic troops like Tilly's. But a great sickness spread throughout the overcrowded village and many died. Rinkart outlived all the other ministers and found himself conducting upwards of fifty funerals a day."

Mr. Pipes set his hymnal on the bench and walked over to the edge of the wall. He thrust his hands into his pockets, and Annie watched a far away expression come over his face; his eyes looked sad as he continued.

"Martin's own wife grew very ill," he took a deep breath and expelled it slowly, "and one day in 1637, she too died."

"Imagine it," said Drew, "on the same day he buried his wife, he probably buried forty-nine other people."

"That wouldn't leave much time for mourning," said Annie softly. "The poor man."

"The pestilence raged on," said Mr. Pipes, "finally taking the lives of some 8,000 people. Meanwhile, outside the walls the Thirty Years' War waged on, food grew short, and—a year later—more of the remaining townsfolk died of starvation. Mr. Rinkart spent nearly all of his own money desperately trying to feed people. To make matters worse, Swedish soldiers surrounded the walls of the town and demanded payment for protection against the imperial forces."

"How could they?" said Annie, her cheeks flushed in anger. Lady Kitty jumped off her shoulder as Annie rose and looked down the stone wall into the moat. Her head began spinning and she quickly backed away.

"To fight," said Mr. Pipes simply, "soldiers must eat. It was expected in those days that villages would give food and housing to soldiers fighting for freedoms the town hoped to enjoy when peace returned."

"But they didn't *have* any food," protested Annie.

"Yes, of course. So it fell to the minister, Mr. Rinkart, to negotiate with the troops. By his courage and good sense, he was able to bring their demands more within the feeble means of the remaining villagers."

Drew leaned against the cannon, a troubled scowl on his face. "Doesn't sound so—so noble," he said.

"What's that, my boy?" asked Mr. Pipes.

"War."

"Ah, the nobility does rather fade when children and wives and mothers die by the thousands. Little nobility in that."

"Yes, but Dinkelsbühl children survived," said Annie, hoping to dispel some of the gloom.

"Indeed."

"Mr. Rinkart's hymn," she went on, "he must have written it after peace returned to Germany?"

"One might expect so," replied Mr. Pipes. "Fact is, Mr. Rinkart found time to write a good deal of poetry, including sixty-six hymns, and a series of Reformation dramas celebrating the centenary of the Reformation; much of it produced while war and disease closed in on every side."

Annie picked up the hymnal and looked again at Rinkart's hymn. "It says next to his name, '1636.' Was the war still going then?" Lady Kitty playfully followed a trail of ants working their way along the wall.

"Yes, war raged on for another twelve years," replied Mr. Pipes.

"How could he write," asked Annie, "'Who wondrous things hath done,' and talk about 'blessed peace' and 'countless gifts of love,' when little children, his own wife, and thousands of people were suffering and dying all around him? I don't get it?"

Mr. Pipes ran his fingers through his white hair, then stroked his chin in thought before answering.

"Peace and joy mean very little, my dear," replied Mr. Pipes, "unless they follow trouble. Mr. Rinkart had his share of trials—that is certain; but his prayer that God would 'guide us when perplexed, and free us from all ills,' is a prayer for faith to see beyond the troubles and trust in God when human understanding fails us. Make sense of a war that some historians say killed off half the population of Germany? You and I can never make sense of that; we must lean not on our own understanding, but trust in God who does all things well. Only then can we with Martin Rinkart offer 'All praise and thanks to God' in every trial—no matter how costly."

Drew stared unblinking at Lady Kitty's play. No one spoke for several minutes.

Finally Annie broke the silence.

"Who was Catherine Winkworth? I've seen her name with Johann Franck, and—oh, let me see—"

"Yeah, Neander, Nicolai, and some others," added Drew.

"Right," said Annie. "Did she help write some of these hymns?"

"In a manner of speaking, my dear," said Mr. Pipes, sitting back down on the bench and crossing his legs. "Catherine Winkworth, born in 1829, contributed to the great literary accomplishments of many other Christians living in Victorian England. It is said that she was a person of remarkable intellectual and social gifts, especially distinguished for her combination of rare ability and great knowledge, charmed with a certain tender and sympathetic refinement. Her spiritual piety, adorned by poetic and foreign language skills, enabled her to become the most well-loved and faithful English translator of German hymns."

"It's gotta be tough translating poetry," said Drew. "The rhyme gets all messed up, doesn't it? I mean, German uses different sounding words than English, so it wouldn't rhyme when she's done translating it, right?"

"I should say so," said Mr. Pipes. "Great hymn translation requires poetic skill of the highest rank and, of course, mastery of foreign language. It takes near genius to convey all the original nuance of meaning while still keeping the poetry intact. I say, not at all an easy task."

"So Catherine Winkworth really did help write Mr. Rinkart's hymn—for English speakers, anyway," said Annie.

"She deserves our admiration," said Mr. Pipes. "We are deeply in her debt for giving us these wonderful hymns in English." He paused, then added, "After a fruitful life, she died near Geneva in 1878."

"Where's Geneva?" asked Drew.

"Switzerland," replied Mr. Pipes, rubbing his hands together and smiling. "Lovely place; I shall take you there soon."

"Oh, look at Lady Kitty playing on the cannon," said Drew with a laugh, pointing at the kitten crouching on the huge barrel. "Fire when ready, sergeant Kitty," he said with a salute.

"Stop!" screamed Annie as the kitten crept gingerly along the shiny bronze barrel toward the notch in the wall. The sheer drop to the watery moat extended below her.

"I say, whatever is that kitten thinking," said Mr. Pipes, hopping up from the bench and joining Annie at the cannon, but just out of reach of the reckless kitten.

"Here, kitty," coaxed Annie. "Drew, do you have anything to eat; maybe she'll come to some food."

"I don't usually have any leftovers," said Drew. "I sure hope she doesn't slip off; she could you know. That metal gets pretty slippery. And, whew, what a drop!"

"Stow it, Drew," said Annie. "Come here, Lady Kitty— *please*!"

"Yeah, come here, kitty," added Drew, really wanting to help. "Don't jump."

"I say, don't be foolish, now," said Mr. Pipes, in reasoning tones.

Annie never talked about what happened next without shuddering and growing pale. A little white butterfly flittered lazily toward Lady Kitty, where she crouched just over the mouth of the cannon. Annie gasped. Lady Kitty lifted her head and followed the dizzying flight of the butterfly. Then, haltingly, ever so haltingly, she lifted a white-tipped paw off the cannon and reached toward the butterfly. Suddenly, she slipped. Her little claws scrambled frantically on the round, unyielding bronze. Annie screamed. Lady Kitty, ears laid flat and tail bristling, clutched frantically at the air with her claws as she plunged down. Annie groaned as her kitten landed in the moat with a pathetic little splash.

Now Thank We All Our God

Now, our God, we give you thanks, and praise your glorious name. 1 Chron. 29:13

1. Now thank we all our God with heart and hands and voic - es,
2. O may this boun - teous God through all our life be near us,
3. All praise and thanks to God the Fa - ther now be giv - en,

who won - drous things hath done, in whom his world re - joic - es;
with ev - er - joy - ful hearts and bless - ed peace to cheer us;
the Son, and him who reigns with them in high - est heav - en—

who from our moth - ers' arms, hath blessed us on our way
and keep us in his grace, and guide us when per - plexed,
the one e - ter - nal God, whom earth and heav'n a - dore;

with count - less gifts of love, and still is ours to - day.
and free us from all ills in this world and the next.
for thus it was, is now, and shall be ev - er - more.

Martin Rinkart, 1636
Tr. by Catherine Winkworth, 1858

NUN DANKET 6.7.6.7.6.6.6.6.
Johann Crüger, 1647

Chapter Ten

Johann Schütz
1640–1690

The Lord forsaketh not His flock,
His chosen generation;
He is their Refuge and their Rock,
Their Peace and their Salvation.

Choking back the tears, Annie turned and bolted down the worn stairs, running as hard as she could through the narrow streets and out the city gate onto the banks of the moat. Drew followed. Mr. Pipes gathered their things, not forgetting his walking stick, and strode rapidly after.

Moments later, he came alongside Annie's hunched form squatting on the grassy banks of the moat and put his arm around her. She stared blankly into the quiet water, numb with grief.

"I'm most awfully sorry, my dear Annie," said Mr. Pipes tenderly.

Annie only sniffled.

Drew, meanwhile, walked right past them, studying the wall and gazing into the moat further down. "Hold on a second," he called. "There's a bunch of cannons up there; they all look the same. But Lady Kitty fell from that one, just over there. I'm sure of it."

Annie felt a surge of hope, but then—how could anything survive a fall from that high wall?

"We must go see," said Mr. Pipes, helping her up.

"Hey! Look!" yelled Drew, tearing off his shirt and sneakers. A big "Sploosh!" followed.

"He's jumped in the moat!" yelled Mr. Pipes. "Come along, Annie!"

What they saw, moments later, was Drew swimming toward the kitten, its eyes wide with terror and its orange fur plastered with water—and only just visible above the surface. He reached Lady Kitty, turned on his back, placing the wet bundle on his chest and, steadying the kitten with one hand, stroked carefully back to the grassy bank with the other.

"I-is she—alive?" stammered Annie as he approached.

"Sure—sploot," said Drew, spitting out some of the moat he'd swallowed. "Just a bit soggy."

"Oh, you naughty kitty," said Annie, taking the kitten from her brother and giving it a long hug. Lady Kitty emitted a sort of gurgling meow, sneezed, hiccuped, and began purring.

"And thank you, Drew," she said, giving her dripping-wet brother a hug.

"It's nothing," said Drew, looking a little embarrassed. "I needed a good dip."

A loud "Rrribut," came from close by.

"What's that?" asked Annie.

Drew dug in the soaked pocket of his cargo pants, and with an enormous grin he pulled out a speckled frog the size of a chicken egg.

"Picked this fellow up when I jumped in. They make great pets, Mr. Pipes. Please say I can keep him?"

"That's all right, then," said Mr. Pipes, shaking his head and laughing heartily. "Though I have simply no idea what Swiss immigration will say about all this. But, for now, it's off to the youth hostel for a warm bath and dinner. One more stop before Switzerland!"

◈ ◈ ◈

The next day, Mr. Pipes, Annie, Lady Kitty, Drew, and the frog he'd named "Rinky-Dink" traveled by train a few miles southwest to the university town of Tübingen.

A short walk from the train station found them in the center of the city.

"This is a beautiful place," said Annie.

"Bigger than Dinkelsbühl," said Drew. "Lots bigger."

"I like Dinkelsbühl, but Tübingen—" Annie frowned in thought, looking around at the rows of solid trees lining the wide walking path, jackdaws cawing high above in their branches, "—well, Tübingen seems just as old, but it has a freshness about it."

"Oh, it is old; the university here was founded in 1477, though the town is older still," said Mr. Pipes. "Lovely place, indeed, and recently voted the German city with the highest quality of life."

Just then a group of young people rode by on bicycles, and to the left of the path under the shade of the giant trees, a family chatted and laughed as they spread out a mid-morning picnic.

Bells rang brightly from the marketplace just visible through the trees.

"That would be the glockenspiel chiming the hour on the Rathaus," said Mr. Pipes, after a glance at his guidebook. "You can just see its red-tile roof and weathered bronze spires through the trees. It dates from before Luther's Ninety-five Theses—1511."

"*Rat house?*" asked Drew. "Some of the names Germans give things!"

Mr. Pipes laughed. "Language consensus is rather important; we've agreed that 'rat' means, well, simply, 'rat,' but Germans have agreed that it means 'counsel.' So Rathaus means 'counsel house' or 'town hall.' Ah, yes, just ahead is the Neckar River; popular place, no doubt, on such a lovely summer morning."

"Swans!" said Annie, spying several large white birds drifting in the calm water. "And look at the reflection of those old houses and that church spire in the blue water. I could sit here and draw all day."

"Boats!" added Drew, watching a near-collision in the middle of the river. "They're all different colors. Could we rent one?"

"I fear others have had much the same idea," said Mr. Pipes. "There's only one left pulled up across the river where it appears they're available for hire."

"Bridge, just ahead," said Drew. "I'll race over and snag the last one."

"Splendid idea, Drew. We'll catch you up."

Moments later, Drew, panting for breath, watched in frustration as a young man paid for the last boat and, picking up the oars, prepared to push off.

"Rats!" said Drew out loud, as he collapsed onto the grass to catch his breath.

"Hello, there," called the young man in near-perfect English, pausing as he readied the boat. "Lovely day for some rowing. Did you vant to go rowing?"

"Well, yes," said Drew. Just then Mr. Pipes and Annie joined him.

"Carry on, friend," said Mr. Pipes, waving at the young man. "We'll simply wait until another boat becomes available. Enjoy your row."

"Von't you join me? It vill be a very long time before another boat is free on such a day as this. Do come; you must. I need to practice my English," he concluded with a laugh.

"If you insist, and with our gratitude," said Mr. Pipes. He introduced himself and the children.

"I am Dietrich," said the tall, blond young man. "Who vould like to row first?"

"You simply must, my friend," said Mr. Pipes.

"Well, now," said Mr. Pipes as Dietrich, with expert strokes, maneuvered the yellow rowing boat into midstream. "We must know more about our benefactor—I say, you are a university student here in Tübingen?"

For the next little while they learned about Dietrich, his family, his aspirations, and his studies.

"—So I decided to study law. Tübingen seemed to be the best place for law," he concluded with a shrug. After a pause he said, "Shame on me, I have done all the talking; what are you doing in Germany—and here in Tübingen? Besides, that is, collecting wildlife—is that a frog?"

They laughed, and Mr. Pipes began explaining how he met the children last summer and about where they had been in Germany so far.

"Wittenberg, Erfurt, Worms—" said Dietrich, reviewing some of their destinations, "—sounds like you have been following Martin Luther around the country."

"Indeed, we have," replied Mr. Pipes.

"Mr. Pipes tells us all kinds of wonderful stories," said Annie, "about German hymn writers—that includes Martin Luther, you know."

"Hymns?" said Dietrich, raising his eyebrows and resting on his oars for a moment. "Like what some people sing—in church? Most people visit Germany for the beer—more of it produced and consumed in Germany than in any other European country—probably than any place in the world. This is a new one on me—you've come for the hymns?" he concluded with a laugh. His English sounded more correct as he spoke.

"Indeed!" said Mr. Pipes.

"So teach me about German hymn writers from Tübingen," said Dietrich, a hint of mockery in his voice.

"Better still," replied Mr. Pipes, ignoring Dietrich's taunt, "I'll tell you about a brilliant and distinguished law student. Annie and Drew, do you remember my mentioning Johann Schütz when we explored Neander's cave?"

"I think so," they replied.

Drew couldn't help noticing how tall and self-assured Dietrich seemed. And he sure rowed well. He caught a glimpse of Dietrich's strong jaw as he turned to look forward down the river. His patronizing smirk made Drew uneasy. He hoped Mr. Pipes wouldn't say something that would embarrass all of them. This sophisticated European student acted like he knew something Mr. Pipes didn't understand. Drew didn't like admitting it, but he was worried. Maybe they should just talk about—well, about the weather. He nudged Rinky-Dink with his finger, and the frog hopped into the air and landed with a splash in a puddle of water sluicing back and forth with the motion of the boat.

"Born in 1640," Mr. Pipes seemed unabashed as he began the story, "Johann Schütz eventually studied at your university, Dietrich, and achieved high honors in both civil and canon law. He quickly gained a reputation in Germany as a man with considerable legal understanding," Mr. Pipes paused, looking over his glasses at Dietrich, "but he is long forgotten for anything achieved in that profession."

"So why teach me of this man?" asked Dietrich.

"Ah, a most interesting question. May I ask you, for what will you be remembered hundreds of years after your legal career is ended by your own death? Johann Schütz's most enduring work—his hymns—are sung in many languages in the Christian Church the world over—I say, not a Sabbath passes where his greatest hymn, 'All Praise to God, Who Reigns Above,' is not sung by faithful Christians. Sung over and over again hundreds of years after his death; truly extraordinary, when one pauses to think on it."

"I suppose I must hear this hymn," replied Dietrich.

Drew groaned inwardly; surely Mr. Pipes wouldn't sing it in front of Dietrich and right here on the river crowded with boats filled with people—and expect Drew to join in? He felt panic rising; maybe some diversion. He looked in the quiet water— falling overboard?

But Mr. Pipes seemed to read Drew's thoughts and, pulling out his hymnal, suggested, "Perhaps I'll simply read it to you, under the circumstances."

With flushed cheeks, Drew listened as Mr. Pipes read:

All praise to God, who reigns above,
The God of all creation,
The God of wonders, pow'r, and love,
The God of our salvation!
With healing balm my soul He fills,
The God who ev'ry sorrow stills,
To God all praise and glory!

Mr. Pipes continued reading about God's almighty power making and keeping all His works in perfect justice; then with feeling he read on:

> I cried to Him in time of need:
> Lord God, O, hear my calling!
> For death He gave me life indeed
> And kept my feet from falling.
> For this my thanks shall endless be;
> O, thank Him, thank our God, with me,
> To God all praise and glory!

Humbled by Johann Schütz's grateful testimony expressed in the hymn, Drew, feeling ashamed, shifted positions on the forward thwart. Dietrich's rowing slowed as Mr. Pipes continued reading, his voice rising and falling, and pausing at just the right moments:

> The Lord forsaketh not His flock,
> His chosen generation;
> He is their Refuge and their Rock,
> Their Peace and their Salvation....
>
> Ye who confess Christ's holy Name,
> To God give praise and glory! ...

His voice rising in a doxology of praise, Mr. Pipes finished reading and quietly closed the hymnal.

There it was again, thought Annie: "His chosen generation." She frowned and began drawing in her sketchbook. After yesterday's near-tragedy, she felt relieved that Lady Kitty seemed only interested in sleeping on the floorboards of the rowboat.

Dietrich finally broke the silence that followed.

"I'm not at all certain what that man was talking about in those lines, but I am certain one has to make some rather enormous assumptions—unfounded assumptions—about God.

And I suppose this Schütz fellow would say he learned those assumptions from the *Bible*, would he not?"

"Undoubtedly, he would say precisely that," said Mr. Pipes. "Though he would not call them 'assumptions.'"

Drew thought he detected a sparkle of anticipation in Mr. Pipes's eyes.

"But, my dear sir," said Dietrich after a pause, "you seem a reasonably intelligent man. How can you possibly believe such—forgive me for saying so—such utter nonsense? The best authorities have proven the Bible to be a veritable minefield of errors and inconsistencies. Surely you are aware of this—sir?"

Drew felt that same uneasiness creeping up his scalp. He had heard his parents say similar things, and it always made him feel so ignorant.

"One does hear such criticisms, from time to time, leveled against the Bible," said Mr. Pipes calmly. "But unless you have a particular error to discuss, may I ask you a question?"

"Ask," replied Dietrich, grinning over his shoulder, stroking with his starboard oar to avoid a bright red rowboat crossing their bow.

"Who do you think Jesus is?"

"Jesus?"

"Yes, the biblical authors, writing over some 1,600 years, devote considerable space to answering that question. One might argue the entire book is devoted to answering this question. To put it in Johann Schütz's words, what does it mean to 'confess Christ's holy Name?'"

Dietrich frowned in thought before replying.

"He was a man," he replied guardedly.

"But you do believe He truly lived, that He was a historical figure in flesh and blood?"

"Yes," replied Dietrich, "but just a man, like you or like me—Oh, perhaps, a bit greater."

"Why greater?"

"Well, it is well accepted that he was a great moral teacher. He taught men to love others—to do good. Ethics, you know."

"What do you mean by 'good'?"

"Well, you know, the golden rule: 'do unto others as you would have them do unto you.' That is all Jesus really taught, now isn't it?" Dietrich concluded a little defensively.

"It seems to me rather odd," said Mr. Pipes, crossing his legs and gripping his knee with his hands, "that they would crucify a man for teaching people to be nice to one another. Doesn't that seem a little strange to you, Dietrich?"

Dietrich suddenly became very concerned about the precise positioning of his oars, but made no reply.

Mr. Pipes took his Bible out and, licking his finger, turned to a text. "You, no doubt, have read the Bible."

"Yes ... well, uh—I've read—*about* it," Dietrich stammered.

Drew listened as Mr. Pipes read text after text declaring that Jesus is in fact God: "I and my Father are one.... Therefore the Jews sought the more to kill him, because he ... said also that God was his Father, making himself equal with God...."[†]

"Now, Dietrich, I am an old man, but even I understand something of basic logic. When forming your understanding of someone who went about claiming to be God, you have but three options: either he was a man hopelessly self-deceived— someone with a deranged mind—a madman. If, for example, I insisted I was God and the only way to eternal life, you would rightly conclude that I was a man, shall we say, rowing with but one oar in the water. Your second option would be that I was intentionally trying to dupe men into believing I was someone that I simply was not. You'd be hard pressed to call anyone 'good' who was either so self-deceived or so intent on deceiving others."

Dietrich's left oar splashed awkwardly. Drew raised his eyes in wonder: this guy had looked like a champion oarsman until now.

The bells from the glockenspiel at the Rathaus rang the hour.

Mr. Pipes glanced at his watch and said, "You must be near starved, Dietrich. Let us buy you some refreshment. After all,

---

† John 10:30, 5:18

you have been so kind allowing us to intrude on your solitude, and you certainly have worked up an appetite with all that rowing. We must continue our discussion over lunch. Do you know of anywhere that serves tea—good English tea?"

◈ ◈ ◈

Dietrich returned the rowboat and led them to an outdoor café nearby.

"Better here, in the open air," he explained, smiling at Annie's kitten and the bulge in Drew's pocket that was Rinky-Dink the frog.

Their waitress, the full skirt of her traditional peasant dress swooshing ahead, escorted them to a table set against a lattice fence bordering the courtyard of the café. They sat down under the shade of a broad maple tree. While Drew studied the menu, Annie looked across to a grassy lawn bathed in sunlight where university students lounged; some reading, some eating, and others kicking a soccer ball.

Dietrich seemed to have regained some of his confidence and smiled indulgently as Mr. Pipes led in prayer. Then, between bites of beef stroganoff, he said with a slight taunt, "So, either he is a madman or a con-artist," he paused. "And I suppose you have one more option for me."

"You are an intelligent young man, Dietrich," replied Mr. Pipes, giving the law student a penetrating look over his glasses. "Logic is Christianity's great ally, my dear man. Why don't you tell *me* what is the only remaining option?"

Dietrich swallowed and fiddled with his fork before answering.

"But how could it be true?" he blurted. For the first time it sounded like a genuine question, and the look in his eye suggested that he wanted a real answer. "How could Jesus really be the Son of God? It cannot be. Everything I have been taught—besides, all religions just point the many different ways to God. Is it not far better to be tolerant of other religious opinions? After all, isn't religious intolerance responsible for all the devastating wars down through history? No, I prefer to tolerate all religions and live at peace."

"Ah, live at peace now—I must remind you of the atheistic twentieth century filled with more bloodshed than the rest of human history can count—but what about when you must answer to a Holy God for your defiance of His truth? How will your tolerance serve you then? Your third option about Jesus is absolutely true," said Mr. Pipes, wiping his mouth with his napkin. "Which of necessity makes all other views," he fixed his kind eyes on Dietrich, and said with a decisive nod of his head, "*false.*" Pushing aside his plate, he opened his Bible. "And this book—true from beginning to end—declares *that* truth to anyone who seeks with all his heart."

A look near panic came over Dietrich's face.

"We are all desperate sinners, Dietrich. But there is hope; Jesus Himself said," continued Mr. Pipes, "'… I am the way, the truth, and the life: no man cometh unto the Father, but by me.'"† Mr. Pipes paused, studying the young man's face.

As if to sweep it all away, Dietrich shook his head vigorously. "No, no, I cannot believe that all other religions are wrong, that Jesus is the only way. It is a monstrous idea; it is—is—" he blustered, looking for the right word.

"—Intolerable?" suggested Mr. Pipes, a little twinkle in his eye.

"Yes, that is it—" Dietrich abruptly stopped. Drew thought he looked like a fox cornered by the hounds.

"You see, Dietrich," said Mr. Pipes, "your ideas about toleration are proven false by your own intolerance. What you dislike in Christianity you practice in your own intolerance *of* Christianity. You don't really believe all ways lead to God; you are prepared to exclude Jesus' teaching as an invalid way. That, my dear friend, is *not* tolerance."

Dietrich did not answer. He drew circles on his plate with his knife.

---

† John 14:6

"You see," went on Mr. Pipes, "you can call Jesus a madman, a deceiver, or you can fall at His feet and call Him Savior and Lord. But you cannot call him a good man. You are a student of law; think legal evidence, my man."

"Y-you have given me a great deal to think about, sir," said Dietrich soberly.

"You must read this book," said Mr. Pipes. "It is the truth, and the truth alone will set you free."

"But how do I know that?" Dietrich ran his fingers through his blond hair. "I've always heard it is so filled with errors."

Mr. Pipes smiled and plopped his guidebook to Germany on the table with a thud. "Keep this; I cannot use it anymore, because—" he opened to Tübingen and found the information on their café, "—the prices are slightly higher on the menu than this book said they would be. There are, no doubt, other errors. It is, therefore, worthless to our travels."

Dietrich smiled. "Yes, yes, of course, I see something of your point."

"Every book you open, Dietrich," said Mr. Pipes, "contains errors, but you continue to consult books. Why? Because they claim to have the information you are looking for. Now open God's Book—the sinner's guidebook to eternal life; read His words of truth and life. Prove to yourself that the Bible, like no other book, is true from beginning to end. Then cry to Jesus in time of need," went on Mr. Pipes, "and He will give you life indeed. Confess Christ's holy name, my friend; confess His name, and give God all praise and glory."

◈ ◈ ◈

Mr. Pipes and Dietrich exchanged addresses, and after warm handshakes all around—including Lady Kitty—he left them.

"Wow!" said Drew, looking at Mr. Pipes with something akin to awe. "Wow!"

Annie glanced around the scattered tables, then said, "I just wish you could have—well, you know—*saved* him."

"I say, Annie," replied the old man, raising his eyebrows in surprise. "The God who reigns above—He alone saves sinners, my dear. God, by His Spirit, must reveal His Son to Dietrich, and without God's sovereign work in his lost soul, no amount of reasoning will open his blind eyes. We must earnestly pray that God will grant Dietrich the gift of saving faith."

Drew opened a little box he'd found and checked on Rinky-Dink. "He seemed so sure of himself—I wondered if you could do it."

"Do what, my boy?"

"Beat him," said Drew, replacing the lid and slamming his fist into his palm.

"Beat him? I had no intention of *beating* him. No, no, my boy. I wanted to demolish his arguments, certainly, but I had no intention of demolishing him. Persuade him, yes. You see, I want Dietrich to know the forgiveness of sin, the freedom of the new birth, and the joy of worshipping and serving God all his days. That, my boy, is not *beating* him—nothing like."

"I wish I knew what to say when ..." Drew frowned, "well, you know, when people say they don't believe in Jesus or the Bible."

"You do, my boy," replied Mr. Pipes. "Tell them what Jesus did for you. And, of course, the more you know the Bible the more you will be able to give an answer to anyone who asks for reasons why you believe."

Annie stroked Lady Kitty and, biting her lower lip, looked across the courtyard nervously.

"What is troubling you, my dear?" asked Mr. Pipes, following her gaze.

"Oh," she began, now biting her knuckle. "Well, maybe it's nothing."

"What is nothing, my dear?" asked Mr. Pipes.

Annie didn't want to point, so she gestured with her head across the courtyard. "But I'm almost sure it's him. And ... h-he's been there the whole time."

"It is 'he,' you mean," said Mr. Pipes, following her gaze through the other guests eating lunch. Then he caught sight of a young man wearing a university-student uniform of sweatshirt and jeans. He paused before continuing. "Hmmm, remove the black leather jacket and boots—"

"—And earrings," added Drew. "And we have found our spy again," he concluded, smiling and rubbing his hands together. "All right, this'll be great, what's our plan?"

Mr. Pipes's eyes narrowed. How could this man repeatedly find them? He must be very good. But why was he after them? And for whom did he work? Mr. Pipes's uneasiness grew. He looked at Annie and Drew—the children might be in danger—real danger.

"Gather your things," he said in even tones. "I seriously doubt that we can throw him off our scent between here and the youth hostel—but we shall try."

A plan began forming in Mr. Pipes's mind as they visited the Hohentübingen Castle that afternoon. Yes, it was a rather bold—perhaps, desperate—plan. But it just might work.

All Praise to God, Who Reigns Above

Let them give thanks to the LORD for his unfailing love and his wonderful deeds for men. Ps. 107:15

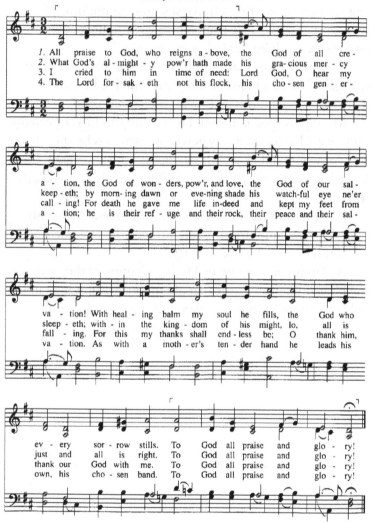

1. All praise to God, who reigns a-bove, the God of all cre-a-tion, the God of won-ders, pow'r, and love, the God of our sal-va-tion! With heal-ing balm my soul he fills, the God who ev-ery sor-row stills. To God all praise and glo-ry!

2. What God's al-might-y pow'r hath made his gra-cious mer-cy keep-eth; by morn-ing dawn or eve-ning shade his watch-ful eye ne'er sleep-eth; with-in the king-dom of his might, lo, all is just and all is right. To God all praise and glo-ry!

3. I cried to him in time of need: Lord God, O hear my call-ing! For death he gave me life in-deed and kept my feet from fall-ing. For this my thanks shall end-less be; O thank our God with me. To God all praise and glo-ry!

4. The Lord for-sak-eth not his flock, his cho-sen gen-er-a-tion; he is their ref-uge and their rock, their peace and their sal-va-tion. As with a moth-er's ten-der hand he leads his own, his cho-sen band. To God all praise and glo-ry!

5. Ye who confess Christ's holy name, to God give praise and glory!
Ye who the Father's pow'r proclaim, to God give praise and glory!
All idols underfoot be trod, the Lord is God! The Lord is God!
To God all praise and glory!

6. Then come before his presence now and banish fear and sadness;
to your Redeemer pay your vow and sing with joy and gladness:
Though great distress my soul befell, the Lord, my God, did all things well.
To God all praise and glory!

Johann J. Schütz, 1675
Tr. by Frances E. Cox, 1864

MIT FREUDEN ZART 8.7.8.7.8.8.7.
Bohemian Brethren's *Gesangbuch*, 1566

Chapter Eleven

John Calvin
1509–1564

French Psalm Singing

They come with sounding cymbals:
The singers first, the minstrels last;
And in among them filing past,
The maidens play their timbrels.

Psalm 68 (versified)

Long after nightfall a soft tapping came at the door of
Annie's room at the Tübingen youth hostel. Fully dressed and
with her knapsack packed, she hopped off her bunk, gathered
up the sleeping Lady Kitty, and tiptoed to the door.

"Come ever so quietly, my dear," hissed Mr. Pipes, his face
somber. Drew grinned beside him, about to burst in anticipation of what lay ahead.

Annie and Drew followed Mr. Pipes down one flight of
stairs into his room on the second floor. He closed the door
soundlessly behind them. In the dim light from the window,
Annie saw a chair wedged under the window frame, a trash can
positioned nearby. Cool night air drifted through the open window. She shuddered, not sure whether to be scared or excited.

"Move to the window," he went on, "but make not a
sound." He quickly signed a note, folded and stuffed it into an
envelope, and placed a wad of Deutsche marks in with it. Licking the flap, he placed the sealed envelope on his sheetless bed.

"There," he whispered, joining the children at the window,
"I've made our apologies and offered payment for any inconve-
nience our night escape might cause. Oh, I do feel most awkward doing this. But the uncertainty of our position leaves me
no option."

Annie felt a little dizzy looking out the window at the blackness below. A knotted bed sheet hung out the window, reaching the ground. It glowed in the moonlight like a narrow shaft of light.

"All right, then," said Mr. Pipes, pulling the sheet up to the knotted loop in its end. He looked encouragingly at Annie. "You will go first, Annie."

Annie gulped and stepped into the sling. Drew handed Lady Kitty to her, and she placed the wide-awake kitten on her lap.

"We have you safely in hand, my dear," said Mr. Pipes.

She felt herself being lowered, by jerking intervals, toward the gravel path below. Her knapsack tugged persistently, and for one terrifying moment she felt herself slipping, about to flip out of the sling. Steadying herself, she held her breath as the window of the room below Mr. Pipes's room grew closer. What if the sleeping occupants heard? What if it was the spy's room? The sheet rope began spinning, and as she wound around in a circle, her foot nearly thumped against the window. Moments later, with a sigh of relief, her feet touched the gravel path; she released her steel-like grip of the sheet and stepped out of the sling.

She watched as Drew poked his head out the window, looking stealthily left and right. He clearly was enjoying himself.

"No heroics, my boy," hissed Mr. Pipes in Drew's ear. "Simply go from knot to knot as quietly as you can, and take no unnecessary risks."

"Boy, I wish I could paint my face all green and black first," said Drew, grinning broadly.

"Off you go, lad."

After a disappointingly uneventful descent, Drew joined his sister and watched in amazement as their elderly friend made his way carefully down the bed sheets.

"He's even doing this with—with—" Drew began softly.

"—dignity," hissed Annie.

"Yeah, something like that."

No sooner did Mr. Pipes reach the ground than he began pulling on the end of a light string hanging down from the window, the other end attached to the bottom end of the bed sheet rope. The improvised rope rose steadily as Mr. Pipes pulled until it disappeared inside the open window.

"How did you do that?" asked Drew.

"I looped this string around the dust bin and used its rounded sides as a pulley," explained Mr. Pipes, giving the string a yank. The string broke free, trailed out the window, and fell softly at their feet. "With the many other windows that will be opened in the morning, no outside evidence remains of our escape—I do regret the untidiness in my room. Can't be helped. Now, we must be away. We've just enough time to catch the night train to Switzerland."

Drew looked at the old man in wonder. "Have you done this kind of thing before?"

◈ ◈ ◈

When Annie awoke early next morning, she rubbed her eyes several times in wonder at what she saw out the window of the train. Could this be heaven? she wondered in the groggy moments between sleeping and waking. With elbows on the windowsill and her chin resting on her hands, she watched the first shafts of brilliant sunlight flash golden on the craggy mountains separated from the train by a great divide. As the sun continued rising, the darkness between the train and the mountains turned to sparkling diamonds floating on a vast lake. With the sun's rising, she realized—with more than a little flutter in her stomach—that the train she rode on raced along a very steep precipice. Row upon row of lush vineyards clung to the plunging hillside. But the beauty of it all overwhelmed her fears, and she closed her eyes for a moment as a beam of sunlight warmed her face.

"More beautiful than words can express," said Mr. Pipes, joining her at the window.

"Yes," was all Annie replied.

With a quiet, "Bon jour," a porter wearing a starched white jacket brought them three trays. Within an instant, Drew's slumbering form began uncurling. He stretched, opened one eye, caught the scent of breakfast, opened the other, and sat up. He looked hungrily at the fresh croissants, the generous wedge of pale cheese with large holes, and the coffee and cream.

"Good morning, Drew," said Mr. Pipes, adjusting his tie and unfolding his napkin on his lap.

Drew threw off his blanket and pulled a tray toward him.

When they finished their breakfast, Annie again looked out the window and said, "Switzerland is gorgeous! Oh, please, Mr. Pipes, tell us everything about it."

Drew plastered his face against the window and stared wide-eyed at the mountains and the vineyards dropping straight down to the lake. "Look at that farmer—there, with the basket. He's got to be part mountain goat to work on these slopes—I do hope this train track is laid well."

"No doubt it is, my boy. Switzerland is a rugged country," said Mr. Pipes. "And that very ruggedness has helped produce

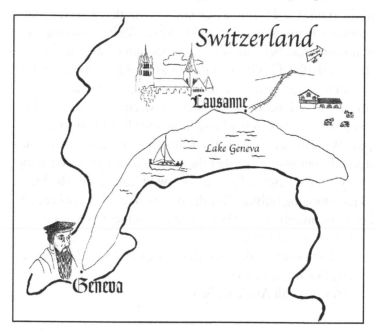

a hardy and highly efficient people. They generally get things done right the first time. And though one of the smallest of European countries, tiny Switzerland has had more impact around the world than perhaps any other place."

"Why's that?" asked Annie, taking the somewhat unhappy Lady Kitty out of the box they had been required to store her in overnight.

"I'll bet it's the banks," said Drew. "Hey, maybe our spy's got something to do with secret bank accounts where criminals stash their loot. Do you think we got rid of the guy, Mr. Pipes?"

"I've seen nothing whatsoever of him," replied Mr. Pipes, glancing both ways down the aisle of the train.

"I think your clever plan got rid of him," said Annie, stroking her kitten.

"I don't know about its cleverness, but I most certainly hope it worked," said Mr. Pipes. "We are days ahead of schedule, which should make for a most enjoyable visit with my niece and her husband on their lovely little farm. That is, if we have seen the last of the spy."

"But why is Switzerland so important?" asked Annie. "It must be because it's such a pretty place."

"It's all of that, my dear. But we must again return to the Reformation to find Switzerland's enduring importance."

The children situated themselves near the window of the speeding train as Mr. Pipes's story began.

"After Luther defied the emperor at Worms, and about the time he finished his German New Testament, a young scholar named John Calvin arrived in Paris to study law. God prepared the way for him by sending His Holy Spirit to work mightily in the hearts and minds of students and professors at the University of Paris. Calvin, a serious-minded and brilliant young man, heard the doctrines of free grace and salvation preached, and soon he, 'by a sudden conversion,' was brought to a 'teachable frame'; he repented and trusted in Christ alone for salvation. Inflamed with an intense desire to make progress in true godliness, Calvin soon found himself writing a speech for a friend to deliver before Roman Catholic dignitaries visiting the university. In it, Calvin exposed the errors of the Church of Rome and contrasted them with the true Reformation doctrines of salvation. After his friend delivered the speech, however, Calvin was a wanted man. Friends helped him escape from Paris by lowering him out a window with bed sheets."

"No kidding!" said Drew. "That's just like us!"

"It is rather like," replied Mr. Pipes, chuckling.

"For the next three years young Calvin wandered as a fugitive around France and Switzerland, Catholic authorities never far behind. While fleeing, he likely met the gifted French poet and Christian, Clément Marot, who would later help versify the Psalms for congregational singing. As he continued fleeing for his life, Calvin studied Holy Scripture and began writing down the Bible's principal teachings. Soon those notes became a book that would, more than any other single book except the Bible, explain Reformation truth."

"What's his book called?" asked Annie.

"*The Institutes of the Christian Religion*," replied Mr. Pipes. "Ministers around Europe received it with joy, and Calvin, its author, was soon seen as the instrument of God's blessing on the newly Reformed churches in Switzerland. Shy Calvin, however, had no intention of leading the world against the Roman Church. He wanted a quiet scholar's life free from the troubles of such a responsibility. Then he stopped overnight in the city of Geneva. William Farel, the fiery leader of the Geneva church, came to see Calvin. Farel had read the *Institutes* and was convinced Calvin was the best man to lead Geneva's Reformation. He pressed Calvin to stay—even calling down a curse from God if he refused. Calvin stayed."

The train slowed. Drew looked across the aisle and through the opposite window at the tidy streets of Lausanne climbing relentlessly uphill.

"Ah," said Mr. Pipes, following Drew's gaze, "the lovely city of Lausanne—a truly gracious place. Gather your things and follow me as we explore."

As they hiked up the narrow, cobblestoned streets, Annie paused and looked behind them several times; no one seemed to be following. She listened to the crowds speaking all around them—French, she thought—and felt a wave of calm at the gentle beauty of the language. Looming above them, the thirteenth-century cathedral seemed to rise out of the top of the hillside like an ancient beacon. Gazing at its flying buttresses and graceful arches, she soon forgot about the spy.

"You know," she said, "French sounds like—well, like talking in cursive."

"C'est vrai, ma cheri," replied Mr. Pipes, cocking his ear and laughing. "How true, my dear."

"It sounds pretty close to music, to me," said Drew.

They arrived at the worn steps of the cathedral entrance. A workman in neatly pressed overalls swept the corners of the stairs with a small whiskbroom.

"In 1536," said Mr. Pipes, leading them through the fluted archway into the stillness of the nave, "Calvin's first year in Geneva, he visited here in Lausanne because the city council had called for a debate between Roman Catholic priests and the Reformers." His clear voice echoed throughout the stone sanctuary. "Roman Catholic priests filled one side of the cathedral—just over there, while Calvin and a small handful of Protestants stood boldly on the other. Farel began the proceedings by demanding that 'Holy Scripture alone be the judge' of the outcome. For three days, timid Calvin said nothing at all, letting Farel and the others do the talking. On the fourth day, a proud priest rose and accused the Reformers of ignorance of St. Augustine and the Church Fathers."

Annie and Drew sat down next to Mr. Pipes at the base of a massive column.

"Calvin," he continued, nodding toward a point a few yards away, "seated about there, stood and fixed his gaze on the haughty accuser. He began freely reciting passage after passage from the vast writings of the Church Fathers—all without a single book opened in front of him. The Catholic priests shrank in their seats in wonder at the accuracy and magnitude of Calvin's memory. He would refer to St. Augustine and preface his recitation with, 'from the twenty-third chapter toward the end,' then quote the whole passage by heart. Calvin applied all these references to prove that Reformed doctrine, not Roman Catholic teaching, agreed with the Early Church."

"I'm loving this guy!" said Drew. "You say he stood about here?" Drew hopped over to a spot on the worn paving stones of the nave.

"Perhaps, there," said Mr. Pipes, with a smile.

"So what did the priests say after all that?" asked Annie, stroking Lady Kitty's orange head.

"Not one of them dared rise for a rebuttal. The villagers watching the debate looked on in wide-eyed wonder, but for some time no one spoke a word. Finally a friar, Jean Tandy, known for his zealous preaching against the Reformers, with pale face, slowly rose to his feet. After stammering out a humble confession of his errors and his acceptance of gospel truth heard in Calvin's words, he concluded with this: 'I defrock myself henceforth to follow Christ and His pure doctrine alone.'"

Annie felt a lump in her throat. Drew looked around from the spot where he imagined Calvin standing 500 years ago. He jutted out his chin and looked triumphantly across the cathedral.

Mr. Pipes went on. "When he recovered himself, Farel sprang to his feet and cried, 'The Lord's name is Wonderful, Counselor, Mighty God. He makes wounds and heals them. Behold and rejoice: The sheep erring among wolves and beasts in the wilderness—He has led it to His pasture!' Over the next weeks, 200 priests from Lausanne and neighboring Swiss cities confessed their faith and declared their support for the Reformation."

"Sounds like the Welsh revivals you told us about last summer," said Annie.

"Very much like, indeed," said Mr. Pipes, "though Calvin and the Swiss Reformation proved to have even further reaching effects. Back down the lake in Geneva, Calvin increasingly took more initiative to reform the church's doctrine and practices. He preached the Scriptures almost daily and gave himself wholly to reforming worship."

"What was so wrong with the Catholic worship?" asked Annie.

"Much, I fear. In the Roman Catholic mass, the congregation just watched; the priest did everything. Calvin believed that Christians should participate in worship, especially by singing praises to God, and what better music to sing to God than His own inspired poetry—the Psalms? But Calvin had a problem: the people in Geneva had never sung in church. What's more, nothing existed for them to sing in French."

"How did he fix that?" asked Drew.

"Like any well-educated and spiritually-minded Christian should," said Mr. Pipes, getting up and leading them around the outer aisle of the cathedral. "He began himself to versify the Psalms in French."

"What does 'versify' mean?" asked Annie.

"Psalms are versified when one takes unrhymed lines and, keeping the content intact, rewrites them in metrical lines that rhyme."

"Huh?" said Drew.

"Let me give you an example," said Mr. Pipes. "Psalm 42 begins 'As the hart panteth after the water brooks, so panteth my soul after thee, O God.' When versified, Psalm 42 sounds like this:

> As pants the hart for cooling streams
> When heated in the chase,
> So longs my soul, O God, for Thee
> And Thy refreshing grace.

"That sounds more—" said Annie, "—more singable."

"Precisely," replied Mr. Pipes. "And so important was congregational singing to the Reformation that Calvin, lacking a gifted poet, began versifying the Psalms on his own. But Geneva was filled with immorality and irreverence for God's Word—preached or sung. Many wanted the benefits of Christianity without true conversion and an obedient life. Calvin's biblical preaching angered many, and the magistrates finally forbade him to preach."

"Did he stop?" asked Drew.

"I'll bet he didn't," said Annie.

"Some came to church armed with swords at their sides, but he preached," said Mr. Pipes. "His opponents threatened him, even sang mocking songs about him, fired shots outside his windows, and named their dogs after him—"

"—What's wrong with that?" asked Annie.

Mr. Pipes's merry laugh rang off the stone vaulted ceiling. "Probably stray dogs, my dear. The mob eventually drove Calvin out of Geneva. But the mob and disorder remained. For the next three years Calvin enjoyed a peaceful ministry in Strasbourg—"

"Wait, you mean the Strasbourg with the giant spire?" said Drew, "that Strasbourg?"

Annie was tempted to say, "Don't you mean the wet Strasbourg," but she bit her tongue instead.

"The same, indeed," said Mr. Pipes. "Strasbourg Christians already sang in worship, so Calvin found enthusiastic support for Psalm singing. The cantor of the Strasbourg Cathedral, a chap by the name of Greiter, composed a wonderfully martial tune for Psalm 68, the battle hymn of the French Reformation. It begins like this:

> God shall arise and by His might
> Put all His enemies to flight....

"It is a magisterial Psalm, extending to many verses," said Mr. Pipes when he'd finished singing the first verse. "French Christians so loved Psalm 68 that they sang it not only in church but at the plow and in the streets. Catholic authorities, angered by their incessant singing, made it a crime to even whistle the tune!"

"How mean," said Annie.

Drew puckered his lips and Mr. Pipes joined him whistling the triumphant melody.

"Do you think we could do it on our Fritz pipes?" said Drew, about to dig his out of his knapsack.

"I rather think not," replied Mr. Pipes with a chuckle.

"What else did Calvin do in Strasbourg?" asked Annie.

"He preached, of course. And during Calvin's ministry there, the French poet, Clément Marot, fleeing persecution in France, joined him. With Marot's help, in 1539 Calvin published his first edition of the French Psalter: thirteen Psalms by Marot and five by Calvin himself. Much work remained, but the first of many editions was now in the hands of Reformed Christians. Soon people from every level of society—from peasant to prince—sang the Psalms of David in French."

"What happened next?" asked Drew.

"Calvin grew quite fond of Strasbourg," said Mr. Pipes, "as well he might."

Mr. Pipes's smile faded as he continued. "A man who had repented and embraced the gospel under Calvin's preaching fell ill—and died. Over time, as Calvin consoled his widow, he fell in love with her."

"Oh, tell us all about it," said Annie. "What was her name?"

Mr. Pipes smiled at Annie. "Her name was Idelette."

"Idelette. I love that name," squealed Annie. "Maybe I'll find another kitten and name it Idelette!"

Blinking rapidly, Mr. Pipes's eyebrows quivered and he couldn't help emitting a slight groan.

"Two cats?" said Drew. "Humph, then I'd get two frogs—at least."

Mr. Pipes composed himself and continued, "Idelette is a beautiful name—for a *woman*, and Calvin loved her dearly."

"Did they have any children?" asked Annie.

"God granted them a son—" Mr. Pipes broke off. "And—then it pleased God to take the child away—much to their sadness."

Annie said nothing for a moment, then asked, "Didn't they have any other children?"

Mr. Pipes wiped his glasses on his necktie before answering. "Well, in a manner of speaking they did. As the years passed, Calvin came to describe all the young refugees who fled persecution and flocked around him for instruction and nurture in their new faith. He liked calling all these his children." Mr. Pipes looked at Annie and Drew in turn, and smiled.

"Meanwhile, the church in Geneva, lacking spiritual leadership, went from bad to worse," continued Mr. Pipes, "until, finally, the city officials begged Calvin to return. Reluctantly, in 1541 he agreed, but under conditions, adding congregational Psalm singing to worship an important one among those conditions."

◈ ◈ ◈

They left the cathedral, boarded the train, Mr. Pipes scanning the other passengers cautiously, and rode to the nearby village of Oron-la-ville.

As the train left them alone at the little station, Mr. Pipes looked around at the rolling green fields speckled with peacefully grazing cows, their bells clanging merrily as they ate. He gave a great sigh of relief.

"By the Lord's help," he said, breathing in the sweet scent of alfalfa, "we have done it—no more spy."

Drew looked around them and said, "Yeah."

"Are you sure?" asked Annie.

"Rather!" said Mr. Pipes. "You see, when *he* found us yet again in Tübingen I rang up a somewhat distant relative—my brother's wife's niece—married to a Swiss dairy farmer—wonderful chap. It is completely not part of our plan to be here. No one can possibly know—yes, yes, here we are safe, indeed, and you shall love it."

They walked through the cobbled main street of the little village; tidy cottages, adorned with flower boxes bursting with red and yellow, lined the short street. Everyone they met gave them a quiet "Bon jour, monsieur" in greeting.

"Is this where we're staying?" asked Drew, moments later, after a short walk from the village. He halted, his imagination doing back flips as he gazed at a broad, chalet-like farmhouse surrounded by fields on three sides and nestled against a little wood on the fourth. Gold and white cattle munched contentedly on the lush greens of a field to the left of the house, and spindly-legged calves bawled and frolicked in a smaller adjoining enclosure.

"It is, indeed," said Mr. Pipes, turning into a narrow lane leading up to the farm.

Suddenly, Lady Kitty bristled and hissed from her perch on Annie's shoulder.

Overflowing the front step and guarding the doorway by nearly filling it, lay the biggest dog the children had ever seen. It lifted its great brown, black, and white head and gave a deep, but not altogether unfriendly, "woof, woof." Rising to its full height, it wagged its shaggy tail in greeting.

"There now, Lady Kitty," said Annie. "See, he's a friendly fellow."

"Ah, what do we have here?" asked Mr. Pipes, stroking the huge head as the dog smiled up at him, blinking its drooping eyes and slobbering from its great lolling tongue.

"I have never seen a dog like it," said Drew, stroking the animal's head that reached higher than Drew's waist. "You could almost ride him."

A tall, sturdy woman, with a quiet dignity about her, appeared in the doorway, wiping work-worn hands on her checkered apron.

"Bon jour, Dame Charrue," said Mr. Pipes, bowing slightly. "Je m'appelle Monsieur Pipes. Enchanté, Madame."

He introduced Annie and Drew and explained to them that Dame Charrue was Pierre's, the farmer's, mother, who lived on the first floor of the farmhouse. Suddenly, from behind Dame Charrue, bursting with shy giggles, four rosy-cheeked children tumbled out onto the front step. A young woman followed. Annie glanced again at the children and back at the woman;

she felt certain she was their mother. Young Madame Charrue approached Mr. Pipes, her uncle by marriage, and Annie and Drew looked on in wonder as they planted two light kisses alternately on each other's cheeks. So much French was spoken in the next few moments that Annie and Drew hardly knew what to make of it all. They met the four children: Pierre, named for his father—he looked about Drew's age; Francois and Paulette, eight-year-old twins; and Henri, who just turned five. The children called the St. Bernard dog, "Bruno."

Little Henri was much more interested in Lady Kitty than in the newcomers. "Le chat, le petit chat!" he kept saying, stroking and kissing Lady Kitty.

Annie and Paulette followed young Madame Charrue into the garden to gather greens and then to feed the chickens scraping and clucking busily behind the house.

Young Pierre led Mr. Pipes and Drew into the barn adjoining the house and below the main living quarters. His father cooed gently in French to an injured cow as he doctored its left rear hoof. The sweet smell of hay and rich cream, and the heartier aroma of cows, mingled in Drew's senses as he gazed around the ancient timbers of the barn. Someone had been milking cows in this place for hundreds of years—maybe even in Mr. Calvin's day. He listened to the farmer humming softly to his cow. Was it Psalm 68? Drew couldn't be sure.

"Voila, voila, Countess," said Monsieur Charrue, rising from the hay and patting the large animal gently on her golden flank.

Drew's mouth fell open as Monsieur Charrue turned and gripped Mr. Pipes's shoulders with his strong dairyman's hands and planted a kiss on each cheek in greeting. The big man turned to Drew. How about a nice American handshake, Drew thought. Before he knew it he was in the farmer's embrace with a kiss lingering on each cheek. Monsieur Charrue, laughing heartily, clapped him on the back in welcome.

They ate a light lunch outdoors in the sunshine at a table in the garden just under Dame Charrue's kitchen window. She passed the hearty fare on plates through the diamond-leaded window.

Pierre showed Drew a pond behind the farm. A little creek emptied from it and snaked its way through the woods. Drew stared hopefully into the dark water.

Drew showed Pierre and Francois his frog, a universal symbol of friendship among boys, and for the next hour they chased and splashed, playing with Rinky-Dink, who seemed (like the boys) to feel very much at home in a Swiss pond.

While feeding the calves, Paulette and Annie "talked" to each other with hand signals and smiles. Annie giggled as the calves nuzzled wet noses against her hand, then encircled her fingers with their rough tongues. Calf slobber foamed on her palm as they smacked and pulled eagerly at her fingers.

The afternoon raced by. Monsieur Charrue's clear voice carried across the pasture as he called his cows in for milking. The cows, like the Swiss people, seemed courteous and orderly as they lined up to enter the barn. On their broad necks, each cow wore a bell, some small and some as large as buckets. These all clanged a different pitch, making, Drew thought, a jumbled sort of music. But Monsieur Charrue cocked his head and listened; hearing each cow's bell, he smiled in satisfaction.

"Those bells make lots of racket," said Drew to Mr. Pipes as they followed the last cow into the barn.

"Ah, but not to Monsieur Charrue," said Mr. Pipes. "His ears are tuned to hear each cow's bell, and thus, to know they are all accounted for. Clever, are these Swiss."

Drew and Annie watched in amazement as each cow, passing other stalls, made its unhurried way to its own place. Pierre, wielding a grown-wood pitchfork, served up generous piles of hay. The cows munched, great puffs of breath coming from their wide, moist nostrils as they ate.

Monsieur Charrue, wearing rubber boots to his knees, walked toward them carrying a large silver bucket; he wore a thick leather belt buckled at his waist across his coveralls. He smiled at them and turned toward the first cow. Annie and Drew nearly broke into laughter. As he turned they saw a large wooden disk strapped to his backside with the belt, and a single stool leg extending from the middle of the seat. The farmer moved into position next to the cow and promptly sat down, balancing on the one-legged stool.

"Get a load of that!" said Drew. "The Swiss really are clever! It's a one-legged stool attached with a belt so he keeps his hands free to work."

"Looks a little silly at first," added Annie. "But what could be better?"

Mr. Pipes spoke with Monsieur Charrue in French. He laughed heartily as he worked. He called to Pierre, who took another milking stool down from a hook on the wall and helped strap it on Drew.

"Hey! Now I'm the real thing!" said Drew.

Annie laughed as Drew turned, admiring himself, and whacked his stool leg against Mr. Pipes's walking stick.

"Show me what to do!" said Drew.

Monsieur Charrue and Pierre demonstrated how to attach the portable milking machine to the bulging udder of the cow, and soon Drew felt like a real farmer.

They poured the last of the rich, creamy milk into larger milk barrels standing ready in a two-wheeled cart. Lady Kitty lapped up a milky puddle by the cart. Pierre disappeared, then came around the corner of the barn leading Bruno. Annie and Drew watched in excitement as he hitched the huge animal to the cart.

"They actually use Bruno to pull the cart?" asked Annie in amazement.

Mr. Pipes spoke to Monsieur Charrue, then replied to the children, "He says we will eat dinner as soon as you two and Pierre come back from delivering the milk to the *Laterie* in the village."

"Do we ride in the cart?" asked Drew hopefully.

"Pierre will walk," said Mr. Pipes, "but you are welcome to ride with the milk. Bruno looks strong enough for all that."

Bruno wagged his broomlike tail and gave an eager, "woof!"

Annie left Lady Kitty with little Henri and climbed aboard. Drew followed. Dusk began settling over the rolling hills, and the Charrue cowbells clanged merrily as the cows returned to pasture. Annie gave a great sigh and whispered to her brother.

"We won't ever forget this."

"Who'd want to?" Drew agreed.

They smiled at each other, listening to Pierre's lilting voice as he walked along beside Bruno. He gestured to the hills and forests, apparently telling them all about everything—all in French.

❖ ❖ ❖

Seated at the Charrue dinner table, Annie and Drew listened to Monsieur Charrue's earnest prayer of blessing and thanksgiving. "Merci, Seigneur.... Donne-nous chaque jour notre pain quotidien...."

His voice rose and fell with passion as he offered heartfelt thanksgiving for their daily bread and God's kindness to his family.

When he finished, Drew looked hungrily at the plates of pickled onions, baby potatoes, plates of sliced cheese, chunks of beef, and bite-size pieces of bread. Two pots simmered in the center of the table; they sat on portable stoves that kept their contents hot. Drew watched as—ladies first—the family speared chunks of meat and plunged them into one pot, or forked pieces of bread and dipped them into the other. The bread came out dripping with mouth-wateringly fragrant, blended cheeses. Drew paused in anticipation. It was serve yourself, so he could have all he wanted.

Conversation at the leisurely meal was all in French, with Mr. Pipes occasionally translating for the children. When the last crumb disappeared and plates and serving dishes were removed, Monsieur Charrue opened his great Bible and read:

"'Dieu se lève, ses ennemis se dispersent.... Chantez a
Dieu, celebrez son nom!'" He intoned the sacred words with
reverence and feeling—that much Annie and Drew understood.

The whole family began singing. Annie and Drew recog-
nized the tune—Psalm 68. What were the words Mr. Pipes
sang for them in English?

> God shall arise and by His might
> Put all His enemies to flight....

They joined in singing as much as they remembered. Next,
Monsieur Charrue led them in a strong but simple tune. Mr.
Pipes told Drew to collect his *Hymns Ancient and Modern* on
the double.

"It's Psalm 100," he hissed, helping Drew find the page.
"And one of the most defining tunes of all Christian hym-
nody—Louis Bougeois's 'Old Hundredth.' He was Calvin's
musician in Geneva. Wrote many Psalter tunes—this is the
greatest. Here it is; we'll sing along in English."

> All people that on earth do dwell,
> Sing to the Lord with cheerful voice;
> Him serve with fear, His praise forthtell,
> Come ye before Him and rejoice.
>
> The Lord ye know is God indeed;
> Without our aid He did us make;
> We are His folk, He doth us feed,
> And for His sheep He doth us take.
>
> O enter then His gates with praise,
> Approach with joy His courts unto;
> Praise, laud, and bless His Name always....

Drew felt that new surging in his soul; he blinked several
times before continuing.

For why? the Lord our God is good,
His mercy is for ever sure;
His truth at all times firmly stood,
And shall from age to age endure.

◈ ◈ ◈

Drew clasped his hands behind his head and gazed out the open window of the hayloft that would be his bedroom for the next few days. He sighed. This was the spot for him. Calves rustled in their hay beds below, and crickets seemed to be tuning up their chirruping for a nighttime symphony in the pasture.

Feeling for his knapsack, he opened the hymnal Mr. Pipes had given him and by the pale moonlight shining in the window, he carefully read Psalm 100 again: "God is good … mercy is for ever sure … truth at *all times* firmly stood … from *age to age* endure." He felt his heart and faith strangely united with Christians living in another land and at another time, yet united by a common worship—a worship filled with music worthy of God in every place and throughout all ages.

All People That on Earth Do Dwell

Shout for joy to the LORD, all the earth. Ps. 100:1

1. All   peo - ple   that   on   earth   do   dwell,   sing
2. The   Lord   ye   know   is   God   in -   deed;   with -
3. O   en - ter   then   his   gates   with   praise,   ap -
4. For   why?   The   Lord   our   God   is   good,   his

to   the   Lord   with   cheer - ful   voice;   him   serve   with   fear,   his
out   our   aid   he   did   us   make;   we   are   his   folk,   he
proach   with   joy   his   courts   un -   to;   praise,   laud,   and   bless   his
mer - cy   is   for - ev - er   sure;   his   truth   at   all   times

praise   forth - tell,   come   ye   be - fore   him   and   re - joice.
doth   us   feed,   and   for   his   sheep   he   doth   us   take.
name   al - ways,   for   it   is   seem - ly   so   to   do.
firm - ly   stood,   and   shall   from   age   to   age   en - dure.

Psalm 100
William Kethe, 1561

OLD HUNDREDTH L.M.
Louis Bourgeois's *Genevan Psalter,* 1551

Chapter Twelve

The Enduring Psalter
Soli Deo Gloria

I will sing of the Lord's great
love forever;
with my mouth I will make
your faithfulness
known through all
generations.

Psalm 89:1 (NIV)

Mr. Pipes, swinging his walking stick and whistling, strode briskly along the winding pavement returning from the village. As he approached the farm, Annie and Drew came from the barn to meet him. Mr. Pipes's mouth twitched in amusement: Drew—wearing a one-legged milking stool strapped to his middle—looked for all the world like he'd sprouted a tail.

"Good morning!" called Annie, smiling at the way the morning sun glowed on Mr. Pipes's white hair.

"Where have you been?" asked Drew.

"I posted a letter to Dr. Dudley, letting him in on our change of plans—employing guarded language, of course; wouldn't want our spy intercepting the mail. I informed him we would arrive in Geneva for Sunday worship at the Cathedral of *St. Pierre*—where Calvin preached. And from there: England."

"Do we have to leave?" asked Annie. "I mean—I know we do, but so soon?"

"We have several more days," replied Mr. Pipes, "and a lifetime of fond memories for you and the Charrue children, I'm certain of that."

"So," said Drew, "do we take the train to Geneva?"

"Ah, that is where you are wrong," said Mr. Pipes, tapping his stick on the gravel for emphasis. "I made telephone inquiries whilst in the village this morning, and I've hired a wonderful sailing craft for our transport to Geneva. You know it is just down the lake from here?"

"Surrounded by mountains and sparkling like jewels," said Annie. "That will be a voyage to remember!"

"Indeed, it will be, my dear," said Mr. Pipes.

"Boat like *Toplady*?" asked Drew.

"Oh, larger still," said Mr. Pipes. "With accommodations—a wee cabin, you know."

"We'll sleep in it?" asked Annie.

"And eat?" added Drew.

"Yes, yes, all of that," said Mr. Pipes, with a laugh, "while moored snugly at the pier in Geneva."

❖ ❖ ❖

For three more days, Annie and Drew's life on the Charrue farm was filled with work and play. Drew helped Monsieur Charrue, Pierre, and Francois with the milking, delivering the milk—twice daily—to the village *Laterie* in the cart pulled by Bruno. Between milking, he and the boys hefted great bales of hay onto a flatbed cart pulled by the bright blue farm tractor—Monsieur Charrue even let Drew drive, but only in the pasture. Each afternoon, the boys—and Rinky-Dink—played in the woods and fished in the pond.

When Annie and Paulette were not busy making paper dolls, they helped Dame Charrue and kindly Madame Charrue harvest tomatoes and cucumbers in the garden. They chopped and visited together, preparing meals for the hungry family. When they finished feeding the calves, Annie and Dame Charrue arranged flowers for the dinner table. Though Annie understood very little of what Dame Charrue said, she learned French words by pointing at an object or holding up a flower; Dame Charrue would reply with a dignified smile and a sideways nod of her head, "La fleur."

One morning Annie found Dame Charrue alone at her table reading her French Bible. She motioned for Annie to join her. Annie ran quickly upstairs and retrieved her own Bible, and for the next hour Dame Charrue read favorite passages from the sacred pages; Annie followed along in English, her heart growing more in love with the saintly old woman—and with her God.

And they sang Psalms—at morning milking, after breakfast, while doing evening chores, and all together again at evening worship. When Annie and Drew asked Mr. Pipes about the nonstop singing, he replied, "In James' epistle we read, 'Is any merry? Let him sing Psalms.' This is a joyful Christian family, children, and their joy overflows—as it ought to—in praise."

Many kisses were planted on many wet cheeks Saturday morning when it came time to leave. Annie hugged little Henri, and then, not trusting herself to speak, she kissed Lady Kitty and placed her into the pudgy arms of her new master. She felt a sob choking her as she hugged Dame Charrue and said, "Au revoir—until we meet again." But would they? She could only hope.

Drew thrust Rinky-Dink into Francois's hand as he said good-bye. "He's a German frog, but if you'll teach him French he should get along fine with Swiss frogs—he'll pick up French really fast."

"A Dieu!—God be with you!" called the family, waving as Mr. Pipes and Annie and Drew walked away from the farm toward the train. Biting her lip, Annie turned for one last look.

"Woof! Woof!" Bruno called after them.

⬧ ⬧ ⬧

An hour later they stood on the dock at Lausanne, looking at the boat Mr. Pipes had hired.

"She's a beauty!" said Annie, cupping her hands around her face as she peered through a bronze porthole. "Oh, and it's like a dollhouse inside!"

"She looks a seaworthy craft," said Mr. Pipes, striding the length of the vessel with his hands clasped behind his back like an admiral.

"Will it sail faster than *Toplady?*" asked Drew, squinting up at the varnished mast rising high above the deck, "being bigger, and all?"

"I should think so," said Mr. Pipes, swinging his leg over the lifeline. "Give me your hand, Annie dear."

"What's her name?" asked Annie. She ran her hand over the rich wood grain of the teak doors leading below. "—Can I go below?"

"*Minstrel*," said Mr. Pipes, "lovely name for a boat moved by the winds. And you most certainly may go below. Make yourself at home."

"Shall I cast her off, Skipper—sir?" asked Drew.

"Lend a hand unfurling the mainsail first," said Mr. Pipes, "and then heave on the main halyard—we've a lovely easterly."

Moments later, after the frantic rattling and flapping of sails, Mr. Pipes gave the signal; Drew cast off and jumped aboard. Mr. Pipes sheeted in the main; the sail snapped taut and billowed to port; Mr. Pipes eased the sheet. The dockhand waved and called, "Bon voyage!" Annie felt a thrill as *Minstrel* leapt to life, leaving the dock behind and moving swiftly onto the wide, sparkling lake.

"We're sailing!" Drew yelled from the bow where he worked, arm-over-arm, raising the jib halyard. As he pulled, he watched the sail climb higher, flapping in the gathering breeze.

"Annie, mind the tiller," said Mr. Pipes, wrapping the jib sheet on the wench and pulling on it. He leaned over the lifeline, squinted critically at the foresail, until with a nod of satisfaction, he cleated off the sheet and took the tiller from Annie.

"Thank you, my dear," he said, glancing at the bubblelike compass and easing the tiller to starboard.

"Now we're *really* sailing!" said Drew, joining them in the cockpit of the sturdy craft.

"Indeed," agreed Mr. Pipes.

Annie, her hair fluttering in the breeze, gazed at the sunlight shimmering like gold on the patchwork vineyards along the steep shoreline; she turned and watched the jagged mountains rising above the lake on the French side. She listened to the chuckling of the water against *Minstrel*'s planked sides, leaned back against the warm wood of the cockpit combing, and breathed a contented sigh.

"Lovely, isn't it, my dear," said Mr. Pipes, smiling at her. *Minstrel* heeled slightly. The winch rattled as he eased the sheet, and the boat raced along like a hunting pony eager for the chase.

"The wind could not be more perfect for a day on Lake Geneva—*Lac Leman*, the French call it," he added.

As the sun rose higher in the sky they saw more sailboats, their owners enjoying the warm summer day and perfect winds on the deep blue lake.

"Hey! Look at that red sail!" said Annie. "It almost looks like a giant balloon—well, half a balloon." For a fleeting moment she wondered if the spy might be on one of those boats.

"That's a spinnaker," said Mr. Pipes. "Wonderfully power-ful downwind sail."

"It's got a white cross right in the middle," said Drew.

"Swiss flag," said Mr. Pipes. "Fancy that, a sail made to look like their national flag."

"Isn't it about lunch time?" asked Drew a few minutes later.

"If you think it is, my boy," said Mr. Pipes with a laugh. "I seldom feel the need to consult my watch for meal times, Drew, when you are near."

Annie went below and unwrapped the lunch Madame Charrue packed for their voyage. They munched on Swiss cheese sandwiches made with Dame Charrue's hearty wheat bread smothered in sweet-cream butter, raisins grown along the slopes of the lake, sweet yellow pears, juicy and ripe, and washed it all down with bubbly mineral water.

"Aren't the Swiss known for—well, for *chocolate*?" asked Drew after devouring his second sandwich.

"Some of the finest chocolate in the world, most assuredly," said Mr. Pipes.

"Just curious," said Drew, now seated at the tiller and gazing nonchalantly up at the trim of the mainsail as he'd seen Mr. Pipes doing.

"And I happen to have stumbled upon several rather large slabs of the delicacy," said Mr. Pipes, with a merry twinkle in his eyes, "the other day in the village. Hmm, now whatever did I do with it?" He rustled in his pockets, then in his knapsack, feigning a futile search. "Aha! Here we are. Saved it for just such a time as this."

"If you insist!" said Drew, laughing as he broke off a chunk and began chewing the rich, creamy Swiss chocolate.

After several hours, the lake seemed to grow narrower, the steepness on the Swiss side growing more gentle.

"I think we might be getting close to the end of this huge lake," said Annie, gazing forward. "And, I'm pretty sure that looks like a bigger city than anything we've seen so far."

Mr. Pipes consulted the chart. "Indeed, it is Geneva, just ahead."

"What on earth is that giant column of water doing, shooting up in the air like that?" asked Drew as they sailed even closer to the city. "Do they have whales in this lake? It's a big one if they do."

"No, no, my boy," laughed Mr. Pipes. "It is the Jet d'Eau. Genevans converted a former outlet for the city's waterworks into an artificial geyser continuously shooting water hundreds of feet into the sky—a Geneva landmark, one might call it."

"I'll try avoiding it," said Drew, the mist from the waterspout drifting onto his face. "But, uh, where do I go?"

"Do you see that jetty projecting out into the lake?" asked Mr. Pipes. "Just over there, with that lovely lighthouse beacon." He pointed to the right of the waterspout.

Drew eased the tiller to port as they came up alongside an imposing stone promenade. Couples strode arm-in-arm, children raced each other along the waterfront walk, and Annie smiled, watching a dog take its master for a walk.

"Mr. Pipes," said Drew, looking uneasy at the confusing rows of docks and narrow slips filled with a forest of tall masts. "I-I think you'd better take it from here."

"Very well, my boy. You trot forward and lower the mainsail. One doesn't want too much speed when approaching a mooring under sail."

The boat slowed as Drew dropped the mainsail; with Mr. Pipes's guidance he gathered it in pleats on the boom and lashed it with sail ties.

"Now, move to the bow, and with dock line in hand, prepare to step off when I bring us alongside the guest moorage just ahead. We'll tie on the port side."

Annie held her breath; she finally decided to tidy up down below.

Mr. Pipes eased the jib sheet; the sail went slack and *Minstrel* drifted soundlessly toward the dock.

In a calm voice, Mr. Pipes said, "There, now, step ashore and cleat us off, my boy."

Minstrel nudged gently against the dock. Mr. Pipes stepped off and made fast the stern line. In a flurry of activity, they stowed sails and tidied ship.

"What next?" asked Annie, when they'd finished.

"Shore leave," said Mr. Pipes, gathering his walking stick. "And a visit to the grand cathedral in which John Calvin preached 500 years ago. She has a lovely organ," he added, a little wistfully, as they made their way onto the promenade.

※ ※ ※

Afternoon rush hour found Geneva's streets busy with traffic and her sidewalks crowded, but far from chaotic. Geneva, though clearly a very busy place, was an orderly city. Annie, nevertheless, clung to Mr. Pipes's hand as they crossed traffic and made their way into the narrow, winding streets of the Old City. She studied every face. Would the spy find them in Geneva?

The old part of town seemed deserted after the bustle of the business district, and as they wound their way up a cobbled street Annie eased her grip on Mr. Pipes's hand. Moments later, a narrow spire rising high above them flicked into view through a gap in the stone houses lining the street. And then they rounded a wide corner and saw before them the twin Gothic towers and thin brass spire of *St. Pierre*. The Swiss flag flapped lazily from the south tower.

"Ah, here it is," said Mr. Pipes, leading them through the arched entrance. "Much more impressive from inside, isn't it?" he said in hushed tones as they looked down the high-vaulted nave. A shaft of light shone from the upper row of Gothic stained-glass windows and cast a flood of light on the curving stairway leading to an ornately carved pulpit.

"Just there," he pointed to the pulpit, as they walked down the central aisle, their steps echoing softly off the high stone walls and ceiling, "Calvin preached—in this very place, and sometimes every day of the week."

"Why so much preaching?" asked Drew.

"Calvin answered that best himself," replied Mr. Pipes. "He said that biblical preaching is the soul of the Church; it is God 'stretching His hands out to us'; he even called preaching 'the visitation of God.'"

"Pretty important, then," said Annie, running her fingers over the curved wood of the banister leading to the high pulpit.

"And when they gathered here to hear Calvin preach God's Word," said Annie, "they sang Psalms, didn't they?" She looked around at the empty pews and imagined them filled with families like the Charrues lifting their voices in Psalms of praise to God—right in these walls.

"They most certainly did," said Mr. Pipes. "He said singing Psalms in worship 'brings us into the company of angels.'"

Just then, Drew thought he heard wings flapping high overhead in the cathedral.

"What was that?" he said, gazing up at the ribbed vaulting.

"Sparrows, I fear—or swallows," said Mr. Pipes. "And there they are."

Dipping and swooping, several sparrows circled the large central chandelier and landed in a row on the back of one of the pews.

"Do you think we can catch one?" hissed Drew, inching toward the pew.

Mr. Pipes smiled, and said, "Never. But I am reminded of Psalm 84; no doubt, the Psalmist experienced something very like this, only in the Temple. It reads: 'How amiable are thy tabernacles, O Lord of hosts! My soul longeth, yea, even faint-eth for the courts of the Lord.... Yea, the sparrow hath found an house, and the swallow a nest for herself, where she may lay her young, even thine altars....'"

The sparrows twittered merrily on their perch.

Suddenly, the birds stopped singing, and in a flurry of wings, they flittered upward, disappearing under the Gothic arches. Then, with a wild "Yeeow!" a little man holding a broom high over his bald head came running down the aisle, his eyes bulging from his red face.

"Allez-vous! Allez-vous!" he screamed, swinging the broom in frustration as the birds flew to safety. He wiped his balding forehead and, seeing his unexpected guests, said, "Ah, C'est ter-riblement! C'est sacrilege!"

Mr. Pipes spoke briefly with the man, who then, scowling upward and with a shake of his fist at the feathered intruders, turned and swept his way down the aisle, disappearing up a circular staircase in the north transept.

"I take it he doesn't appreciate Psalm 84," said Drew. "At least not the part about the birds."

"I think they're nice," said Annie. "And I'll bet sparrows flew around in here when Calvin preached. Tell us more about him. I think you left off when he and his wife Idelette returned to Geneva—when was it?"

"1541," said Drew.

"Precisely," said Mr. Pipes. "Calvin stepped into that pulpit after his three years of banishment, and everyone wondered on what text he would preach. Would he rail against the mob who drove him out, but now found themselves begging him to return?"

"Yeah!" said Drew, slamming his fist into his palm with a sharp slap that echoed through the nave.

"I-I don't think so," said Annie, sitting down on the bottom step of the curved stairway leading to the pulpit. "But what did he preach on?"

"Calvin opened his Bible," said Mr. Pipes, settling into a nearby pew, "and turned to the exact text where he left off three years before, and expounded God's Word without mention of past wrongs."

"He could have nailed 'em," said Drew.

"Yes, but Calvin's sole concern was the glory of God in all of life. For the next twenty-five years, Calvin preached, taught, and wrote commentaries and letters encouraging and instructing saints all over Europe. Under Calvin's wise and godly leadership, Geneva soon became a refuge for Christians fleeing persecution. John Knox, the Scottish Reformer, called Geneva the most perfect school of Christ since the days of the apostles. And French Huguenots came to study at Calvin's knee in the *Academia*—now the University of Geneva—and then returned to France as missionaries, many to die martyrs' deaths for loyalty to Christ."

"Did all those refugees learn Psalm singing in Geneva?" asked Drew.

"Indeed, they did," said Mr. Pipes. "Among the English and Scottish refugees, fleeing the persecutions of Bloody Mary, was a young man named William Kethe. He and others began translating and versifying the Psalms in English. When they returned to Britain, they sang many of them to the Geneva 'Jiggs,' as critics liked to call Calvin's congregational singing. Psalm 100 is one of Kethe's Psalm versifications sung to Louis Bourgeois's tune, 'Old Hundredth.' Anglicans, Scottish Presbyterians, and American Puritans sang only the Psalter for generations—Calvin's Geneva Psalter was the model for their singing."

"We sang 'Old Hundredth' at the farm," said Drew. "'Old' doesn't mean out of date and useless, does it?" he added.

"No, indeed, my boy. 'Old' when applied to a great hymn or Psalm means a treasure—a lasting treasure. You see, the worth of what we sing in worship is not based on age; worth is determined by what is true and beautiful."

"I think I understand what you mean," said Annie. "Could you teach us one of Calvin's Psalms," she went on, "one that he versified?"

"That poses a bit of a problem, my dears. For you see, Calvin's battle cry was, *Soli Deo Gloria*, to God alone the glory. In that spirit, Calvin didn't sign any Psalms and hymns he might have written. However, some ascribe to Calvin a hymn that appeared in the Strasbourg Psalter. No one knows for sure if he wrote it, but it certainly is in keeping with his reverence for God, and he was in Strasbourg encouraging congregational singing when it first appeared."

He pulled out his hymnal. "Here it is, my dears," he said, pressing back the page with his fingers. "It rather reminds me of Luther's 'A Mighty Fortress,' but this is less martial, with a touch of sweetness and near-perfect gentleness—qualities that critics of Calvin would never ascribe to him."

His clear voice rang off the walls as he read:

> I greet Thee, who my sure Redeemer art,
> My only trust and Saviour of my heart,
> Who pain didst undergo for my poor sake;
> I pray Thee from our hearts all cares to take.

> Thou art the King of mercy and of grace,
> Reigning omnipotent in ev'ry place:
> So come, O King, and our whole being sway;
> Shine on us with the light of Thy pure day.

> Thou art the Life, by which alone we live,
> And all our substance and our strength receive;
> O comfort us in death's approaching hour,
> Strong-hearted then to face it by Thy pow'r.

Thou hast the true and perfect gentleness,
No harshness hast Thou and no bitterness:
Make us to taste the sweet grace found in Thee
And ever stay in Thy sweet unity.

Our hope is in no other save in Thee;
Our faith is built upon Thy promise free;
O grant to us such stronger hope and sure
That we can boldly conquer and endure.

Out of the stillness when he finished reading, Annie said, "If it was Calvin, he was a better poet than he admitted." She looked over Mr. Pipes's shoulder at the words. "I love the way he organized each verse."

"How is that, my dear?" asked Mr. Pipes, smiling at her.

Drew came over for a look.

"Well, in each verse he makes a statement—" her eyes ran down the page, "—a statement about God or our relationship with God."

"Hey, you're right," said Drew. "He's our Savior, King, our Life—"

"And He has true and perfect gentleness, and sweet grace is found in Him," said Annie.

"And thus," added Mr. Pipes, "our faith and hope rests in God alone."

"And the second part of each verse," Annie continued, "is a prayer for something."

"Well observed, my dears," Mr. Pipes beamed at them. "You see, this hymn follows the biblical model of adoration and worship: the theological truth must come first, then the prayer of faith to God who, by His sweet grace, makes us to boldly conquer and endure. Calvin understood the essential importance of theology—he was even called the Theologian of the Reformation, and through his writing and the Psalter, biblical Christianity flourished and spread the world over."

Mr. Pipes rose, and the children followed him out of the cathedral and down the steps. "I have one more thing to show you before we retire to *Minstrel* for the night. Tomorrow we shall come back here and worship," he paused on the steps, looking back at the Gothic façade of the church, "here, where Calvin preached and where Christians have sung Psalms and hymns for centuries."

As if on cue, the bells from the tower of the cathedral suddenly began a slow gonging, echoing down the winding streets.

"Wait! It sounds like a tune," said Drew, listening. "—Hey! It is! It's 'A Mighty Fortress'—Luther's hymn! Here in Geneva."

"The bells of St. Pierre are tuned to *Ein' Feste Burg*, Luther's grand melody, because it is the battle hymn of the entire Reformation, Lutheran or Calvinist."

They listened until the weighty music ended.

"Maybe we'll sing Luther's hymn in church tomorrow," said Drew.

"Maybe we'll sing Calvin's hymn," said Annie.

"T'would be lovely," said Mr. Pipes.

After several minutes walking along the bumpy cobblestones of the streets, Drew suddenly stopped.

"'*Rue Jean-Calvin*,'" he read from the street sign. "Wasn't that the street we left our boat on in Strasbourg?"

"Indeed, it was," said Mr. Pipes. "Remember, Calvin left his influence there, as well. And just ahead I'll show you a monument to his world-wide influence."

◈ ◈ ◈

A wide, grassy park, nearly as long as a football field, spread along paving stones. Rising above these stones, four bearded figures, all carved out of solid rock, stood in long flowing robes.

"They're giants," said Annie.

Drew moved closer and read, "'Calvin, Farel, Beza, and Knox.'" He frowned up at the statues. "Who was Beza?"

"Ah, a most important fellow," replied Mr. Pipes. "He was an accomplished poet and theologian who joined Calvin in preaching the gospel. After Calvin's death in 1564, Beza became the pastor of the Genevan Church—his successor at St. Pierre."

"A poet?" said Annie.

"Yes," said Mr. Pipes. "The great poet, Marot, died without completing the Psalter, leaving Calvin with only forty-nine Psalms in French when he returned to Geneva. Beza, preaching in Lausanne, in 1551, added thirty-four more Psalms to Marot's. In his introduction—a poetic classic in its own right—Beza called for poets, those with 'minds of heavenly birth,' to turn their pens to spiritual themes, to write enduring verse with which all the Church might worship God. Later, when persecution of French Christians grew worse, Beza's poetic way with words is seen in bold lines written to the French King: 'the Church of God is indeed an anvil to receive and not strike blows, but an anvil that has worn out many hammers.'"

Drew walked over and touched the warm granite of one of Beza's giant feet. Next to Beza, he looked up at Calvin, rising a dozen feet or more above.

"They were giants," he said simply.

"Spreading in both directions of this statue," continued Mr. Pipes, "one sees the influence of Calvinism in England, Scotland, Holland—and in your America, just here."

Drew followed Mr. Pipes to the right and read: "'... *we doe by these present solemnly and mutually in the presence of God, and one of another, convenant and combine ourselves togeather into a civill body politick.... Anno Domini 1620....*'"

"That's the Mayflower Compact!" said Annie. "We learned that in school."

"Not only did Calvin formulate and restore biblical theology," said Mr. Pipes, "his reforms here in Geneva have affected politics—even as far away as America. You must read more about him. But now we must buy what food we shall require on the Lord's Day and retire to our ship."

◈ ◈ ◈

Annie wriggled in excitement. It was the first time she and Drew had ever slept in a boat. She ran her fingers over the finely fitted rows of polished teak lining her berth; leaning on her elbow, she peered out the porthole at the twinkling lights of the harbor shimmering on the dark water.

Nearby, Drew listened to the soft lapping of Lake Geneva against *Minstrel's* hull. The boat rocked gently.

"Good night, my dears," whispered Mr. Pipes a few moments later from his berth in the forecastle.

There was no reply.

⬧ ⬧ ⬧

"What do the Swiss call these?" asked Drew the next morning, staring hungrily at a plate of large buns hollowed out and filled with whipped cream.

"*Gugelhopf,* popular all over Switzerland," replied Mr. Pipes.

"*Gugelhopf* ! What a name!" said Annie, after they gave thanks. She bit into the sweet pastry.

"Umph ... mmm ... gulp ... Is there enough for seconds?" asked Drew.

"Indeed! Finished already?" said Mr. Pipes from across the ship's dining table. "My lad, don't bolt your food; one must chew. Hmm, I do, however, want to arrive plenty early for worship."

After they cleared up their breakfast dishes, Mr. Pipes watched Drew's awkward attempts at tying his necktie. "Allow me, Drew," said Mr. Pipes, untangling the wadded tie and knotting it smartly.

⬧ ⬧ ⬧

The nave of the great cathedral was nearly empty when the threesome arrived forty minutes early for worship.

"There's the bird hater," said Drew, pointing to the little red-faced man who stood wringing his hands in the narthex of the cathedral.

"Looks pretty upset about something," said Annie.

"Let's find out what troubles him," said Mr. Pipes.

As Mr. Pipes talked in French with the agitated man, the children watched his face and tried to figure out the problem. Mr. Pipes first looked sympathetic, then puzzled; then he shook his head as if dismissing something out of hand. Then a faraway twinkle came to his eyes; he broke into a smile and nod-

ded his head in agreement. The little man suddenly grabbed
Mr. Pipes by the shoulders and planted a kiss on each cheek.
Turning to the children, Mr. Pipes said, "Well, that's settled,
then. Follow us."

Annie and Drew scurried to keep up with the birdman
and Mr. Pipes. Puzzled, they mounted a staircase winding up a
narrow stone shaft. It reminded Drew of Coburg Castle where
they spent the night in Luther's room. Suddenly, they stepped
out onto a narrow gallery, the nave of the cathedral sprawling
far below. As the children admired the view, the birdman led
Mr. Pipes to the organ console. Drew turned and saw rank
upon rank of pipes rising above the keyboard.

"What's going on?" asked Drew.

"Monsieur Balayeur needs an organist," Mr. Pipes
explained. "The organist of the cathedral is *tres malade*—
unwell, sick; that is to say, he cannot play for morning worship."

"And you'll do it, won't you, Mr. Pipes?" said Annie.

"I have consented to fill in," said Mr. Pipes, positioning his
glasses on his nose and sitting at the organ console. He shifted
the bench, then began pulling stops and stretching his arms and
feet out, getting a feel for the instrument. "Monsieur Balayeur
has asked me—us—to select the Psalms and hymns for worship. It is truly the minister's task, but he insists that we must
do it. What would you two suggest?"

Annie and Drew began listing a torrent of favorite hymns.

Mr. Pipes lifted his hands. "Hold, hold, my dears. The
liturgy includes but four hymns. May I suggest we begin with
a German hymn, then two French, and conclude with, again, a
German hymn. How does that sound?"

After much discussion they finally agreed on four hymns.
Mr. Pipes played a quiet prelude, blending the melodies of all
four. The children stayed up in the gallery by the organ, peering
over the rail at the service below when not singing.

"This is what I call a bird's eye view," Drew whispered in
Annie's ear.

They sang along in English, using Mr. Pipes's hymnal:

> All praise to God, who reigns above....
> ... The Lord forsaketh not His flock
> His chosen generation;
> He is their Refuge and their Rock,
> Their Peace and their Salvation....

After a corporate confession of their sins they sang Psalm 68 to the rousing tune, *Greiter:*

> God shall arise and by His might
> Put all His enemies to flight....

Then in French the minister, wearing a plain black gown with white collar, led the congregation in reading Exodus 20.

After several more minutes passed the congregation rose and sang:

> I greet Thee, who my sure Redeemer art,...
> ... Thou art the King of mercy and of grace,
> Reigning omnipotent in ev'ry place: ...
> ... Make us to taste the sweet grace found in Thee ...
> ... Our faith is built upon Thy promise free; ...

The minister preached a sermon, during which Mr. Pipes—his face moving from earnest consent to brow-furrowing sadness and even alarm—whispered occasional translations.

Then came the final hymn; the organ swelled with the manly tune of *Ein' Feste Burg:*

> A mighty Fortress is our God,
> A Bulwark never failing; ...
> ... Were not the right Man on our side,
> The Man of God's own choosing....
> ... Christ Jesus it is He,
> Lord Sabaoth His Name,
> From age to age the same, ...

... God's truth abideth still;
His kingdom is for ever.

Annie and Drew wanted it never to end.

The minister pronounced the benediction. When the service ended, Mr. Pipes clicked at switches and stops, putting things in order at the organ console.

"Grandeur, my dears, grandeur," he said, plunking the last stop in place. "And it is all ours, from age to age, and throughout all eternity—this grandeur is yours."

◈ ◈ ◈

Monsieur Balayeur pumped Mr. Pipes's hand and introduced him to the minister, who expressed his gratitude for Mr. Pipes's organ playing.

As they walked down the steps of the cathedral, a tall gentleman with a mustache and black leather medical case firmly in hand, stopped them.

"Well, now, if I may make so bold, I say, dashed awfully good to see you—hmm, looking tolerably. I say, may I take your blood pressure? 'Twill only take a moment."

"Dr. Dudley, himself!" said Mr. Pipes, wringing his friend's hand. "But, Martin, whatever are you doing here? Hang my blood pressure! Oh, do greet the children."

"Hello," he said, turning briefly to Annie and Drew.

"Shall we say," he continued to Mr. Pipes, "let's just say that my communication with you was somewhat interrupted. When I received your letter—at last—I felt very much the need to determine for myself if you were still—well, alive. Absolutely dropped off the planet, you did, sir."

"Martin, as so frequently happens in my conversation with you, I don't have the slightest idea what you are talking about."

Suddenly, Annie's fingernails dug into Drew's arm and she hissed in his ear. "It's him! Coming up the steps toward us!" She cowered behind her brother.

Drew tried to be brave. Maybe this was it—the showdown—the spy had finally cornered his prey, and....

Drew tugged on Mr. Pipes's sleeve viciously. "Mr. P—"

The spy strode up and stopped abruptly next to Dr. Dudley. Drew swallowed hard. He watched the spy's hands—*if he reaches inside his jacket, I'll ... I'll ...*

Catching sight of the man, recognition quickly spread across Mr. Pipes's face. He fixed his eyes steadily on the spy and positioned himself in front of the children, his arms spread, protecting them as best he could.

"Ah, yes," said Dr. Dudley. "My nephew Brentwood, just returning from making my call to the Geneva police. You see, when I didn't find you in church this morning—by the by, where were you? Never mind—when you didn't show for services, I made my decision and put an all-points bulletin out on you as a missing person—the children, too, of course. There will be notices all over the city by nightfall—no doubt the next round of milk cartons will feature your pictures. 'Tis dashed inconvenient now I've found you. I do hope you're not disappointed with the photographs I've chosen—"

"H-he is your nephew?" said Annie.

"Brentwood's the name," said the spy, extending his hand and smiling warmly.

Mr. Pipes just stared.

When he did find his voice, he said, "Martin, your care of me is boundless—and, I fear, forgive me for saying so, somewhat *mindless* at times."

"I beg your pardon, sir!" said Dr. Dudley.

"Your nephew can fill you in on all the *hazards* we underwent trying desperately to evade your surveillance, believing him to be—" It suddenly seemed all rather silly to Mr. Pipes, and he hesitated before admitting, "—believing him to be.... well, to be a-a *spy*."

"A *what!*" said Dr. Dudley. "My dear man, have you again taken entire leave of your senses? The need for my constant oversight, my dear fellow, is now more clearly established than ever. A *spy?* I say, did these little blighters put such a notion in your hoary head?"

Annie cowered behind Mr. Pipes.

"My dear Martin, I assure you that had you been with us, tracked and hounded as we were by your—by your *kindness*, you would have concluded very much the same about our situation."

"I thought it was great," Drew chimed in. "We jumped ship, ducked in and out of back streets at breakneck speed— even climbed out a window on a rope made of bed sheets. Sure, it was a little dangerous—but what a lot of fun you made for us, Dr. Dudley. Thanks."

"What!— Humph—I never—!" Dr. Dudley spluttered.

Annie squinted, looking closely at Brentwood's face. "So, I am glad to see you didn't actually pierce your nose," she said. "Must have been a clip-on. Oh, and hair grows back, you know. But how can I ever thank you for catching Lady Kitty like you did?"

"Yeah, that was some catch," said Drew, "how'd you do it?"

"Oh, that. I play a bit of rugby at Oxford," said Brentwood modestly.

"You must do a bit of swimming, too," said Mr. Pipes, "swimming to shore in Rhine River current as you did. Wise of you to leave behind the combat boots and leather jacket."

Brentwood just smiled. "I needed work for the summer holidays; Uncle Martin enlisted my help. It was all very fun. In fact, when is your next adventure?"

"Oh, no," said Dr. Dudley decisively. "Clearly I will need to be personally in charge of future surveillance of my most incorrigible patient. Why did not I go into veterinary surgery? Now then, I propose we get out of Geneva before your pictures are posted everywhere. But first, my dear man, how about that blood pressure?"

I Greet Thee, Who My Sure Redeemer Art

Who gave himself for our sins to rescue us from the present evil age. Gal. 1:4

1. I greet thee, who my sure Re-deem-er art, my on-ly
2. Thou art the King of mer-cy and of grace, reign-ing om-
3. Thou art the Life, by which a-lone we live, and all our
4. Thou hast the true and per-fect gen-tle-ness, no harsh-ness
5. Our hope is in no oth-er save in thee; our faith is

trust and Sav-ior of my heart, who pain didst un-der-
nip-o-tent in ev-'ry place: so come, O King, and
• sub-stance and our strength re-ceive; O com-fort us in
hast thou and no bit-ter-ness: make us to taste the
built up-on thy prom-ise free; O grant to us such

go for my poor sake; I pray thee from our hearts all cares to take.
our whole be-ing sway; shine on us with the light of thy pure day.
• death's ap-proach-ing hour, strong-heart-ed then to face it by thy pow'r.
sweet grace found in thee and ev-er stay in thy sweet u-ni-ty.
strong-er hope and sure that we can bold-ly con-quer and en-dure.

Strasbourg Psalter, 1545
Tr. by Elizabeth L. Smith, 1868; alt. 1961

TOULON 10.10.10.10
Genevan Psalter, 1551

ML　　8-15